WOLF Rider

Praise for *Raven Quest*
winner of the Silver Birch Award

"[A] terrific animal fantasy. . . . Tok, called Skydancer as he loves to wheel and dive in the sky, . . . grows from a terrified, ashamed youngster to a wise, compassionate, determined leader. Listening to others, caring for others, holding firm to his search, Tok is the ultimate hero. . . . Stewart brings even minor characters to life with telling dialogue and action-packed scenes. The real life of wolves and ravens is blended effortlessly with her fictional world in which animal groups boast a proud and ancient mythology complete with riddles, proverbs, lore, songs, myths and sayings."
— *Canadian Materials*

"Driven by . . . powerful underlying messages of honour, respect, honesty, and open-mindedness."
— *Resource Links*

Shortlisted for the Manitoba Young Reader's Choice Award 2005, British Columbia's Red Cedar Award 2005–2006 and Alberta's Rocky Mountain Book Award 2005.

WOLF Rider

Sharon Stewart

Cover by Caroline Bochud
Vignettes by Heidi Taillefer

Scholastic Canada Ltd.
Toronto New York London Auckland Sydney
Mexico City New Delhi Hong Kong Buenos Aires

Scholastic Canada Ltd.
604 King Street West, Toronto, Ontario M5V 1E1, Canada

Scholastic Inc.
557 Broadway, New York, NY 10012, USA

Scholastic Australia Pty Limited
PO Box 579, Gosford, NSW 2250, Australia

Scholastic New Zealand Limited
Private Bag 94407, Greenmount, Auckland, New Zealand

Scholastic Children's Books
Euston House, 24 Eversholt Street, London NW1 1DB, UK

Library and Archives Canada Cataloguing in Publication
Stewart, Sharon (Sharon Roberta), 1944-
    Wolf rider / Sharon Stewart.

Sequel to: Raven quest.
ISBN 978-0-439-93646-0

    I. Title.

PS8587.T4895W64 2008   jC813'.54   C2008-900857-X

ISBN-10 0-439-93646-2

6 5 4 3 2 1   Printed in Canada   08 09 10 11 12 13

To Kevin, because he asked me.
And to Roderick, for all the reasons.

Prologue

The world was burning. The sky glowed, and a terrible roar filled the air. Selaks laid her ears back, and her nose twitched at the stench of charring wood. Suddenly a great pine beside her burst into flowers of flame, showering her with sparks. Panicked, she ran, the ground scorching her paws. Then a blazing branch crashed down upon her, searing into her muzzle. She cried out in pain and fear . . . then awoke to clean cold and the feather touch of snowflakes.

Part 1

The Terror

Chapter 1

Sorrow is colder than snow.

— Raven proverb

Tok stretched his wings and tilted them against the gusty wind. Tightening his claws around the topmost branch of his favourite spruce, he rode the gale. It was a strange, spring-like wind for the Moon of Nestlings. Good weather for sky dancing, but he had no heart for it. There was no joy in dancing or anything else now, with Tarkah gone.

Just a year ago they had had their second nesting, raising a fine brood that spring and watching them disperse the following autumn. But after the young-sters were gone, Tarkah had grown restless.

"My heart longs to go a-journeying, as we once did," she had said. "Why not fly east or south this autumn?"

"And abandon our territory?" Tok had asked, aston-ished.

Tarkah had given him a pleading glance. "I don't mean abandon it forever. We can come back in the spring," she countered.

"No ravenlord abandons his chosen holding," Tok had protested. "It would be *unkora!*"

"Would it?" she had asked wistfully. After that she said no more about journeys.

And then . . .

Not many days afterward he had left her foraging at the edge of a pond, while he flew in pursuit of a mob of strange ravens who had invaded their territory. They had swooped insultingly close overhead, then, ignoring his challenges, had fled. Enraged, he had taken wing and followed them far, so far that darkness had forced him to roost overnight. When he got back the next morning his mate was nowhere to be found.

"Tarkah?" he called, sure she must be somewhere nearby. Perhaps she was hiding, to punish him for having left her for so long, he thought. "Come out, Tarkah!" But still she didn't answer. He took wing, calling and circling, thinking that perhaps she had followed him and that they had somehow missed each other in the air. But the skies were empty. Deciding she must have gone to forage in the forest, he descended and flew among the trees, still calling, his voice growing sharp with panic. At last he found her in a glade, or what was left of her. She had been torn to pieces, every delicate bone and glossy feather broken, and scattered across the floor of the forest.

"Tarkah!" he screamed. But only echoes answered. Numbly, he covered her remains with dead leaves. For days he perched, fasting, on a branch overhead, sunk in grief, his mind turning in helpless circles. What could have killed her? No owl or eagle, or any other predator he knew would have smashed and broken her body but eaten nothing. And behind his grief loomed the darker shadow of guilt. No ravenlord should leave his lady, exposing her to harm. One who did was without *kora* and deserved to be a lord no longer.

Somehow Tok had survived the bleak winter that followed. Now other ravens would be busying themselves with their nests. Soon eggs would be laid, and new life would begin. But such things could never be again, for him. His heart swelled with sorrow. If he had listened to Tarkah, gone on a journey as she had asked, she would be alive today!

Suddenly harsh croaking sounds drifted down the wind, breaking into his thoughts, and he glared upward. Ravens, high overhead, flying north in an angled flight, like a flock of geese. Tok roused his feathers angrily. It was the same formation he had seen on the terrible day Tarkah died! Could they be the same birds? And why were ravens flying like geese? It was *unkora,* he told himself. With a furious quork, he launched himself on the wind, angling his flight feathers to gain height, pulling himself upward with powerful beats of his great wings. He had failed to catch the strange flight of ravens before. This time he would succeed, and if Tarkah's murderers were among them, he would kill them! He willed himself onward, into the teeth of the wind, which grew stronger the higher he rose. The flight was wavering, and when the leader dropped back, letting another bird take his place, Tok caught up with him. As he had guessed, the bird was a stranger to him.

"I am Tok, son of Rokan! I am a lord of these hills," he screamed into the gale. "My mate has been killed. Do you know anything of this?"

The other bird gave him an insolent stare, and flapped on.

Losing his temper, Tok gave the bird a buffet with his wing. "Answer me!" he demanded.

The other struck out savagely with his claws, then with a half-roll shot off across the angle of the wind to rejoin the flight, which beat on toward the north.

What use to pursue them? thought Tok, his rage cooling. They would not answer, and he could not fight them all. Sullenly, he glided down the wind, heading for the last of a gut pile left where a Two-Legs had killed a deer in the Moon of Hunters. He made a sparse meal at it, then as the light failed, returned to roost among the boughs of the spruce. Though what did *his* spruce, *his* territory matter now, without Tarkah? Here he and she had ridden out many a winter blizzard, telling stories, or talking of their previous year's offspring, since dispersed, and wondering where they were in the world. Or saying nothing at all, but simply dozing pressed against each others' sides. Now all his nights and days were lonely.

Morning dawned clear and bright. Tok noticed that at least it felt decently cold for once. He felt little hunger, so he only satisfied his thirst at a place he knew where a spring bubbled up among the roots of a pine tree. The water had never once frozen over this winter, he reflected. A creeping sense of unease added to the weight on his wings, a feeling that something was wrong with the world around him. He mounted the wind, and soared, thinking about it.

Three years had passed since Tok had led the wolves from the Lost Hills to the Raven Mountains. After that, he and Tarkah had departed eastward in search of a new territory, as *kora* required. For according to ravenlaw, young ravens must leave the territories where they had fledged. The first summer he and his mate had spent in these eastern hills had been perfect, but in the second summer the land had sweltered under a blanket of heat. There had been little snow the preceding winter, so creek levels fell and beaver ponds dried up. The leaves of the maples showed brown edges by mid-season, and living creatures panted for water. But there was almost none. The next year had been warmer still, and all the small forage of frogs and fish began to fail, though deer were plentiful because of the mild winters. But without wolves to kill them, what good were deer to ravens?

Now the only time of plenty was in the Moon of Hunters when the hills echoed to the boom of the Two-Legs' firesticks, and the carcasses and gut piles left from their kills provided feasts for ravens, foxes and coyotes. But the rest of the year, ravens knew hunger.

If only the wolves had come as they had promised! When Rokah and Parvah, his first-fledged son and daughter, had set out to claim their own territories, Tok had sent them to the Raven Mountains to find the wolf leaders Selaks and Durnál and beg them to bring their wolf pack here — the other wolves would follow their *vór* and *vóra*. But another year had passed and they had not reappeared.

The wolves had failed him, Tok thought bitterly, despite the friendship and gratitude they had shown him for leading them from a place of hardship to a land of plenty. As for the other ravens of the hills, they seemed a tame lot, with no thoughts beyond the cares of nest and young. He had tried to organize a Kort and find Tellers to keep the old ways alive, as they were kept in the Raven Mountains, but there was little interest. Then, as times grew harder, ravens began to vanish from the hills. Great swaths of territory fell empty, with no one to claim lordship. Ravens no longer danced in the skies, only flapped north in the strange-shaped flights.

It was an insult to Skyah, who had given them wings for dancing, thought Tok. And he was no better than the rest. No longer would anyone call him Skydancer, for he too danced no more. Brooding on this, he forced himself to swoop and roll in the air. Then he dove steeply, the wind keening through his flight feathers, and circled up again. Remembering Tarkah's dancing, he imitated her glides and twirls, then added his own movements, trying to weave the two of them together as an offering to Skyah. But his wings felt as heavy as his heart.

So absorbed was he that he did not at first notice the approach of a solitary raven who watched him make a twirling dive like a falling leaf and waited for him to rise again.

"Lord Tok?" said the other, when they came together. "Can I be lucky enough to have found you so quickly? Those who sent me said you would be dancing."

By his voice and the tinge of brown in his feathers, Tok knew the newcomer was a ravenet. "I am Tok, son of Rokan," he replied. "Who are you, and who has sent you?"

The ravenet did a neat little wing dip in the air. "Barek, son of Karek, at your service," he said eagerly. "Selaks, *vóra* of the Mount Storm wolf pack, has sent me. She and her *vór*, Durnál, beg you to return to the Raven Mountains."

Tok shook his wings impatiently. "I *cannot!*" he snapped. "A lord may not abandon his territory. Do you know nothing of ravenlaw?"

"Not much," Barek admitted cheerfully.

"Even if I could leave," Tok went on, "why should I? Long ago I sent to the *vór* and *vóra* to come here, as was agreed between us, but they failed me. Why should I do their bidding now?"

"I know nothing of that," Barek replied. "But the *vóra* said it was urgent, a matter of life or death."

"When did you leave the Raven Mountains?" Tok asked.

"Five days ago."

"Then you have flown fast. It took me and my mate much longer to reach these hills. Come, you must feed and rest before we talk more."

Down in the forest, Tok led Barek to the gut pile. While the ravenet stuffed himself on the last scraps, Tok stalked and killed a red squirrel, which the two of them shared.

"I must think more about the *vóra's* request," he told Barek. "Go, forage more. You can usually find me near that tallest spruce."

Later, as they settled in to roost, Tok asked many questions about the Raven Mountains and how things were there.

"I have only lately come there," the ravenet replied. "So I cannot speak of changes. There are many Two-Legs, as there were in the place where I was fledged. But the living is good. The wolves kill plenty of deer, and when they eat, we eat."

"Many Two-Legs? Then the Mountains have

changed much indeed," said Tok. "But sleep now. We'll talk more in the morning."

The ravenet tucked his head under his wing. But Tok remained awake, his mind seething with questions. Why had Selaks sent for him now? Did she not realize that he could not come? He shook his feathers. No, of course she didn't know. She knew nothing of ravenlaw. That law demanded that he stay here and hope someday to find another mate. But his heart shrank from that. It was his fault Tarkah was dead. He did not deserve or want another mate.

He drifted off to sleep at last, but some sixth sense woke him in the dead of night. Through the branches of the spruce he glimpsed moonlight glinting on lightly-falling snow. Then, startled, he roused his feathers. For at the end of the bough on which he perched sat another raven. It was purest white, and the light of the moon seemed to shine through it. Tok nudged Barek, perched on the other side of him, but the ravenet slumbered on.

The white raven gazed at him out of dark-shadowed eyes. "The Change is upon us," it said in a silvery voice. "The world you know is ending. Go north."

"I'm dreaming!" muttered Tok.

The white raven stretched its shimmering wings. "North," it said again. "Remember." And then it dissolved into crystals of snow.

Chapter 2

*I A ravenlord may not abandon his chosen
territory on pain of forfeiting his lordship and his kora.*

*II No ravenlord may by his actions endanger
the life of his mate.*

— from "The Laws of Lordship,"
Dooms of the Kort

At dawn, Tok left Barek to forage alone and flew to
the glade where Tarkah had died. It was drifted over
with snow now, with no sign of the violence that had
occurred there. Shoulders hunched, he perched on a
bare limb, brooding. He had been urged to do the
unthinkable, leave his territory. He shivered at the
thought. Were he to do such a thing, he would
become no better than an outcast, doomed to life on
the margin of ravenkind. And yet Selaks had said it
was a matter of life or death. . . .

Unbidden, his old fondness for the great white she-wolf stirred within him. She was a Snow Seer of the Lanna, and he had never known her to speak falsely. And then there was the matter of the white raven. It, too, urged him to go. But was it real, or no more than a strange trick of moonlight on falling snow?

His sharp ears caught the tiniest noise, the scrape of claws on bark. He froze and looked around. Nothing. Yet he had the feeling that he was being watched.

"Barek?" he called, thinking the ravenet might have followed him into the forest. But there was no reply. He was imagining things, he told himself.

Launching himself into the air, he flapped away with heavy wingbeats, his heart colder than the snow below him. A thermal was building over the hills, and he rode it upward, hoping to feel closer to Tarkah's bright spirit in the clean blue of the air. Soaring in circles, he gazed down upon the wooded hills and valleys of his territory. He felt a sudden surge of loathing for it. For *that* he had refused the last thing Tarkah had asked of him, he told himself. For that and his *kora*. But by exposing Tarkah to danger he had forfeited his *kora* anyway. Suddenly he knew what he would do. He would take the weight of his guilt and sorrow on his wings. He would fly west.

After a while, Barek came up to join him.

"I will go to the Raven Mountains," Tok said, abruptly.

With a delighted quork, Barek turned a tight victory roll in the air. The youngster was no mean flyer, Tok noticed. So he flew an inside roll and a back flip, just to show he was up to it himself, though he mocked himself for his vanity.

"I'll go back with you," said Barek, when they flew side by side again. "That is, if you'll accept my company. It will be something to tell my fledglings someday."

"Why?"

"Every bird in the Raven Mountains and even far beyond knows the story of Tok Skydancer, and how he brought the Grey Lords back from the Lost Hills to save ravenkind. You're a hero, my lord."

"Hero, am I?" Tok uttered a croak of bitter laughter. "You might ask the *vóra* who sent you. She could tell you a few less heroic parts of the story. And just call me Tok. For I will be a lord no longer once I leave these hills."

Barek dipped a wing respectfully, but his glance was puzzled.

Putting the sun at their backs, they headed west. After they had been travelling for some time, Tok noticed the hills had grown taller, like standing blue waves. His heart yearned ahead for the sight of high mountains. When the sun stood highest, they went down to rest and forage, but soon rose again. The sky was still clear, and above them Tok saw two angled flights of birds too small to be geese. Ravens.

"Have you ever seen ravens fly like that?" he asked

Barek, pointing with his beak in the direction of the strange flights.

"It happens all the time nowadays," Barek replied. "They're mostly young birds like me. Many are leaving the Raven Mountains. Most stay away, but those who return flock together and fly . . . like that!" he finished, with a contemptuous flip of his wing.

"I've seen many such groups, but when I caught up to one of them I learned nothing," Tok said. "They wouldn't speak to me. But they seem always to be flying north."

"Not this lot, though," said Barek.

"You're right," Tok exclaimed. For the two flights had turned sharply in their direction. "Well, perhaps they have something to say after all."

Wings bent back, the raven formation plunged downward toward them through the air. Tok and Barek held their course, and in moments the strangers were all around them. But there were no words, just a vicious attack, silent except for the whine of wind through flight feathers and the sound of blows. A mass of black bodies drove Tok and Barek apart, and Tok lost sight of the ravenet. Surrounded, he himself was struck and buffeted by many wings. They seemed to be trying to drive him in a direction they had chosen.

Tok did the only thing he could think of. Folding his wings, he dropped like a stone from the sky. By the time his attackers had sorted themselves out, he had gained precious distance. He plunged through the roof of the forest, and dodged some way through the trees before burying himself at last among the thick boughs of a hemlock. Scarcely breathing, he listened to the heavy *whick-whick-whick* of raven wingbeats growing nearer, then passing him. Then he heard his pursuers turn back, baffled.

"We must capture this raven called Tok," he heard one of them croak. "The Master's orders. He said to bring him at all costs."

"Why? What has he done?"

"Who cares?" the other replied. "Orders are orders."

Their voices faded into the distance. Tok sat frozen to his branch while his pursuers searched the forest. At last all sounds died away, but still he sat unmoving as the light faded and the moon rose. He dozed as darkness thickened around him, then roused to find the white raven on the branch beside him.

"Stay here," it said. "For now. They will search again at dawn. They must not find you."

"Who are you?" demanded Tok. "*What* are you?"

"I am Tunavik," it said. "I am the Messenger."

Already the outline of the strange creature was fading, but in the last moment of its going, Tok realized something. From the way it carried itself, the tones of its voice, he knew the white raven must be a female.

At dawn, it was as his strange visitor had said. Suddenly Tok heard wingbeats all around him again, as his pursuers made another search. He kept still, grateful for the warning he had received. If he had taken to the air at first light, he would surely be a prisoner now. But an hour after sunrise, hearing nothing more, he ventured to poke his head out from among the hemlock boughs.

The daytime life of the forest was stirring all around him. He flew down onto the snow and listened for mice stirring in their tunnels under the frozen crust. If only he had a wolf to help him, he thought, remembering his mouse-hunting with the young wolf Timmax. Never had he caught so many mice as then. Still . . . He cocked his head, listening to the scrabble of mouse feet just below the surface. Then he plunged his head and beak into the snow and pulled out a squeaking prize. Hungrily, he pulped it and bolted it down. Only a morsel, but better than nothing.

But he had to find Barek. He flew to the top of a tall evergreen and scanned the sky. No enemy flights, no Barek. He rose into the air and began to quork, flying in low circles over the trees. It wasn't long before he heard an answering kark from below, and Barek rose to meet him. His brownish-black feathers were dishevelled and there was a wobble in his flight.

"You're looking the worse for wear," said Tok. "How badly have they hurt you?"

"Knocked the wind out of me and roughed me up, no more," replied Barek. "But I need a good preening."

"It'll have to wait. We should try to cover a lot of distance fast, in case they come back looking for us."

They circled higher and headed west again, keeping a wary eye out for marauding flights of ravens. But the rest of the journey passed uneventfully. On the fifth morning, Tok saw a familiar three-cornered peak looming in the blue distance and his heart leaped. Mount Storm! There he had fledged, only to be driven away later by false accusations of dishonour. There he had returned with the wolves to clear his name, face death, and in the end be saved by the timely arrival of Selaks and the rest of the pack.

Eagerly, he scanned the sky for dancers. Where were all the ravens? On such a day the sky should be full of shaggy shapes. And what had happened to the mountains? Many of the slopes had been denuded of trees, creating great swaths of open white among the snow-tipped black and grey of the forest. It resembled the Lost Hills where he had first found Selaks and her family, where the Two-Legs had felled most of the trees and dragged them away with their big *grawls*. Things did not look as bad as that here. Not yet.

"You say there are many Two-Legs here now," he said to Barek. "They take the trees?"

"More and more every year. It is good for us, though."

"Good?" Tok repeated. "How could losing the forest be good?"

"Ravens here tell me there are more deer than ever before. Few die of cold now that the winters are warmer, so there are fewer of those carcasses to eat.

But that doesn't matter because the wolves kill the deer easily, and we feed too. And the deer seem to like the open clearings better than deep forest. Easy pickings for the wolves — and us."

"So you have an easy life," Tok said. Yet he hated to think of the snarling roar of the Two-Legs' *grawls* echoing among these mountains, and the crash of falling trees.

"It has been good for me," Barek replied. "But I am a newcomer. Others tell me, though, that things are not as they were. That in summer, death stalks the Raven Mountains. More they will not say."

By midday, the two ravens were battling gusty winds over the Black Ridge. They shot down into the valley below, then angled toward the glade at the foot of Mount Storm where the great Kort Tree stood. Circling once, they descended and lit on a branch. Below them, a small grey wolf lay curled up in the snow. When it saw them it jumped to its feet.

"Would one of you be Lord Tok?" it asked, staring up at them with its ears pricked.

"I am Tok."

At once the wolf threw back its head and howled. From deep in the woods many voices answered. Minutes passed, then a pack came bounding, leaping, flowing among the trees. Deep in Tok's frozen heart, something stirred. He had forgotten the sheer joy and beauty of wolves, running.

Chapter 3

Nothing, not even home, remains the same.

— Wisdom of the Tellers

Tok recognized Selaks at once, though the white she-wolf looked larger and more powerful than he remembered. At her side paced her mate, Durnál, big and black. They were followed by eight more wolves Tok did not know.

"Well met, Skydancer," said Selaks.

"Greetings, *vóra.*"

She showed her fangs, grinning. "There are ravens aplenty here, but since you left none has ever dared to land on my back."

Tok stared bleakly down at her, remembering how often he had ridden on her shoulders. But he did not take up her challenge. "Why didn't you come as you said you would?" he demanded.

She looked puzzled. "It is you who broke your

word," she protested. "You didn't send for us. For ourselves, we have no need to move. There are many deer in these mountains."

"But I *did* send for you!" cried Tok. "Rokah and Parvah, my first-fledged, came here to find you."

The *vóra's* eyes narrowed. "We know nothing of them." And Durnál gave a bark of assent.

Tok felt a pang of fear. Had the biggest and boldest of all his children been harmed by attackers like the ones who had set upon him and Barek? But no, he comforted himself. It wasn't likely. For from the day he fledged, Rokah had been restless, impatient of advice and eager to prove himself. He had grown to be a powerful bird, larger even than Tok, well able to take care of himself and guard Parvah. He would not have fallen easy prey to lesser birds.

Tok gazed down into Selaks's golden eyes, and his heart warmed at the thought that she had not betrayed him after all. Relenting, he fluttered down and lit on her back.

"Oof!" she growled, and Tok felt the warm rumble of her voice even through her thick fur. "I'd forgotten how much you weigh."

"You're big enough to take it," he teased. "Fatter too. You must be eating a lot of deer. And these?" he went on, his eyes moving from one wolf face to another. "Can all of them be your children?" he asked.

"They are," she said. "We are the Mount Storm pack."

"I once told you wolves have large families," said Durnál. "Now you see that I was right."

Selaks pricked her ears and her deep ruff stood up around her face. "These are my first-born — Adánik and Rekshana . . . " she began. A heavyset grey male drew his lips back in a grin that showed his sharp white teeth. A silver-white female, only a little smaller than her brother, stared up at Tok with cold pale eyes.

"This daughter is very like your mother," he said, remembering the proud she-wolf Bervenna who had hated him so passionately.

"Like her in more than looks," said Selaks, with a quelling glance at Rekshana. Then she went on, "And here are their litter-mates, Barator and Araxa." A tall brown wolf returned Tok's gaze curiously, the tip of his tail waving slightly, but the tawny female beside him was biting at a flea on her hind leg and scarcely glanced up.

"And these," Selaks went on, "are my second-born — Kimmik, Fornál, Vikka and Tulik."

Among the younger group of wolves, Tok's eyes were drawn at once to Kimmik, a black female who lifted her head at the sound of her name. She was the image of Durnál, except that she had her mother's golden eyes. Her brother Fornál was lean and shadow-grey. His bright eyes travelled between Selaks and Tok, as if he were trying to solve a puzzle. A chubby brown female and the little grey wolf that had waited below the Kort Tree hung back behind their larger brother and sister, as if afraid to put themselves forward.

"But where are Timmax and Sirva?" Tok asked. "Has something happened to them?"

Selaks shook her head. "Last year my brother took Sirva as his mate and they budded off to form their own family. They and their offspring are now the Black Ridge pack." Turning to Adánik, she added, "Go find them. We have need of a council." At once the big wolf bounded away among the trees.

"The rest of you hunt or sleep as you please," added Durnál. "The *vóra* and I wish to speak with Lord Tok."

The other wolves trotted off, and Barek, ever hungry, flapped hopefully after them.

With a sigh, Tok fluttered down and lit on the snow before the *vór* and *vóra*. "Do not call me Lord Tok," he said. "Not any more. Tarkah is dead, and I have broken ravenlaw. I have abandoned my territory."

"Tarkah dead? No!" rumbled Durnál. For Tok's mate had been his rider, and the two had shared a bond as close as Tok's with Selaks.

"It happened some time ago, in the Moon of the Hunters," Tok replied. "I found only her feathers. Something tore her to pieces."

Selaks whined and nudged Tok gently with her nose. "We grieve with you, Tok," she said softly.

"Her death was my fault," he said bitterly. "Last autumn Tarkah wished to travel, to leave the territory I had claimed. But I refused, telling her it would be *unkora*. Not long after, I left her to pursue strangers invading my territory. I had no right to leave her! And while I was away, something killed her."

"You must not blame yourself, Tok," said the *vór*. "*Numon* is *numon*."

Tok bowed his head. "So you wolves always say. But by my own actions I have destroyed everything that matters to me. I am *unkora*."

The pupils of the *vóra's* eyes widened into pools of darkness. "I cannot believe that, Tok," she said. "*Kora* has ever been your strength, though it has always cost you dear."

"I can tell you only what I feel," replied Tok. "My heart has turned to ice."

Selaks sat down in the snow, curling her brushy tail around her paws. "Forgive me, Tok. We did not know ravenlaw forbids you to leave your territory. Had we not sent for you, you would not have abandoned it. You would have spared yourself that sorrow at least."

"I think I would have left in any case," Tok replied. "Ravenlaw or no ravenlaw, I could not bear to live there now. But tell me why you sent for me."

"I have had a Seeing," said the *vóra*.

"A Snow Seeing? Like Alkara's?" For Alkara, Selaks's grandmother, had been a Snow Seer of the Lanna, the great family of wolves.

"Yes. Though I am not as great a Seer as she was. Only once or twice has it happened to me since we came here. This last time, it was terrifying. I Saw the world burning, Tok. We must leave here soon, or our family will die."

"Leave the Raven Mountains?" Tok was thunder-struck. "But . . . you journeyed so far, through so many dangers, to get here!"

"Still, I think we must leave," said Durnál. "I believe in Selaks's Seeing. And many other things tell me that something is going wrong here, very wrong."

"You mean the tree-cutting? But that's just the Two-Legs. And Barek told me that the deer are more plentiful than ever!"

"Almost too plentiful." Durnál gave a bark of laughter. "A strange wolf am I to think there could be too many deer. But though we wolves do our part by killing what we need to live on, the new growth in the tree-cut lands favours the deer — for now. They swarm like maggots in a carcass."

"But why is that bad?"

"Because it cannot last. Last season was very dry, and the season before that. Not just no rain, but little snow in winter. New growth in the forest is drying up. With so many deer, there soon will not be enough food for them. They are devouring all the browse in the forest. Soon most of them will starve to death."

"All the more food for wolves, then. And ravens!" Tok smacked his beak. It was long since he had tasted the juicy flesh of fresh-killed deer.

"True. But after that, what? First the deer will die

23

off. Then it will be the wolves' turn to die, for we have large families to feed. We cannot wait for that to happen. And now Selaks has Seen the forest consumed by fire. It is only too likely, with the trees so dry. I think we should go. Perhaps farther north we will find a land with more water, more snow. A place where everything does not feel wrong, as it does here."

"I sent for you, Tok, because we want you to guide us again, as you did before," said Selaks. "Without your help we would never have reached these mountains."

Green and gold, two pairs of wolf eyes watched him narrowly.

"North," mused Tok. "I have had strange dreams," he said to them at last. "If they *were* dreams. Twice I have seen a white raven. She said the Change is upon us and told me to go north."

"The Change well describes what is happening here," said Durnál.

"But . . . a white raven?" said Selaks. "Is there such a thing?"

"Not that I have ever seen before. But this one orders me to go north."

"Then come with us!" With an eager yelp, Selaks bounced to her feet.

"But your territory, Tok," said Durnál soberly. "Could you not return to it, become a lord again and restore your *kora?*"

"Going back would not change the fact that I have broken the law," said Tok. "But even were I to return, it seems to me that the Change is happening there too. Little rain. Scant snow. Burning summers with low water and poor forage. But what causes these things?"

"We do not know," said Selaks. "Only that we must leave."

"We mean to try to reach the Cold Forest, far to the north where I was born," added Durnál. "There is much game there, enough for many wolf families. But I do not know the way from here to there."

"Help us, Tok," pleaded Selaks.

Tok gazed from one eager face to the other. "I will," he promised.

Selaks gave a cry of triumph, and from the forest behind them came answering voices.

Durnál pricked up his ears. "The Black Ridge pack," he said. "It is time for council."

Tok stared hard at the big brindled wolf that came bounding through the trees with three others running at its heels. Then, "Timmax!" he cried.

The wolf ran out his tongue, laughing. "It's Tok Skydancer, isn't it?" he demanded. "I'd know your quork anywhere!"

"And this is your pack, you old mouse-hunter!"

Timmax grinned. "Sirva you already know," he said, turning toward his mate. She, too, had changed, thought Tok. Gone was the timid little brownish wolf who had slunk at the back of the pack. Now her fur glistened and she held her plumy tail proudly. Though he noticed she kept close to her mate, and well away from Selaks.

"Greetings, Tok," said Sirva. "These are our first-born, Taxin and Minnek," she added proudly. The two young wolves gazed up at Tok, their eyes bright with curiosity. Tok noticed that Selaks's eyes rested on Taxin with a faraway expression in them. And no wonder, he thought, for Timmax's big son with the cloud-and-shadow coat was the image of Selaks's father, Adanax. He had been *vór* of the Lost Hills pack, and she had loved him with all her heart.

The rest of the Mount Storm wolves joined them. Adánik and the others of Selaks's family gave nose licks and shoulder bunts to their Black Ridge cousins, while the senior wolves exchanged ritual sniffs. Then they all gathered in a rough circle, some sitting, some standing.

Durnál looked around the circle. "I have called a council, Timmax, because Selaks has had a Seeing that affects the future of all of us," he said. "That is why we have summoned Tok from the eastern hills. We have asked him to guide us once more, and he has agreed."

"Guide you where?" demanded Timmax. "Where are you going? What has Selaks Seen?"

"Death and destruction," replied Selaks. "The world in flames. My heart tells me that this Seeing means we must leave the Raven Mountains. We may all die if we don't."

"Leave?" Timmax jumped to his feet. "Leave the Raven Mountains? Never! This land is a paradise for wolves, just as Tok promised us long ago. Why, the hills swarm with deer — "

"You are right, Timmax," Durnál cut in. "But you must have seen how they are destroying the forest. Soon there will be no food left, and most of them will die. What then?"

"And what about the danger of fire in this dry forest?" put in Selaks. "You can see for yourself how little snow there is this winter, Timmax. What if next summer is as hot as the last ones have been?"

Timmax shook his ears. "What then? What if? Why, there was fire on the Black Ridge last summer, but it was no threat to us. Bones! I say the two of you are getting old and cautious," he teased. "You worry too much. If the summer is bad, if the deer die, then there will be plenty of time to act."

Sirva glanced at him fondly. "I think as my *vór* does," she said. "He and I suffered much on our journey here from the Lost Hills. This land is our home now. I will not leave it!"

"Nor I! Nor I!" chorused Taxin and Minnek.

"So the Black Ridge pack stays," said Timmax. "I'll be happy to take over your territory, Durnál."

"Then the Mount Storm pack goes north alone," announced Selaks, getting to her feet.

At this, her big grey son Adánik spoke. "Not I, *vóra*. I agree with *Vór* Timmax. You and my father are too cautious. I am not afraid of your Seeing. There is no need to leave these mountains we love."

Araxa, his younger sister, sidled over to him. "I, too, will stay," she said. "If Vór Timmax will accept us. I would not want to hunt alone."

Timmax grinned, showing his sharp teeth. "Stay, and welcome," he said.

"And the rest of you?" Durnál turned toward his other children. They crowded around him, biting his muzzle and rolling around his feet like a pack of pups.

"I follow you anywhere, my vór." Rekshana's pale eyes gleamed in her white face.

"And I," rumbled Barator, in a voice almost as deep as his father's.

"And I! And I! And I!" yelped Fornál, Kimmik and Vikka. Even Tulik, who seemed to fear the rest of them, added his voice.

Durnál raised his muzzle and howled. Selaks chimed in, then Timmax and Sirva and the rest of the two packs lifted their voices one by one. Each wolf sang its own song, yet all were part of the great harmony of the pack that echoed among the mountains.

Tok shivered, and his feathers prickled in delight. It was long since he had heard wolf music, and he remembered how he had first heard of creatures called the Singers, and believed them to be birds, only to discover that they were wolves, the Grey Lords of the Tellers' tales. As the last notes died away down the long valley below Mount Storm, Selaks and Timmax stared gravely into each other's eyes.

"Farewell, sister," said Timmax. "Perhaps we will meet again."

"Surely," replied Selaks. "If not in this world, then on the Wolf Trail among the stars. Good hunting, brother."

Now Adánik and Araxa pranced around her and Durnál, biting their muzzles and rubbing against them one last time.

"Change your minds, my son, my daughter," pleaded Selaks. "Come with us!"

Adánik leaned against her for a moment, then leaped gaily away. "No, my *vóra*. It's time and past time I chose my own trail." Araxa said nothing, but she followed her older brother. The two of them trotted after Timmax as the Black Ridge pack bounded away in the gathering dusk. Selaks watched them out of sight, then lifted her head and howled her loss.

Chapter 4

In the First Time, the Maker created just one being.
But the world was too lonely. So from the One,
Skyah made all the creatures of the land,
the air and the waters. That is why,
though we are many, we are also One.

— from "The Myth of the One,"
Tales of the Tellers

"Now that the wolves have decided, the ravens must be told. I need a Kort," Tok told Selaks.

The wolves had hunted down a deer. Having gorged themselves, they lay about in the snow, dozing or gnawing bones. Tok had fed with them, and Barek and several other ravens were now stripping flesh from the almost-bare carcass.

Selaks licked blood from her muzzle with a long pink tongue. "There are fewer ravens here now than there used to be," she said.

"Though still enough to plague us at our kills," put in Durnál, baring his teeth in a grin.

Heavy with meat, Tok flapped over to the feasting ravens. "I am Tok, son of Rokan," he told them. "I wish to summon a Kort."

"Why should we care who you are?" asked one of the group, bolting a gobbet of juicy red flesh. "And what's a Kort?"

But a larger bird bowed to Tok. "I am honoured, my lord," he said. Then he turned and gave the other bird a buffet with his wing. "Ignoramus!" he quorked. "This is Lord Tok, the hero who brought the wolves to the Raven Mountains. Thanks to him and to them, we all live well."

"Many of the wolves are going to leave," said Tok. "At least, some are. Can you summon a Kort? For tomorrow, when the sun is at its highest?"

"There has been no Kort for many a season now," the other replied. "But I can try. I know a few lords and ladies, and they will know others. Come on," he added, knocking another bird off its perch on the deer's rib cage. "You've feasted enough. If the wolves are leaving, that's something all ravens should know."

"I'll help spread the word," offered Barek.

The three of them lifted off, and Tok returned to the wolves.

Selaks's gaze was stern. "Whatever the ravens say, Tok, this pack is leaving the Raven Mountains. And soon."

"Won't you wait for the snow to melt?" countered Tok. "Travel will be much easier for you then."

The white wolf, Rekshana, had pricked up her ears, and now gave a bark of amusement. "How little you know of wolves," she sneered. "The Lanna can travel in any conditions."

Selaks turned, wrinkling her muzzle in a warning snarl. "It is not for you, daughter, to give Lord Tok lessons in wolf lore. He knows more than you think."

Rekshana flattened her ears and lowered her head. "Yes, my *vóra*," she said submissively. But Tok saw a cold glint in her pale grey eyes.

"The answer to your question is no, Tok," Selaks went on. "We must leave now. We will wait for your Kort, but no longer."

That night, Tok found a roost near the Kort Tree. He waited in vain for a noisy horde of ravens to flock in for gossip and stories and companionship, but only a few birds arrived. He told them of the Kort he had called for the next day, and of the decision of the wolves. The more who know, the better, he thought, listening to them discussing the news.

Just as dark fell, a latecomer swooped in. Landing clumsily near Tok, it brushed him with its wingtip. "Excuse me, my lord," it muttered, stepping quickly away to the end of the branch.

"Come closer," invited Tok. "I have news to tell."

"I cannot," replied the other. "I am Shunned."

At that, the other birds set up a clatter and edged

to the farthest places in the roost.

"Shunned?" echoed Tok. "What is that?"

"It is the Death," hissed one of the other birds. "Those who have it must stay apart."

"It is true I had the Death," croaked the shunned one. "But I survived. No one dies the Death in winter. You all know that! So I cannot harm you now."

"I have heard that death stalks the Raven Mountains in the summer," said Tok, remembering the words of Barek. "But what does that mean?"

"The Death is a terrible sickness," said the shunned one. "I know. I had it. One day my wings began to tremble, and I fell from the sky. My body shook and I panted with fever. My eyes blurred, and I suffered burning pain. I found a pond where I could at least drink, and somehow I survived. But many do not. In the first year of the Death, the ground was black with bodies."

The other birds croaked and karked their agreement.

Tok shuddered. So that was why the skies above the Raven Mountains were empty of ravens, and why there was no Kort! He put his head under his wing, but it was long before he slept.

Before leaving the roost at dawn, he asked after his mother. None of the birds knew Karah, but they told him of other roosts where birds might remember her. But at each the awakening birds knew nothing.

"A Teller?" asked one. "It is long since I have heard

a Teller. What good are tales anyway? They cannot save you from the Death."

But they can teach you to summon your *kora* to face it, thought Tok, though he said nothing.

Still well fed from the wolves' kill, he felt no need to forage. Instead he searched out his parents' old territory on the slopes of Mount Storm. Here, at the top of a tall pine, beneath a looming cliff, Karah and Rokan, his father, had nested. Here he himself had fledged. And then, after his father's murder, his mother had taken a new mate, Lord Groh, who became Tok's bitter enemy. In the end, Groh's crimes had been discovered, and the Kort had exiled him forever from the Raven Mountains. And Karah had become a Teller, a guardian of raven traditions.

A few sticks from the old nest still clung among the branches, and Tok perched there long, remembering. Suddenly he heard the swish of raven wings, then a voice shrieked, "Rokan!" and Karah swooped past him. She lit on a branch below and peered up at him. "Rokan?" she said, less certainly. Then, "No, it cannot be. I know that, but . . . "

"It's Tok, mother."

She stared at him. "You are the image of your father," she said at last, settling her feathers. She was still handsome, Tok thought, though he noticed grey feathers in her wings.

"I've been looking for you," he told her. "But nobody knew where to find you."

"No one cares for Tellers," she replied. "Not anymore. Our old territory has remained empty — the Death has seen to that. So I make my home here, remembering." She cocked her head, observing him closely, then, "But what are you doing here, Tok? Did you and Tarkah not find a territory after all? I see sorrow in you — you are not as you were."

"Tarkah is dead," said Tok, feeling the splinter of ice stab his heart as it always did when he thought of her.

Karah roused her feathers in surprise. "Young Tarkah dead? But how?" She listened while he told her what had happened.

"And so it is my fault she was killed," Tok finished. "And I have abandoned my territory."

There was a long silence. Then, "What you have done is against ravenlaw," Karah said slowly. "You were wrong to leave your mate defenceless against harm. And no lord may abandon his territory. Any Kort would find you guilty. But I would not have you despair, my son."

"Despair and I are comrades now," replied Tok. "I once thought I could not exist without *kora*. Yet somehow I go on living." He gave a bitter quork of laughter.

"You return to us in an evil time," his mother said. "Mysterious cruel deaths happen here too. And nest-breakings. The driving of lords and ladies from their territories. We call these things the Terror."

"The Terror? I have heard only of the Death."

"That is part of it, but not all. The Death is a sickness, dreadful but not cruel. But all fear it, and with the dread of the Terror it is too much. Ravens are fleeing these mountains."

Tok's feathers prickled. "They travel in angled flights like geese?" he demanded.

"No, not those who flee. Those who fly so are the raiders, the despoilers. They acknowledge no *kora*, no Kort, no traditions of ravenkind. But it is said — " Here Karah paused and glanced around, as if afraid that the very trees had ears. "It is said that they obey one master, who calls himself the Overlord."

Tok told Karah of the attack on him and Barek during their flight westward, and how he had overhead two birds speak of a master.

She nodded. "The marauders rule the skies now. Nothing moves without their knowledge. Their sheer numbers let them do as they please. Sometimes they do no worse than swoop down and drive other ravens from kills, picking the bones bare before travelling on. But other times they attack to kill. For no reason. A raven need not have done anything more than skydance to be destroyed. No one knows where or when the attackers will appear. This is the Terror."

They sat together in silence, looking out across the mountains. Then, "I have more bad news," Tok confessed. "The wolves have summoned me here because they are leaving the Raven Mountains. At least, some of them are. And he told her of the wolves' fear of the

Change and his own calling of the Kort.

"It will be the end for us, if the wolves go," Karah said. "Already we are under siege by the raiders. This will be the final feather to fall."

"I have promised to go with them," said Tok, "to help them find a new home. I too have had warnings about the Change — visions of a white raven called Tunavik. She tells me to go north."

"A white raven!" Karah's voice was sharp with interest.

"Yes. A strange creature with eyes that are un-raven. She calls herself the Messenger."

"I know a Telling about such a white raven," said Karah. "It has to do with the Later Time, after Skyah created many animals. Because all had come from the One, many creatures still understood each other, as we and the wolves do to this day. And the white raven was ever the Messenger between Skyah's creatures."

"But could such things happen now?" asked Tok.

Karah half-spread her wings. "I do not know. The world has changed much since the Later Time."

"Will you come with me when I leave with the wolves, Mother?" asked Tok.

Karah's eyes brightened. "Gladly, if you will have me. For here there is nothing but sorrow and death."

"We must go to the Kort . . . " began Tok. Then he froze, gazing up at the sky. High above, three angled flights of ravens were heading south over the Raven Mountains.

When the sun stood high in the sky, they made their way to the Kort Tree. Even knowing what he did about the Terror and the Death, Tok was amazed to see how few lords and ladies had answered his call. Only a few noble pairs perched in the branches of the great Kort Tree. They scanned the skies as if afraid that some punishment would fall on them. And where were the masses of young ravenets who had once bent the branches of the lesser trees that lined the glade? Only Barek and a few others perched there now. The rest must have joined the Overlord, Tok told himself. Either that, or they were dead.

A large, handsome ravenlord unknown to Tok flew to perch on the Speaker's Branch. "I am Gloran, son of Glordak. My mate and I have held territory here the longest," he announced. "Does anyone contest my right to be Speaker of this Kort?" After stirrings and head shakings among the lords and ladies, he went on. "It is Tok, son of Rokan, who has summoned us."

"Lord Tok, the hero, the wolf rider!" someone shouted and there was an outburst of excited quorking and the rattle of claws on branches as the news flew around the glade.

When the noise died down, Gloran bowed gravely to Tok. "Speak now, my lord," he said. With a flap of his wings, Tok joined him on the branch. "I have heard about the evils you are suffering, the Terror and the Death," he said, turning to meet the gaze of the lords and ladies. "Now I must tell you that the wolves have met in council. The Mount Storm pack is leaving these mountains."

There was a chorus of karks and quorks from the assembled ravens.

"Leaving? But why?" demanded Lord Gloran.

"They fear the Change — the warm winters we have now, the burning summers. Their *vóra*, Selaks, has had a Seeing in which the forests are destroyed by fire. She is leading her pack northward to escape this doom."

There were more cries of protest but Tok raised his voice over the clamour. "Listen! All is not lost! The Black Ridge pack has chosen to remain. In time, their numbers will replace the Mount Storm pack."

"There are fewer ravens to go hungry now," Lord Gloran said, when the clamour had died down a little. "But even so, some of us will surely starve next winter."

"The wolves will not wait," Tok warned the assembled ravens. "You must choose to stay or to go."

Another babble of anguished voices.

"Go? Leave our territories? Break ravenlaw?"

"*Unkora! Unkora!*"

Tok raised his voice above the protests. "Know that I myself have faced this decision, though for other reasons. I have left my territory. I am a lord no longer."

A shocked hush fell over the glade and the

assembled ravens stared at him.

"Tok the hero *unkora?* A lord no longer?" protested a solitary voice.

Gloran gazed long at Tok. Then he said soberly, "You must have had reasons to do as you did. We cannot judge you, for you are not one of us. But surely, Tok, there will already be ravens in the north. If we go there we will be lawbreakers, outlanders. We will never hold territory again."

Tok spoke into the silence. "Ravens, you must face this doom. Stay and endure the Change, the Terror and the Death, or go north with the pack."

"Pluck your twigs," announced Gloran at last. "We will decide the matter in the raven way." When all in the Kort Tree had twigs, he went on. "Those who would go, drop your twigs. Those who would stay, keep them."

Only his twig and one or two others dropped to the snow.

"The Kort has chosen to remain," said Gloran. "That decision binds all lords and ladies. Any ravenets or birds without territory are free to do as they please."

Then, just as the lords and ladies began to wing away, a feathered horde broke from the concealing woods and fell upon them.

"Raiders!" croaked Gloran, as he disappeared under a mob of attackers. "Flee for your lives!" The rest of the Kort scattered, with the enemy in pursuit.

Chapter 5

*The Terror went beyond fear. It was
the destruction of hope.*

— from The Annals of the Kort

"Stay out of sight!" Tok shouted to Karah, who shrank
back into the dense foliage near the trunk of the tree
she had perched in. He shot into the air and plunged
headlong into the fight. The attackers had Gloran
down, pummelling him with their wings and hacking at
him with their beaks. Tok struck left and right, slashing
necks and wings with his claws. Feathers showered into
the air, and the attackers turned on him.

"Back against the Kort Tree!" Tok yelled at Gloran.
"We'll stand them off there!" With powerful flaps of
their wings, he and the Speaker broke through the
ring of their attackers. Placing their backs to the
broad trunk of the Kort Tree, they screamed defiance,
stabbing with their beaks and lashing out with their

claws. But the attackers were many. Then, just as it seemed that they would surely be overwhelmed, there came from far above a long drawn-out scream, shrill as an eagle's. At once the attack broke off, and the marauders lifted away over the trees.

Tok and Gloran watched them go, shaking out their battered feathers.

"My thanks," said the Speaker. "They had me, and without you it would have been the end. The raiders do not always kill, but this time they meant to. Come quickly, for I must find my mate. Kordah, my lady, stayed with our eggs. May Skyah have kept her from harm!"

High above them, the attackers were re-forming, this time heading north.

"It is always like this," said Gloran, as they headed west with rapid wingbeats. "The raiders attack us, steal our food, smash our nests. Even kill our young if they can, the brutes. But they never stay."

"The Terror," said Tok. "But why?"

"No one knows. Look, here is my territory."

Tok saw the rugged mass of a nest in the top of a lofty fir. A dishevelled female raven perched on the edge of it. "Gone, all gone. Smashed, destroyed," she croaked when she saw them. And Tok could see that the nest was stained with patches of yellow and white.

"Kordah!" cried Gloran, landing beside her and trying to smooth her feathers. "Did they hurt you?"

"Me? Not much. But what does that matter?" she

said. "They found me — six of them. Beat me and drove me off the nest. Then they . . . they . . . " She broke off.

"Smashed our eggs!" cried Gloran.

Kordah bowed her head. "Worse," she whispered. "They cracked them and they . . . ate them!"

Tok shuddered. Ravens never ate the eggs of their own kind, any more than they would pick the bones of a dead raven. It was unthinkable! For the first time he fully felt the force of the Terror. It was worse than fear. It was a sickness in the heart.

"Listen," said Gloran. From far and near over the slopes of Mount Storm came the sound of raven voices, grieving. "It must have been very bad this time," he went on, after a moment. "The attacks are becoming more vicious."

"Someone is trying to destroy ravenkind," said Tok. "Or at least those of us who live in the Raven Mountains."

"They say it is the Overlord who commands the Terror," replied Gloran. "Though no one knows who he is, or why he attacks us."

"The attackers are well organized," Tok mused. "Did you see how they broke off the fight when someone screamed from above?" He gazed at Gloran and Kordah. "What will you do now?" he asked.

Gloran turned to his mate. "The Kort voted to stay, even though Tok says many of the wolves are leaving the Raven Mountains."

Kordah trembled. "I will not stay, Kort or no Kort. I

cannot," she said. "What use to start over here? The evil ones will only find us again."

"The vote of the Kort is binding on us all," said Gloran. "And there will never be another Kort. To gather in numbers is too risky now." He gazed into the distance, pondering. Then he drew himself up and said, "I know all the lords and ladies, every one of them. I am the Speaker of the last Kort of these mountains. I will take it upon my *kora* to release them from the votes they made, if they so desire. I will find them all, and tell them so."

"And you?" asked Tok. "What will *you* do?"

Gloran stropped his beak nervously on the branch he sat on. "I, the last Speaker, will become a law-breaker," he replied at last. "My mate has spoken, and she is right. I will leave my territory."

Tok's heart went out to him. "It is a bitter decision," he said. "One I had to make myself. *Kora* dies, but somehow one survives."

Gloran met his gaze. "You offer hard comfort," he said, spreading his wings.

"I can take Kordah to my mother, near the Kort Tree," offered Tok. "I must meet with the wolves."

"I will find you there," said Gloran as he lifted off. From the measured beat of his wings Tok could read the heaviness of his heart.

"My mate is noble," said Kordah. "It is a terrible thing for him to go against the ruling of the Kort and to break the law."

"I understand," said Tok. "Only too well." Then, half to himself he added, with a shiver, "For if we break with our traditions, who are we?"

They found Karah with Selaks and her wolves at the foot of the Kort Tree. Tok could see from their bright eyes and waving tails that the pack was excited.

"Your mother had the good sense to fly to us when she was attacked," said Selaks. "Some of the raiders came too close, so we taught them to respect wolf jaws," she added, grinning. "I'm still spitting out tail feathers!"

"And I nipped a wingtip off one of them," boasted her big son, Barator.

"As for me, I have found myself a new companion," said Durnál. Turning his head, he nudged Karah, who was perched on his back with her claws sunk deep in his mane. Then, with a quick glance at Tok he added, "Not that I will ever forget my first rider, your brave Tarkah."

Tok told the *vór* and *vóra* of the Kort's decision. "But perhaps this attack will make some of them change their minds," he went on. "Gloran has gone to ask."

"Let them follow us, then," said Selaks. "We can wait for no more raven meetings."

Once more the pack gathered around their leaders, rubbing against them and mouthing their muzzles in a demonstration of love and loyalty. Then, lifting their heads, they began to sing. Even Tok could tell it was a song of leaving, but also of joy. As they moved off, an answering song rose from the Black Ridge.

Selaks turned her head, listening. "Farewell, Timmax," she growled under her breath. Then she plunged ahead down the slope of the mountain.

For a time they followed well-marked trails through the forest, then emerged into the open where a great swath of trees had been shorn from the mountainside. Tok mounted into the air, looking eagerly for other ravens. At last, far to the west, he saw shaggy shapes approaching and flew to meet them.

"Barek! Gloran!" he cried. There were others too, a small group of ravens and ravenets he did not know.

"These are all who would come," said Gloran, wheeling to meet him. "But who — "

He broke off as a big, glossy raven swept up on powerful wings, carved an inside back circle in the air and pulled up wingtip to wingtip with Tok.

Tok stared wildly at the familiar shape. Something about the beauty of the newcomer, the easy grace of its movements . . . Then, "Rokah!" he cried joyously. "Rokah, my son!"

Chapter 6

Old griefs make for dubious beginnings.

— Raven proverb

Three days later, the wolves reached the top of the pass that led north from the Raven Mountains. Panting, they threw themselves down. They had fed well before they began their climb, and soon they were dozing in the afternoon sun. Even here, high among the peaks, the sun felt warm and the snow was crusted from thawing and refreezing. Gloran and the other ravens perched among the rocks, resting and preening. But Tok took to his wings and circled upward. Below him and to the south, the Raven Mountains rolled away, range on range, blue on blue. In the farthest distance rose the three-cornered peak of Mount Storm. Tok felt a pang in his heart. So much of his life's story had played out on its slopes. Now he would never see it again.

Another raven was rising to join him. Rokah, he thought. Surely it was Skyah's gift that this boldest of all his offspring should join him and the wolves on their journey. He noticed a warmth in his heart that he had not felt since Tarkah died.

"Will you really leave these mountains forever?" his son asked, as they angled their wings against the wind.

"I have promised the wolves that I would help them reach the Cold Forest," replied Tok. "And as I told you, I have abandoned my territory."

Rokah fixed his gleaming amber eyes on Tok. "A desperate thing for a ravenlord to do, surely?" he asked. "It is hard to believe that you, the great Lord Tok, could be so *unkora*. And to lead the others to do the same."

"I lead no one!" Tok replied sharply. "Gloran and the rest chose for themselves. It is almost certain death to remain in the Raven Mountains now. As for me, I left my territory because Selaks summoned me. With your mother dead, I could not bear to stay there. Not even for *kora*."

"A strange event, my mother's death. As you tell it."

"So it was. No enemy I can imagine would do such a thing." Bitterness welled up in Tok's throat. "And I blame myself. If only I had agreed to go journeying when she asked me to. If only I had not left her to face death alone!"

"Indeed." Rokah's tone was cold, and Tok glanced at him in surprise. But Rokah was staring into the distance.

After a moment Rokah went on. "Karah said you have seen a white raven. Tell me more about that."

"I know nothing more, really. Twice I have seen her, and once she saved me from the followers of the Overlord. Both times she told me to go north."

Rokah looked thoughtful. But after a moment he shot away across the wind. Rolling on his back, he flew that way for a moment, then righted himself with a flip of one wing, challenging Tok to follow. The sun warm on their feathers, the two of them tumbled in the sky. It was almost like having Tarkah back, Tok thought wistfully.

But Rokah was not finished talking. "What do you know about the Overlord?" he asked, when they were flying side by side again.

"What do *you* know?" countered Tok. "And where have you been all this time? Why didn't you deliver my message to Selaks?" For the latter question had troubled him.

"Parvah and I couldn't find Mount Storm or the *vóra*," said Rokah. "We must have flown too far south after we left your territory. Then she and I parted, and I have not seen her since. I have only just arrived in the Raven Mountains."

Tok was puzzled. The peak of Mount Storm was a landmark that could be seen for many thousands of wingbeats. How could keen-eyed ravens have missed it?

But Rokah was speaking again. "As to the Overlord," he said, "I have heard only that he is a powerful leader. His followers obey him without question and work together for their common good."

"To plunder and murder!" snapped Tok. Then he checked himself. Surely Rokah, who had only just arrived in the Raven Mountains, knew little of the Terror. How could he understand the evil done by the Overlord? In a calmer tone he went on, "That's another reason I want to go north. To find the Overlord. His flights always come from that direction and return there. So he, too, must be in the north."

"It could be dangerous," said Rokah, glancing at him. "It is said that none who seek the Overlord unasked return to tell the tale."

"Then I must accept the danger," said Tok. "But enough of this. Let's stretch our wings."

By the time they descended, the wolves were stirring. Tok flew to Selaks, who stood nose into the wind, as if savouring the scents of the land they were leaving.

"I am saying farewell to the land you led us to, Tok," she said, as he settled on her back. "It was indeed everything you promised it would be long ago."

"But it is not as it once was," he replied. "Even in a few days I have been able to see that. The Change has come upon it quickly."

"May we find a safe haven in the Cold Forest," said Durnál, who had come to stand beside them. "Meanwhile, should we not discuss where we are going? Your ravens do not have the same cares that we do, Tok, and may not want to follow us so far."

"They are not 'my' ravens," protested Tok. "If they follow anyone, it's Gloran, who was their Speaker."

"If you say so," replied Durnál, but there was a glint of mockery in his green eyes.

At the *vór's* summons, the pack gathered around them, while the ravens flew and hopped onto nearby rocks.

"We have come this far," Durnál said to them all, "but there is still time for you ravens to turn back. Our plan is to seek the Cold Forest far to the north. But there may be many dangers that lie between here and there."

"Raven fears are different from wolf fears," said Tok. "You fear fire. We seek safety from the Death that stalks these mountains, and also from the Terror of the Overlord." He turned his gaze from one pair of raven eyes to the next. "But I want you to understand that on this journey we are going toward danger rather than away from it."

There was an uneasy stirring among the ravens. "You mean," said Gloran, "that the wolves are going north, and that is where the followers of the Overlord come from."

"That is so," said Tok. "My way lies north with the

wolves, for I have promised to help them. But my reason for going has become more than that. As some of you already know, I have seen a white raven who warns me of the Change and bids me to go north. But I have also seen with my own eyes the Terror of the Overlord, and how he threatens the raven way. I am alone now, without mate or territory, a lord no longer. Someone must find this Overlord and confront him. I am going to try to do it."

There was an outburst of karks and quorks.

"Why you?"

"Why stir up trouble? All we want is peace."

"I wouldn't have come if I'd thought it would be more dangerous than staying!"

Tok flapped his wings and shouted to make himself heard over the hubbub. "That's exactly why I am telling you now what I plan to do. You are free to come with me or go back now or whenever you please."

Several birds looked sullenly back at the Raven Mountains, but none flew away.

"Very well, then," said Durnál. "We go together — for now. But so far we have moved only by day, Tok. As you know, we wolves often travel and hunt at night as well. When the ravens roost, how will they find us again?"

At that, Karah spoke up. "Easily, vór. Tok or I can stay with you while others roost. I am not afraid of night journeys. In the morning we can soar to show the others the way."

"Good!" said Selaks. "Let us go." Turning, she followed the trail among the rocks until she came to the place where her grandmother, the *vóra* Alkara, had died. She put her nose to the snow and snuffed, as though seeking *skiffet*. There was no vestige of bone or fur, just the voice of the wind singing among the crags that loomed above.

"I still miss Alkara's wisdom, Tok," said Selaks after a moment. "I am not as great a Seer as she was." Then she faced north, where the trail wound down through tumbled scree to the first thin fringe of forest far below. "But I must trust the Seeing I have been granted. May it truly come from the Lanna, and may they protect us on our journey."

Tok felt her shoulder muscles bunch under his claws, then she bounded forward, with the pack streaming after her. Above them, the other ravens lifted into the air and slid down the wind toward the valley below.

It took the wolves two days to descend from the heights, and they found little game along the way. By the time they reached the floor of the valley, both wolves and ravens were hungry.

"We must keep tight control, Selaks," warned Durnál. "We are not far from the dwelling of the Two-Legs. Remember how it was before."

Selaks's eyes were bright with sorrow. Tok knew she was remembering how Malik, her favourite brother, had attacked the animals of the Two-Legs only to be killed himself by their firesticks. She turned her fierce golden gaze on the pack. "You have heard your *vór*," she said sternly. "Great evil comes to wolves in this valley. Hungry or not hungry, we must pass far along it before we can hunt. Keep away from the beasts of the cursed Two-Legs!"

The young wolves looked puzzled, but chorused their obedience.

They dozed in the woods until dusk, then set off under a moon veiled in low cloud. Light snow began to fall, and the wolves rolled in it and licked at the snowflakes. Near the middle of the night, they passed the dwellings of the Two-Legs, and the wolves' noses twitched at the meat smell of the beasts they kept in fields nearby. But Durnál and Selaks picked up the pace, and the pack soon left the danger behind. Well before dawn, they curled up to sleep in thick woods on the west side of the valley.

Tok flapped onto a low branch and allowed himself to doze off. He was wakened by a gentle shaking of the branch. His eyes flew open and he saw that Durnál had reared up and was tugging the end of it with his teeth. Tok dropped down onto the *vór's* back, and without a word they set off toward the edge of the trees. Durnál trod silently, careful not to rouse the sleeping pack. As they came out into the fields, Tok saw clearly before them a set of tracks leading back the way they had come. Tracks with one three-toed forepaw, that could only be left by the *vóra* who had long ago lost one toe in a trap.

"Selaks!" he said into Durnál's ear.

"I woke and found her gone," the *vór* rumbled. "I feared something like this!"

"She would dare to attack the beasts of the Two-Legs? After all she said?"

"Their beasts, no. But she still broods over her brother. She has not forgotten Malik's death here." Durnál lengthened his stride, flowing over the snow like a shadow.

Tok lifted off, peering ahead in the half-light. His heart sickened as he saw that the tracks led straight toward the roost of the Two-Legs. He, too, knew the depth of Selaks's grief for her brother. Would it drive her to attack the Two-Legs, to endanger her life and her pack? He swooped toward the roost. He had to get there fast, he thought, lest Durnál in his fear for Selaks get into trouble himself.

The tracks veered toward a second, larger structure that his ears told him held beasts inside. There was a disturbance in the snow, as if a struggle had taken place right in front of it. Then more tracks led away. But they were no longer clear. Something half-obscured them, and the lightly sifting snow was rapidly filling them in. The tracks led toward the east wall of the valley, but after a time he lost them and turned back to find Durnál.

"She went there, but she has gone on to the east woods," Tok cried, wheeling over the *vór's* head. "The snow is wiping out her tracks, so the Two-Legs won't be able to follow her. Come, we must return to the pack. You must not leave them alone. Selaks knows where to find us."

Reluctantly the *vór* turned back, and they retraced the way they had come. Then as dawn broke and the clouds lifted, they saw a figure bounding across the valley, white against the whiter snow.

"Selaks!" growled Durnál, as she came up to them, panting from her long run. "How dare you endanger us all!"

Never had Tok heard the *vór* use such a tone to his mate.

Her eyes flashed defiance. "Can you not trust me?" she snapped. "I did what I had to do!" Then her tail drooped, and she lowered her head. "I Saw, Durnál. When the snow came last night. I Saw Malik!"

Chapter 7

Shall I forget you, blood of my own blood?
Through snow and shadow,
and the long trail's running
I swear I will not forget you!

— from "Selaks's Vow," Songs of the Lanna

"Malik is dead, Selaks," said Tok. "I saw him die!"

"Dead indeed!" cried Selaks. "But I Saw . . . I Saw a horror." She closed her eyes for a moment, as if trying to block out an unbearable sight. Then, in a lower voice she went on, "His *hide*, Durnál! The Two-Legs had his hide fastened to the side of their beast-shelter."

The *vór's* eyes widened. Then he stepped forward and nuzzled her.

Trembling, she pressed against his flank. "*That* is what I went for," she went on. "To rescue the thing-that-was-Malik, and keep it from the Two-Legs. I tore it down and dragged it into the east woods. Then I ripped it to shreds and buried it in snow. I *had* to do it, Durnál. I had to! I could not leave him so!"

"You did well, my *vóra*." Durnál's tone was gentle. "Now come, we must find the pack."

The rest of that day they travelled fast up the valley, trying to put as much distance as they could between themselves and the Two-Legs. The young wolves, ravenous now, grumbled as they ran.

Tok took to the air, with Rokah and Gloran behind him. "There used to be elk in this valley," he told them. "We must find them. Then all of us can eat."

But although the three of them quartered the north end of the valley and the lower slopes of the mountains, they found no elk. Then as they passed over a long ridge they saw a single raven flapping toward them.

"None of ours," said Gloran.

The four of them came together, circling in midair. The strange raven eyed them half fearfully, half hopefully. Something about its looks pricked Tok's memory. Its small size and rumpled feathers; its sharp eyes and eager gaze.

"Do you serve the Overlord?" it demanded, and its voice told Tok that it was a female. She swooped impertinently close, peering at him. Then, "Tok!" she cried. "Can it really be you?"

For a moment, Tok hesitated. Then, "Is it . . . Brekka?" he asked.

"It *is* you!" The little female turned a delighted somersault in the air.

"But . . . how did you get here?" he asked. "I last saw you many seasons ago, far west of these mountains, on the Hills of Plenty."

"The Hills of Shame, you mean, where ravens feast on the waste of the Two-Legs," she replied. "I could not stand the life there anymore, so I left. I have been in this valley nearly a year. I tried to cross the mountains to the south, but time and again the followers of the Overlord drove me back. But you — what are you doing here?"

"I have left the Raven Mountains. I am travelling with wolves and it is long since they made a kill. Have you seen elk or other game?"

"Elk? I do not know what that is," she replied. "Deer there are. A large herd of them are browsing in the woods."

"Show us the way," said Tok, "and we all will feast."

With a flip of her wings, she wheeled west.

The deer were browsing in a frozen-over cedar swamp, well screened by the trees. Tok and Brekka perched above them while Rokah and Gloran flew over the ridge to bring the wolves and the other ravens.

"I found the Grey Lords after all," Tok told her.

"So did I."

"You? But how?"

"I took care of Old Craal for two moons after you

left. But then she died, and the Hills of Shame became hateful to me. So I decided to follow you, seeking the Lost Hills that Craal had told you about. I found them, and the Grey Lords too. But you had already gone. So I flew east, as you told me, searching for the Raven Mountains." Brekka fluffed her feathers. "I failed, but now I have found you again," she finished, bowing.

Tok squirmed under her bright-eyed gaze. She did not know about Tarkah, or that he was a lawbreaker and *unkora*. But now was not the time to tell her. "Look!" he said. "Here come the wolves."

Below them the pack, silent as shadows, were gliding among the trees. Tok and Brekka took wing, joining the other ravens, and from the air they could see the wolves' strategy. Approaching downwind of the deer, Selaks and Durnál formed the ends of a line, with Vikka, Tulik and Fornál in between them. Crouching low to the ground, they hid themselves among rocks and bushes. Suddenly Rekshana, Kimmik and Barator appeared from upwind, and charged straight for the deer. Panicked, the herd turned and fled — right into the line of hidden wolves. The line parted, allowing the biggest and strongest animals through. Then the wolves closed in. They attacked two of the slower animals, springing for their rumps and hindquarters and dragging them down. One doe kicked Tulik, sending him tail over nose in the snow, then both deer went down under the slashing fangs of the wolves. In moments their blood and entrails steamed in the snow, and the pack began to feed.

Durnál and Selaks settled in on one of the carcasses, warning the rest of the pack away with bared teeth. Tok swooped in boldly to snatch a beakful of guts from their kill. After a moment Brekka too grabbed a share, while the other ravens, not so bold, settled hungrily in the trees. The rest of the pack fell upon the second carcass. Rekshana, her muzzle streaked with blood, snapped at her brothers and sisters, and Tok noticed that only Barator dared to contest the kill with her. Fornál, Kimmik and Vikka darted in, snatching bones and scraps of meat as best they could, while Tulik, limping from the kick from the deer's hoof, paced hungrily in the background. Only when the others had gorged themselves was he allowed to creep forward and satisfy his hunger.

When the wolves withdrew from their kill, the raven band descended on it in a noisy black cloud. Gloran claimed the place of honour atop the carcass, while the others quarrelled over scraps and buffeted each other with their wings.

"Pretty manners your friends have, Tok," teased Selaks, who was stretched out under a cedar, licking blood from her fur, while Durnál dozed beside her.

"Wolves should talk!" he replied. "Poor Tulik scarcely got a bite to eat, thanks to his brothers and sisters. Why are they so cruel to him?"

Selaks yawned widely, showing her red throat and

blood-streaked teeth. "*Karlán* is *karlán*," she said. "I told you about that long ago, remember? How *karlán* means honour and rank in the pack. Well, Tulik is *karlás*."

"*Karlás?*"

"The wolf with least *karlán*. He eats last, or chews only bones if the kill is small. We're all fond of Tulik, but he's *karlás* and that's that. Now let me sleep." Curling up, she closed her eyes and swept her tail over her nose.

Full of meat, Tok tried to doze too. He closed his eyes, but something kept him awake. And it was not just the presence of Brekka, who had perched cozily on the same branch. It was a prickle at the base of his feathers, like the feeling of an approaching storm. He took wing and flew over to where Rokah kept watch at the top of a tall tree. "Something is wrong," he told him. "Don't you feel it?"

"I've seen nothing, heard nothing," said Rokah. "I took a quick flight a few minutes ago. Nothing is stirring in the valley."

But even as he spoke, there was a crackle of branches, and a black cloud of ravens burst from the surrounding woods and fell upon the birds still picking the carcasses in the clearing. Those who tried to take to the air were driven back down. On the ground, mobs attacked single birds, pummelling and pecking. Tok saw Gloran fighting off five attackers, while his mate Kordah cowered nearby. Karah and Brekka were screaming and slashing at a mob of ravenets that were closing around them. The raiders even attacked the wolves that leaped and snapped savagely at them.

With a scream of rage, Tok hurled himself down into the thick of the battle just as Karah disappeared under a wave of ravenets. Brekka was fighting them off as best she could, but she was beaten back by sheer numbers. Tok flew straight into the mob, hurling birds aside by main force, slashing with beak and claws at any who resisted. He fought his way to his mother, who lay still on the ground. With Brekka guarding his back, he stood off the ravenets. Then Barek swooped in and helped Tok rout them.

Springing back into the air, Tok wheeled toward a party of ravens who were attacking the wolves. The biggest raider flew straight at Durnál and slashed at his eyes with his claws, opening a long gash on the side of Durnál's face. With a mighty snap, Durnál seized the raven in his jaws and shook him. Flinging the body aside, he bared his teeth and faced the next attacker. Selaks, lighter on her feet, leaped high into the air and plucked a huge raven on the wing. Tok heard the crunch of teeth through bone. She spat out the mangled body and leaped after another victim.

Now Tok and Gloran were fighting side by side. But even as they defeated one attacker, another would take its place. "There are too many, Tok!" cried Gloran, over the din of shrieks, snarls and growls.

Suddenly, from high above came a piercing call. At

once the attackers began to lift off, flapping skyward. Tok and his companions watched wearily as two great flights formed high overhead and the attackers turned north.

Silence fell on the glade, which was strewn with black bodies. Three of their own ravenets lay among the dead, broken and pierced with the blows of many heavy beaks. Most of the rest of the company were bruised and had bald patches where feathers had been torn out. They set to work preening and ordering their plumage. Meanwhile, the young wolves, still excited by the battle, sniffed the bodies of the dead ravens, then wrestled and played in the snow.

Tok flew straight to where Brekka stood beside Karah, and Gloran and Barek followed. His mother had been badly battered and one of her shoulders was twisted, the wing drooping useless at her side.

"I cannot move it, Tok," said Karah. "I fear it is broken."

"No!" he cried. They stared into one other's eyes, both knowing that a broken wing meant death for any bird.

"Never fear, Tok," said Durnál, who had come up behind him with Selaks. "Your mother can always ride with me. Surely her wing will heal."

Sick at heart, Tok looked from one to another of the company.

"It was the same as before," muttered Gloran, wincing as he stretched a stiff wing. "A planned attack, broken off at a signal. Ravens have never fought so."

"They could have killed us all," said Tok. "Why didn't they?"

"Another thing," said Durnál. "Since when have ravens ever attacked wolves?"

Selaks tossed her head. "Well, we taught them to fear us," she boasted. "Though I hate the taste of them. And you, my *vór*, were lucky not to lose an eye." She sniffed the gash on Durnál's face, then licked it thoroughly.

"These are ravens like no others," said Tok. "Whoever trains them and leads them has made them so."

"The Overlord?" said Gloran.

There was a long silence. Then Tok shook his feathers into place. "At least most of us survived," he said. "And you all fought well. You should be proud." He looked around at the battered company. "But — where is Rokah?" he cried.

Chapter 8

Out of darkness, out of moonlight
Wove the white raven a spell of healing.

— from "The Saga of Tok Wolf Rider,"
Sagas of the Tellers

"I did not see him in the battle," said Gloran.

"Me either," said Barek.

Panic gripped Tok. He spread his wings and swooped down to the dead bodies strewn about the glade. Was Rokah among them? One by one, he, Gloran and Barek hopped to and fro, inspecting the dead.

"He's not here," Gloran assured him, when all the bodies had been checked. "But he may have fought and died in the woods. Or he may have been taken by the enemy."

Tok's heart sank. Rokah was bold and outspoken. He would not last long in the claws of the Overlord.

"This one's alive!" shouted Barek, as one of the enemy ravenets twitched, then tried to struggle to its feet.

"I'll finish him!" said Selaks, bounding over.

"Wait!" cried Tok, trying to think through his anguish about Rokah. "He may know something that could help us. Hold him, and let's see if he will talk!"

Selaks flipped the struggling ravenet onto its back and put one furry paw on its chest, pressing down none too gently. "Well," she demanded, baring her teeth. "Have you anything to say? Or shall I just nip your head off?"

"Why did you attack us?" demanded Tok. "Why did the others leave?"

"We attacked as ordered," the ravenet said sullenly. "You are enemies of our master, the Overlord, so you deserve to die. We have shadowed you all the way from the Raven Mountains, waiting our chance."

Tok, Gloran and Barek exchanged glances. None of them had seen so much as a wingtip of any other ravens except for Brekka. The attackers had moved cleverly indeed.

"So why didn't you finish the job, then?" asked Gloran.

"We did not know the wolves would fight for you. And then . . . I heard the Call just before I was knocked to the ground. That we obey without question."

"What kind of ravens are you to do such things?" Tok demanded. "Flying like flocks of geese, attacking in mobs, wrecking and killing at will?"

Frightened though he was, the young raven's eyes gleamed. "It is the True Way," he gasped, as Selaks's paw pressed more heavily on his chest. "The Overlord has promised us there will be no more lords and ladies chasing us from their territories. No more Korts where ravenets have no say. All, all are equal under him. He has taught us how to make war and take what we want. Now we are feared, and no one dares drive ravenets away from a kill!"

"Let him up, Selaks," said Tok, with an angry snap of his beak. "Now at least we know what this is about, what has cost the life of Rokah."

"Rokah?" said the enemy raven, struggling to his feet as the wolf stepped back. "But — "

"Rokah is here!" said a voice from behind them. And there he was, just folding his wings.

Joy and relief swept over Tok. "We thought you dead," he said, struggling to appear calm. "Or captured."

"Neither," replied Rokah. "I decided to follow the Overlord's raiders some distance to make sure they were really leaving, not about to sneak back and attack again."

"Good thinking," agreed Gloran.

"I did not realize you would think me dead," added Rokah, turning to Tok. "I'm sorry. I should have told you my intention."

"You are safe. That is all that matters," said Tok

gladly. Then, "Let's set a guard on this prisoner until we decide what to do with him. I must see to Karah."

He found his mother trembling with pain. "I cannot travel, Tok," she said. "Not even on Durnál's back. You will have to leave me behind."

"No!" said Tok. But in his heart he feared she was right. It might be weeks before Karah's wing healed, or perhaps it never would. And they dared not stay long in the valley of the Two-Legs.

Wolves and ravens fed again on the carcasses toward dusk. Then the ravens roosted and the wolves curled up among the trees. "Don't worry, Tok," Selaks had told him. "There is no need to travel tonight. Perhaps Karah's wing will be better tomorrow." But Tok felt in his heart that it would not be so.

With Durnál's help, Tok got his mother onto the lowest branch of a bush, so she at least did not have to roost on the ground. Brekka and Kordah perched nearby, though even in the midst of his worry, Tok noticed how Kordah drew her shining feathers tightly around her body, avoiding contact with the scruffy little newcomer. Meanwhile, Rokah arranged a series of guards to watch the prisoner. Tok stayed by Karah until he saw her head droop in sleep, then found a more comfortable branch to roost on. The wind was up, and the branch swayed gently beneath him. The night was cloudy-bright, with the moon appearing and disappearing.

Tok's mind raced, trying to find a way out of his

trouble. Leaving Karah behind was unthinkable. He had asked her to come with him, brought her into this danger. How could he leave her to suffer a lonely death? But the Two-Legs were bound to discover wolf tracks in the valley soon. And then . . . He shuddered, remembering the horror of the Two-Legs chasing Malik and his pack in their snow-*grawls*. Malik had been shot and the rest had barely escaped with their lives.

The moon appeared again and, heavy hearted, he gazed at the shadowy shape of the raven on it. He could not abandon Karah, he thought bleakly. He could not — not even to keep his promise to Selaks and the wolves. It was not just that Karah was his mother — she was the last of the Tellers of the Raven Mountains. She alone knew all the tales and traditions that taught how ravens came to be, and what they were. She was the memory of their kind. The wolves must go on without him. He would stay with Karah and try to protect her. His journey was over though it had barely begun.

"You need not give up," said a voice beside him. And even before he turned he knew who it must be. For who else could have read his thoughts?

Tok stared for a long moment at the white raven's snowy shape and shadowy eyes, so unlike the eyes of other ravens. "You seem to know all, Tunavik," he said.

"There is a way to help Karah and still continue

your journey," she said. "But you must trust me and do as I tell you."

"What other choice do I have?"

"Even though what I tell you to do is something no raven has done before?"

"Even then."

"Good." Tunavik stepped closer along the branch, then went on. "The first thing you must know is that her wing is not broken."

"But — the pain? And her shoulder is twisted strangely."

"The bone of the wing has been jarred out of its place. You must put it back."

"Tell me how," said Tok. But his eyes grew wide when he heard what he would have to do. "This is . . . un-raven," he said, struggling to find a word.

"I told you no raven has ever done it," replied the white raven. "But that is no reason why you cannot do it."

"I will try," said Tok. Then, "Tunavik, wait!" he cried, as the shape beside him began to fade. "Will you not stay with us?" he pleaded. "Help us on our journey?"

Moonlight reflected in the dark pools of Tunavik's eyes. "I cannot stay, Tok," she replied. "I fly between the worlds, but belong to none."

"At least tell me, then, if we will reach the Cold Forest."

"I have freed you to make this journey, with its

many perils," said the white raven. "That is all I can do. You and the wolves may win through, or you may fail. But if you survive, you and I will meet again at the Gates of the North."

Then Tok was alone with the wind and the moonlight.

In the morning, Karah's wing was no better. She would eat nothing but a beakful of snow, and her eyes were glazed with pain. Tok called the wolves and ravens together and told them that the white raven had taught him a way to save Karah.

Brekka's eyes grew sharp with suspicion when she heard about the mysterious visitor. "Who is she?" she demanded.

"Her name is Tunavik. I know only that she is the Messenger," replied Tok. "I begged her to stay, but she could not. Still, I have no choice but to trust her."

"Let me help, Tok," offered Durnál. Gently, he closed his great jaws around Karah, lifting her from the branch and placing her on the ground.

"Brekka, Gloran, you must hold her on her back while I stretch her injured wing," said Tok. Gloran put his weight on Karah's chest, while Brekka's claws held Karah's good shoulder firmly to the ground. Taking a deep breath, Tok grasped the injured wing in his beak and hopped backward, stretching it as far as it would go. Karah screamed in pain, and after a few seconds he let go.

"Not enough," he muttered, feeling sick at her suffering. "I must try again." This time he clamped the wing harder in his beak and threw his full weight backward, flapping his wings to give himself more pull.

Karah shrieked, then gasped, "Something shifted. I felt it!"

At once Tok let go, and Karah slowly drew the damaged wing closed. Quieting his wildly thumping heart, Tok said, "Now, a vine. One that will bend easily."

It took them some time to find a vine in the winter woods that was thin and flexible. It was Tulik who paraded proudly back to the glade trailing a long strand of tough ivy that he had found clinging to a tree trunk. The other wolves greeted him boisterously, then watched, their eyes widening, as Tok stripped the leaves from it and snipped it to a shorter length. Then he wound it round and round Karah, binding the injured wing tightly to her body. The end he prodded awkwardly with his beak until he managed to poke it firmly under the binding.

"I hope that holds," said Tok. "She must be bound for days, to keep the wing from slipping out of place again." Then he looked at the circle of wolf and raven faces staring at him and said, "What's the matter?"

"Nothing at all," said Selaks. "Except that we've just seen a wonder. All this tugging and binding — never have wolves tried to cure themselves so."

"Nor ravens!" said Gloran.

"It's another tale in the saga of Tok the Wolf Rider,"

said Karah weakly. "I'm going to start thinking how to Tell it right away."

"Nonsense!" Tok protested. "You can't tell stories about me. I am *unkora*. Besides, I only did what the white raven told me to do."

As he spoke, a shrill yell split the air, and Barek, who had been guarding the prisoner, wheeled overhead. "Something hit me from behind," he cried. "The enemy has escaped!"

Part 2

The Not-World

Chapter 9

*More dangerous than the enemy without
is the enemy within.*

— Wisdom of the Tellers

The ravens scrambled into the air, some diving among the trees, the rest swooping low over the forest. But the captive had disappeared.

"It's no use," said Tok after they had searched for a few moments. "He must have hidden himself in the woods. We could look forever and not find him."

"I don't understand how he escaped," complained Gloran.

"Indeed," said Rokah. "How could you have been so stupid as to turn your back on him, Barek?"

"I didn't!" protested Barek. "I was looking right at him when something hit me from behind and knocked me off my perch. By the time I recovered, the prisoner — and whoever helped him — were gone."

"Either more of the enemy are hidden in the woods," said Tok, "or . . ."

"Or we have a traitor in our midst," finished Gloran.

When all the ravens had gathered again, Tok told them what Barek had said. There was a burst of karking and quorking as they argued about the possibilities.

At last one of the ravenlords who had joined them made himself heard over the noise. "Whether surrounded by enemies or betrayed by someone among us, we are in danger. I say we have not left the Terror behind — we have brought it with us!"

There was a loud chorus of agreement.

"Very well, what then?" asked Tok. "You need not go farther. You can still go back to the Raven Mountains, or stay here in this valley if you choose. The Two-Legs here are a danger to the wolves, but not to you."

"Tok's right. We can still go back," one of the ravens said.

"Back to the Death, as well as the Terror? Not I!" cried another.

"Why not stay here then, as he suggests?"

"But the enemy knows we are here. They might come back and kill us all!"

As the argument continued, Rokah snapped his beak in annoyance. "They don't know their own minds!" he complained to Tok. "They need you to tell them what to do. Why don't you?"

"I can't!" Tok protested. "I'm no leader. They must decide for themselves."

"Bah!" muttered Rokah. But he said no more.

But now the wolves grew restless. "We must move on, Tok," said Selaks. "We cannot remain here near the Two-Legs, no matter what the rest of you do." She moved to the edge of the glade, and the rest of the pack followed her. "We go north," she announced.

"I, too," said Karah, taking a tight grip on Durnál's mane.

Tok sprang into the air and circled once over the quarrelling ravens. "Come with me or not. I go north with the wolves!" he called as he flapped off over the trees with Rokah behind him.

"Wait for me!" cried Brekka, winging after them, and Barek, Gloran and Kordah followed, too. The rest of the company took off as well, still quorking, and circled in the air. At last three of them turned south and headed back down the valley. The rest of the ravens and ravenets turned north.

It was good to feel the sun on his back, thought Tok, and to hear the heavy swish of Rokah's wings behind him as they circled higher.

"I'm glad you choose to stay with me," he told his son. "Back there when you disappeared and I thought you had been killed or captured, I felt a great despair."

"And yet it is not the raven way for parents and offspring to remain together long," Rokah pointed out.

"That's true. Yet here I am travelling not only with

my son but with my mother too."

"So the Overlord is not the only one who changes raven traditions," said Rokah, with a sly glance at him. "Perhaps Karah will put all this into her saga."

"I do not seek to change tradition," Tok protested. "Tradition is what I live by."

"So you say," returned Rokah. "Yet here you are, a lawbreaker and *unkora* too, leading a mob of other outlaws."

Tok winced, flicking his whitelids. Did Rokah have to be so blunt about it?

Below, far down the valley now, the wolves were emerging from the woods. Leaving Rokah and the rest of the ravens to soar in the sun, Tok circled down and dropped onto Selaks's back.

"Oof!" she grunted, breaking stride. "I never get used to you dropping down out of the blue like that."

"We must find a different pass from the western one we used before," he said. "That leads to the open lands where it is dangerous to go. I'll see if I can find a way due north."

"Good," she said, picking up the pace. "We will wait for you in the woods, wherever this valley ends."

Lifting off again, Tok watched them flowing across the floor of the valley — Selaks and Durnál in the lead, then Barator, Rekshana, Fornál, Kimmik and Vikka, with Tulik bringing up the rear. They run in the order they live, he thought. *Karlán* ruled the wolves in everything.

Leaving the other ravens behind, he sped far down the valley, toward the range of snowy peaks that barred their way northward. Skimming up over the forest, he angled along steep heights above the tree line. The wall of rock was broken here and there by stony promontories and frowning ridges. Even the sure-footed wolves could not scale these sheer summits, thought Tok. And he saw no pass. He mounted higher and higher, soaring across the crest of the mountain range and giddily riding a downdraft that shot him along the other side. For a few moments, sheer joy seized him, and he twirled like a falling leaf, dropping swiftly through the air.

When he righted himself, he saw another, lower range of mountains some distance ahead. No problem about a pass there, as the summits stood well apart, with broad valleys between them. Mounting higher again, he glimpsed rolling wooded hills beyond. There surely would be much game there, and the wolves would be able to hunt. How many days' running it would be for them to get there he could not guess. It was hard to judge distance, because the hills were veiled in haze — strange for this early in the year, he thought.

But he still had to find a way through the first range of peaks. Angling his wings, he veered east along the northern side, his wings carving the air in a long dizzying glide across the face of the rocky heights below him. But he still saw no pass. Then, just when he was about to turn back, he glimpsed a vertical line of shadow between the shoulders of two summits. He descended toward it and gave a cry of glee when he saw that it was a narrow cleft. Descending farther, he plunged into the gap, then checked his speed as steep walls closed in on both sides of him, at times narrowing to just beyond the tips of his outstretched wings. The cleft lay deep in shadow, with only a thread of daylight high above, and its floor was littered with rocks. Its dank dimness weighed on Tok, and his heart lifted when after many wingbeats he saw daylight ahead of him.

With a joyous quork he shot out into the late afternoon sunshine of the valley beyond. Clouds were building up to the south, and the rising wind felt damp on his feathers. There will be snow, he thought happily, snow to cover the wolves' tracks in case the Two-Legs were stirring.

He retraced his route and found the pack foraging in the woods at the north end of the valley. Above them perched the ravens and ravenets, hungry and hopeful.

"You found a way through?" asked Selaks, as he lit on a branch above her.

"I did, but you won't like it," Tok replied. "It's narrow, deep and dark. But it's the only pass through the northern mountains."

"What we must do, we can do," said Durnál.

The wolves had found no more deer, but the young

wolves were amusing themselves by chasing a snow-shoe hare they had flushed from a thicket, cheered on by the ravens. The hare zigged and zagged, turning nimbly under the very jaws of the wolves, and dashed toward the shelter of another thicket. But Rekshana got there first and, turning, pounced upon the hare and dispatched it with one snap of her jaws.

The *vór* and *vóra* made no attempt to deprive her of her catch. Durnál ran out his tongue, laughing. "Well-caught, Rekshana!" he barked, and the white wolf's grey eyes gleamed as she glanced at him.

The other young wolves sniffed wistfully at the few drops of blood scattered on the snow, but left Rek-shana to her meal. Barator, Fornál and Kimmik wandered off in different directions, followed by ravens who flapped from tree to tree. Vikka and Tulik sat near Rekshana as she ate, saliva drooling from their jaws. When she strolled off, leaving only a few bones and scraps of fur, Vikka fell upon them and snarled savagely at Tulik when her brother tried to snatch a mouthful too.

As the light began to fade, the ravens, realizing they would get nothing, began to look for comfortable spots for roosting and preening. Tok checked Karah's binding to make sure her wing was still held firmly in place, then he flew up beside Brekka, who was perched nearby.

"You may know something that might interest the *vóra*," he said. "You told me you found the Grey Lords in the Lost Hills. Did you speak with their *vór*, Adanax?"

Below them, Selaks pricked up her ears and fixed her eyes on Brekka.

"The *vór*'s name was Mantor," said Brekka. "And the *vóra* was called Bervenna."

Selaks jumped to her feet. "It can't be!" she protested. "Was there no big brindled wolf, much larger than Mantor?"

Brekka bobbed her head. "There was one such," she said, "though no one told me his name. He had only three legs, having been wounded by the Two-Legs. A firestick, they told me. He had a hard time of it, and always ate last and least."

"*Karlás!*" howled Selaks. "Mantor and Bervenna have made my father *karlás!*" Throwing back her head, she uttered a cry of rage and pain that echoed off the sunset peaks above them.

Chapter 10

Water is a seeker.

— Lore of the Lanna

Just as Tok had thought, it soon began to snow, yet the temperature fell only a little. By nightfall the snow had turned to sleet and then to freezing rain. Worried about Selaks, Tok did not roost with the other ravens, but dozed on the branch over her head, awakened now and then by her restless movements. Before dawn, she was up and pacing, while the rest of the pack still slept.

"I must go to the Lost Hills!" he heard her say to Durnál. "My father needs me!"

"Forgive my cruelty in saying so, my *vóra*, but your father is dead," Durnál replied. "He must be. No three-legged wolf could last long near the Two-Legs. We can only hope the Lanna granted him a quick end."

"What Durnál says is surely true, Selaks," said Tok. "Brekka was in the Lost Hills not long after we left. She has been travelling for years, on her way here. Whatever happened to Adanax is past — long past."

"I tell you I cannot rest, thinking of him!" cried Selaks.

"You may not go," said Durnál sternly. "You cannot. *And you know why!*"

Selaks's eyes blazed at him for a moment, then she lowered her head. Flattening her ears, she rubbed her muzzle under his. "You are right, my *vór*," she said sadly.

Then Karah spoke up. "You are a Snow Seer, *vóra*, or so Tok tells me. Look, it is snowing again. Can you See nothing that will ease your heart?"

Above them, the clouds were rolling away from the heights, beginning to reveal patches of clear sky. As the rim of the sun appeared above the horizon, millions of snow crystals flashed fiery rainbows in the air, and the animals gazed upon a forest transformed. Every limb and twig of the bare trees, every needle of the evergreens, was coated with a glittering sheath of ice. The coats of Selaks and Durnál flashed a thousand points of light, and the black feathers of Tok, Brekka and Karah sparkled white with frost.

Selaks walked away, a wolf of light in that radiant morning. The last snowflakes swirled around her as she stood gazing west in the direction of the faraway Lost Hills that had once been her home. Long she stood, until the sun rose higher, the colours faded, and the south wind swept the clouds away. Then she turned and came back to the others.

She looked from one to another of them, and her eyes were no longer tormented. "I Saw the Wolf Trail in the sky," she said. "The Trail we all must run when our time is finished. And it seemed to me that Adanax was there, and that we will meet again, at the end of things."

"It is good, my *vóra*," said Durnál. "May the Seeing bring you peace."

"But I Saw more," she said, turning her glowing eyes on him. "I Saw a valley with towering mountains beyond, one of them cloven from crest to base. And a mighty river winding through the valley. My heart tells me that this will be our new home."

"Where is this valley?" asked Tok. "Is it in the Cold Forest?"

Selaks shook her head. "I do not know. But I fear that it is far."

By now, the rest of the pack had gathered around them. It was agreed that Tok would lead the wolves while the other ravens flew ahead over the mountains to await them. Brekka alone insisted on going with Tok.

"But why?" he said impatiently. "There is nothing you can do to help us. You'll be better off with the other ravens."

Brekka fluffed her feathers defiantly. "I can keep

watch for enemies," she insisted.

There seemed no way to get rid of her. So they took to the air together, while the pack moved off in single file up the steep wooded slope of the mountain, heading for the tree line. The air was warming fast, and Tok and Brekka climbed easily on the thermals forming above the shoulders of the mountains. Rokah and the rest of the ravens had already vanished over the peaks ahead of them.

"It's as warm as spring!" Brekka cried, dancing a few lively turns.

"Too warm," replied Tok. "See how much snow is already gone from the heights!" For the rocky crests below them were wet and bare. Angling his wings, he shot away across the face of the mountain, searching for the shadow of the cleft. Everywhere he could hear the voices of meltwater, dripping and trickling among the rocks, plunging with a roar down precipices. Far below, the forest had cast off its mantle of white, showing its silver and dark green colours.

Brekka had turned nimbly in the air, and flapped after him. "It's only a thaw," she said. "What are you worried about?"

"A thaw *here*, Brekka? On the tops of these mountains? It should be winter up here for two moons yet." Then, "There it is," he added. "That dark blue line between the peaks. That's the wolves' way through."

They descended to the tree line to await the pack, and passed the time by stalking mice, which were no longer concealed by their snow tunnels. Hardly a feast, but something to put in their stomachs, thought Tok.

"You're good at this," he said, noticing that she was catching more than he was.

"It was hard to learn," Brekka admitted. "In the Hills of Shame there was endless food. In the Lost Hills, the wolves killed deer, and I shared their kills. Either way, I never had to wonder where my next meal was coming from. But since, on my own, I have had slim pickings."

For the first time he thought of all she must have gone through. Many moons of journeying. The loneliness and hunger. "So why didn't you stay in the Lost Hills, then?" he asked.

Brekka roused her feathers and settled them again. "I came here because of you," she said, giving him a bright-eyed glance.

"Me?" he asked, startled. "What do I have to do with it?"

"Everything! Remember how you told me about the life of *kora* in the Raven Mountains? How it was a place where ravens had traditions and knew who they were? We had forgotten all of that in the Hills of Shame. So when I found you had left the Lost Hills, and gone nobody knew where, I decided to find the Raven Mountains myself. I hoped to find you there, and that you would help me be the kind of raven I wanted to be. Not what I was, a greedy little grubber."

"You were never that," Tok told her, remembering her compassion for the old raven Craal. But Brekka was small and rumpled, still like the ragged ravenet she had been when he had first met her. Nothing like his beautiful Tarkah. At the thought of his mate, lost because of him, his heart clenched with pain. "Be the best you can be, Brekka," he said. "But do not look to me. For I am no better than the ravens of the Hills of Shame. I am *unkora*." Then he took wing, leaving her behind.

At last the wolves emerged from the trees. Tok led them higher up the slopes until they stood staring into the dark slot between the rocky summits.

"Through *that?*" asked Durnál. "It's hardly wide enough for a wolf to walk through."

"It's the only way. And it's wider than my wing-spread all the way through."

"Well, you said I would not like it," said Selaks. "And I don't. But as we must venture it, let's go!" Without a backward glance, she plunged into the opening and disappeared into the darkness. Tok flapped after her, and lit on her shoulders. Durnál followed with Karah, and the rest of the pack stepped cautiously after him.

Inside the cleft was a dim half-light. High above, a thin strand of blue showed the sun was still shining, and from time to time Tok glimpsed a black dot that was Brekka circling watchfully overhead. The footing was slippery, with small stones skittering treacherously under the wolves' feet. Water from the heights above trickled down the walls, which were worn smooth, offering no footholds. Heads down, the wolves sloshed grimly forward. Much time passed, and then yet more.

"What made this place?" asked Rekshana from her place in the line.

"Water, most likely," replied Durnál. "Perhaps a stream flowed here long ago."

Water. Tok's mind suddenly pictured the heights above, running with meltwater from the sudden thaw. Water, trickling through crevices, rushing down channels, ever seeking a way downward . . . Ahead of them, a shower of rocks clattered down into the cleft, echoing and booming, and the wolves flinched. Fear clenched Tok's heart, and he wished he had thought to ask Brekka to call down a warning of loose rock on the slopes above. The thaw was shifting earth on the mountainside as well as water.

"Faster!" he urged Selaks. "I don't like the feel of this. There's too much water."

"Slow to notice things, aren't you?" she joked. Even as she picked up the pace, more rocks crashed down on them with bruising force. There were yelps of protest as the wolves tried to dodge in the narrow passage. Then a rock struck Kimmik squarely between the ears. She stumbled and fell, and Vikka and Tulik tumbled over her. The three of them scrambled up and ran on, blood streaming from a cut on Kimmik's head.

The wolves were going flat out now, ears laid back, eating distance with every bound. Tok strained his eyes, hoping to see light at the end of the gap. But what had taken him only a few minutes to fly had already cost the wolves much time.

Selaks laid back her ears. "Do you hear something?" she panted. "Behind us?"

Tok's ears were less keen, but soon he heard it too. A low rumble that echoed off the rock walls around them and at last grew to an unmistakable roar. And only then did he realize the deadly truth. The cleft was not just a crevice between the shoulders of the mountain. It was a channel carved into the rock by the raging floods of spring thaws.

Beneath the pads of the wolves' paws, the water level was rising fast. Soon it came halfway up their legs, as they floundered desperately forward. Higher and higher it rose, until the wolves were paddling. Then, with a roar, the full force of the torrent thundered down on them. Tok glanced back to see a towering wave surging down the gap after them, tumbling rocks with it as it came. He heard cries from the wolves as the wall of water and rock hit them, then they vanished beneath it. Tok tried desperately to outfly the flood, but he had left it too late. In moments, the crest of the wave was upon him. He caught a last glimpse of Selaks tumbling tail over nose as she was swept away, then the water smashed him into the smooth stone of the cleft and everything went dark.

Chapter 11

Through flood, in fear, fled they,
Terror behind them and peril before.

— from "The Saga of Tok Wolf Rider," Sagas of
the Tellers

Tok opened his eyes as memory slowly returned. The
onrushing torrent, the wolves swept away, the impact
of the rock as he was thrown against it. But — he
could not see! Had he been blinded by the blow?
Blinking in panic, he tried to get his feet under him,
but fell back onto his side. It felt as if every bone in his
body had been broken. Where were the wolves? And
Karah? At last he struggled to his feet. Slowly his
vision cleared a bit and he poked with his beak at his
sodden feathers. He was coated with mud. Anxiously
he stretched one wing, then the other. They were
unbroken. But he would not be able to fly, not with
his flight feathers glued together like this.

Behind him was the north end of the deadly cleft. The full force of the flood had passed, but a steady stream of water still poured from the mouth of the opening. Tok shivered. Did the wolves lie drowned inside? Or had they, too, been swept clear? He began to hop among the loose rocks, croaking, but heard no answer. Finding a large boulder, he claw-flapped his way to the top of it.

Moments later, there was a flurry of wings, and Brekka landed beside him.

"Are you all right?" she cried. "I was waiting for you on this side, then a great flood burst from the mouth of the cleft. I though you had all drowned!"

"Near enough," said Tok grimly. "Where are Rokah and the others? And can you see Karah and the wolves? My eyes are full of mud."

"I saw ravens in the far distance. Not an angled flight, so they must be ours. As for the wolves, Durnál is far down the slope with two others, one of them lying down," she replied.

"Durnál?" yelled Tok, putting all the strength he had into his voice.

"Tok!" came the reply. "Selaks and Rekshana are here. I can't see Karah. Can you see any of the others?" His voice held a desolate note that chilled Tok's heart.

Still blinking mud from his eyes, Tok scanned the mountainside. Not far away, two large brownish lumps were beginning to stir. Barator and Fornál, he thought. He had missed seeing them before because of their coating of mud. "I see Barator and Fornál," he yelled. "They seem all right. But there is no sign of the others."

It's my fault, he told himself. I led them into that deathtrap. And Karah, bound and helpless, where is she?

Then, from behind, Tok heard plashing footsteps, accompanied by whines and sneezes. From the mouth of the cleft emerged a sorry procession of half-drowned wolves. Once out in the sunshine, Kimmik, Vikka and Tulik shook themselves thoroughly from nose to tail, sending showers of muddy water in all directions.

"Here they are, Durnál," Tok yelled. "They're all right!"

"If you call being pounded to pulp and half-drowned all right," grunted Kimmik, wincing as she stretched her battered body. But seeing Tok hopping toward her and realizing he could not fly, she added, "Come, Tok, ride on me until we find Selaks."

"She's down below with Durnál. All the wolves are safe," he said, clambering up onto her shoulders. "But Karah is missing."

"We'll find her," promised Kimmik. "Spread out along the slope as we go down," she told Vikka and Tulik. "We'll look for Karah on our way."

Together they combed the slope, with Brekka scanning the ground from the air. But it was not until they were nearly down to Durnál that Tok spotted a soggy bundle of feathers lying at the foot of a rock. It was Karah. Like Tok, she was covered with mud, and she seemed dazed.

"I'll carry her," offered Kimmik. Delicately, she picked Karah up between her teeth and carried her down the slope. They found Durnál standing over Selaks. Rekshana, cowed for once, hovered anxiously behind him.

Selaks lay stretched out on the ground with her eyes closed. There was a trickle of blood at the corner of her mouth, and only the gentle rise and fall of her flanks showed that she was still alive.

"There are no wounds on her," said Durnál. "But she doesn't wake up."

Tok's heart sank. "Perhaps she was dashed against the rock wall in the cleft," he said.

"She must recover," said the *vór* sombrely. "Much depends on her. What of Karah?"

Tok turned to inspect his mother's shoulder. Although the ivy binding had been torn away, the wing was not drooping out of position and Karah could stretch it. "I can't tell how bad it is," she said to Tok, "because now I ache all over!"

"I must bind her wing again," Tok told Durnál. "But what can we do for Selaks?"

"I'll stay with her," he replied. "The sun is getting low and the pack should go down below the tree line. They must forage."

"Barator and I can lead them," offered Kimmik.

At once Rekshana turned on her, her eyes flashing fury. "*You?*" she snarled. "Barator and *I* will lead the hunt!"

For a moment their eyes locked, then Kimmik lowered hers. "As you wish, sister," she replied. "I shall help Tok and Karah."

Tulik's ears pricked, and he stepped eagerly forward. "Karah can ride with me if she likes," he said. "I'm not as big as Kimmik, so it's easier to get up on me."

The other young wolves bounded away down the slope, eager for the hunt.

"I don't like to leave you, *vór*," said Tok. "I blame myself for Selaks's hurt."

The *vór* gazed at him out of calm green eyes. "Don't, Tok. *Numon* is *numon*. Selaks foresaw this journey, and in my heart I cannot believe it ends on this mountainside. She is strong, though she is vulnerable right now. I'll keep her warm through the night, and surely she will recover by morning."

Vulnerable? thought Tok. Selaks?

Down in the forest, Tok and Brekka found a vine to bind Karah's shoulder. But first the three ravens had to rid their feathers of the clinging mud that clogged them. They managed to locate a patch of half-melted snow that had escaped the thaw, and in this they rolled, leaving as much mud as possible behind. Then, perched in a low bush, they preened each other, feather by feather, until they were glossy black again. Then Tok wound the vine in place, so that it held

Karah's wing snugly against her side again.

"How I long for the day when I can move my wings freely," she said.

"Perhaps it will be only a few days more," Tok replied. For it seemed to him that as the shoulder had not been harmed by Karah's rough passage through the rock channel, it must be nearly healed.

Kimmik and Tulik went after the pack, which seemed to have roamed some distance away. Meanwhile, Brekka caught mice and shared them with Karah, and Tok contributed an unwary flying squirrel that he had caught foraging in the dusk. With her stomach full, Karah fell asleep, while Tok and Brekka took it in turns to watch over her through the night.

"I thank you for your care of my mother," said Tok, when Brekka roused him to take his turn.

Brekka shuffled her feet on the branch. "I am honoured to help her," she replied. "She is a raven of great *kora*. Not a nobody like me." Then, "Tok!" she added, as he moved away.

"Well?"

"I want you to know that I don't believe what you told me before. That you are *unkora*." She put her head under her wing.

At dawn there was still no sign of the other ravens. Soon the wolves came trooping back. They had killed a deer, and were full of meat and delighted with their first independent hunt. Tulik told everyone several times how it had been he who first scented the deer, in time for them to move around upwind and take it by surprise. For his boasting, Rekshana and Kimmik rolled him on the ground, then fell to play wrestling with Barator and Fornál. Their high spirits lifted Tok's heart too.

Now if only Selaks is safe, he thought, I might begin to forgive myself for having led them all into danger.

Suddenly the wolves broke off their playing and pricked up their ears. From the slopes high above the forest came a long, quavering howl.

"Selaks!" said Kimmik, as the rest of the pack answered with happy barks and yelps. They all dashed pell-mell through the trees and up the slope to greet their *vór* and *vóra*, who came bounding down to meet them. From the eaves of the forest, the ravens watched the pack throw itself upon its leaders, biting their muzzles, licking their fur and pressing against them.

"All is well, *vóra*?" Tok asked anxiously, as Selaks came up to the tree where he was perched. "What happened to you?"

"I am stiff and sore, Tok," she said. "All I remember is being hit on the head by something as the wave took me. I knew nothing more until I woke up this morning." Her golden eyes gleamed up at him, with no shadow in them.

"Come," Durnál urged her. "I hear there's a deer carcass for the picking. That is, if our greedy children have left anything for us!" Throwing himself down, he allowed Karah to mount his shoulders. Then with Tok and Brekka swooping ahead, the pack streamed away through the forest.

Later, with the carcass reduced to a few scraps of hide and bone, Tok and Brekka took to the air while the wolves ran onward.

"I can't understand why Rokah and the others were not waiting on this side of the mountains for us," said Tok.

"Perhaps there is the answer," replied Brekka, who had been scanning the horizon. For in the sky ahead of them, though much higher up, the Overlord's raiders were heading north.

"Skyah grant that they didn't attack our ravens," said Tok. "Let's go lower and call. Keep an eye on the raiders just in case."

But their enemies continued out of sight, heading northwest. After an anxious time of circling and calling over the forest, Tok's heart lifted when Gloran's voice answered him, and he and Barek and the rest of the ravens rose from the treetops to meet them.

"Where's Rokah?" asked Tok, as they came together and circled.

"Gone to scout ahead. At least that's what he said," replied Gloran. "We were waiting for you nearer the mountains, but those cursed raiders found us and we retreated to the forest. They didn't try to attack this time. It was almost as if they just wanted to know where we are. But we took no chances, and moved north under cover of the forest yesterday."

Not long afterward, Rokah appeared and flew toward them with rapid wingbeats. He told them of a river ahead that the wolves would have to cross, so Tok decided to wait for them there.

But the river, when they found it, was swollen with run-off waters from the thaw, and full of logs and debris washed away upstream.

"The wolves can never swim across that," said Tok. "Is there no way around?"

"None that I could see," said Rokah.

"Then they'll have to wait until the water goes down."

As the sun rose in the sky, the ravens and ravenets spread out through the forest, foraging. Tok and Brekka, who had fed well at the wolves' kill, sunned themselves on a bare tree stub not far from the river. It wasn't long before the pack emerged from the forest. They reached the water's edge and stood gazing across it.

"We can't cross that," said Durnál, turning to Tok, who had flown down to land on Selaks's back. "The debris makes it too dangerous. How long do you think it will take the water to fall?"

"A day — or days, perhaps," replied Tok.

"The forest swarms with deer," Barator put in. "We might as well hunt them."

"Yes. Let Tulik show his prowess again," teased Kimmik, giving the *karlás* wolf a playful nip on the rump. He bounded away, then play-bowed, and at once the pack began to chase him. Selaks and Durnál stood aside, laughing. Only when Tulik had been caught and rolled about thoroughly did the young wolves course off after Barator in search of game, followed by a group of eager ravens. Durnál let Karah hop down from his back, then raced after them.

Selaks made no move to follow. "Aren't you hungry?" Tok asked her.

She stretched herself, yawning widely, as Tok flapped down beside Karah. "I'm always hungry, as you very well know," Selaks replied. "But Durnál and I have decided that just now I should rest sometimes, especially when we have been travelling all day. If they kill, there will be plenty left over for me." She put her head down on her paws and closed her eyes.

Tok cocked his head, puzzled. Selaks content with leftovers? he thought.

The run-off had not slackened the next day or the next, so the wolves and ravens remained on the south bank of the river. Tok decided to remove Karah's binding, and she managed a few shaky flaps.

"The wing is much better," she said, "but it's still very weak."

Meanwhile, the wolves killed, then killed again later and everyone feasted.

"I like this place!" said Tulik, as the pack, bellies bulging, lay stretched out in the afternoon sun. From the forest behind them came the squawks of the ravenets, who were happily picking at the most recent carcass.

"I, too," said Barator. "Why not stay here?" he added, turning to Selaks and Durnál, who lay side by side watching the river. The other wolves pricked up their ears, and there were growls of agreement.

"No!" said Selaks. "This is not the place for us. Who has ever heard of spring floods at this time of year? By mid-summer this forest will be dry as an old deer bone."

"It is the same here as in the Raven Mountains," Durnál put in. "Except that there are no Two-Legs."

"I can't say that I miss them," joked Kimmik, and the pack yelped with laughter.

"And there's another reason not to stay," said Selaks. "This place smells strange."

"It does?" said Tok, who had not noticed anything.

"Selaks is right," said Durnál. "I smell it too. It's faint, but there's something wrong about it. Not a scent I've ever smelled before."

"Did you see anything unusual when you scouted ahead?" Tok asked Rokah.

"No, but I didn't go farther than the nearest line of mountains."

"Our turn to stretch our wings," Tok said to Gloran and Barek. "It can't hurt to see what lies ahead of us. The high water has to go down sometime."

"Me too!" called Brekka, flapping after them. The four of them circled higher, turning north. They crossed the line of separated peaks, and soared over the lightly-wooded foothills beyond. As before, the distance was cloaked in yellowish haze. After a time, the air seemed to thicken around them, and though the sun still shone, they lost sight of the ground below them.

"What is this stuff?" asked Gloran, peering through the murk.

"There's something harsh and prickly in my nostrils," added Brekka. "Is it the mist?"

"This must be what the wolves smelled," said Tok. "Let's go lower."

Tilting their wings, they planed swiftly down the sky. The mist thinned around them and suddenly the ground came into view. Tok shuddered as he saw what lay before them, and he heard Brekka croak in terror. As far as his eyes could see, towering objects loomed through the haze, and between them the earth was crusted over with strange-shaped structures.

"What under Skyah is it?" cried Gloran, flapping frantically to gain more height.

"It is a many-roosts," said Tok. "A monstrous home of the Two-Legs."

Chapter 12

Not-earth, not-sky,
Where not-paths run and not-birds fly,
Not field or forest, plain or glade,
This not-world that the Two-Legs made.

— Wisdom of the Tellers

The ravens and wolves peered through the haze at the strange structures sprawled across the plain ahead of them. After the run-off from the thaw subsided, the wolves had crossed the river and then coursed north for days through the lightly-wooded foothills. Now they had reached the obstacle that blocked their way.

"I can see no more than a blur," said Selaks. "But what I can smell terrifies me."

"Just as well you can't see it," replied Brekka. "It's horribly ugly."

"Days ago, Gloran, Barek and I scouted thousands of wingbeats east and then back toward the west,"

Tok reminded them. "But there was no end in sight to this many-roosts. No matter which direction we take, it will cost us much journeying before we can turn north again."

"There is no time," said Selaks. "Despite its fearfulness, we must go through this place, not around it."

"But you can't!" cried Tok. "You don't know what it's like. I nearly died once, trying to get through a many-roosts, and I was flying. For wolves on the ground it will be certain death!"

"Nevertheless, Selaks is right," said Durnál, with a glance at his mate. "We have no time to make a long detour. We must risk the direct way."

"Our *numon* is not your *numon*, Tok," said Selaks. "Our reasons for trying the direct crossing are ours alone. Let you and the other ravens fly ahead and wait for us north of this place. Surely you will be able to find us if we get through."

"You are forgetting Karah," said Tok. "Though her wing is much better, she cannot fly great distances yet. So she must ride with you sometimes, and where she goes, I go."

"And I," insisted Brekka.

"I am glad," said Durnál, "though it is selfish of me to wish it. Our chances are much greater if you are with us."

Tok turned to Gloran and Rokah. "It's up to the two of you to lead the others beyond the many-roosts and keep them together," he said. "In a day or two, look out for Brekka or me soaring somewhere due north of where the dwellings of the Two-Legs end." He hesitated, then added, "If we do not come, then you must make your own decisions."

"We will wait for you," promised Gloran, as the ravens lifted away into the sky. They circled higher and higher, vanishing at last into the murk that hung over the many-roosts.

Durnál turned to the pack. "Know that we would not ask this of you if it were not necessary," he said.

The young wolves, their eyes bright with excitement, rallied around their *vór* and *vóra*, eagerly demonstrating their love and loyalty. Durnál and Selaks raised their muzzles and began to sing, and the rest joined in, their voices intertwining like strands in a silver rope. Then the pack bounded down the slope of the last foothill and out onto the plain.

"We must go silently, and by night once we reach the many-roosts," Tok warned Selaks.

The sun was at the horizon as they approached the southern edge of the great dwelling place of the Two-Legs. Here, squat structures dotted the plain, each with an open space around it. As they went on, the space gradually became less and the structures crowded closer together. The pack took shelter in a belt of trees, waiting for dark before venturing father.

"Fly, Tok, while there's still enough light," said Durnál. "See if you can find the best route to take. And someplace we can hide in case of need."

Tok flew straight toward the many-roosts, every wingbeat weighted by the fear that gripped him. Below stretched a web of hard paths crowded with creeping lines of the shiny *grawls* the Two-Legs travelled in, each with its two round eyes blazing in the dusk. One of these paths was broader than the rest, and was clearly the most direct route north. But it was also the most dangerous, he told himself, for it had the most *grawls*. It led into the cluster of tall, cliff-like structures that stood at the heart of the many-roosts. Not far beyond, he could see trees lining what looked like a ravine that cut across the landscape in a north-westerly direction. That might provide the shelter the wolves will need in daylight, he thought. If they can reach it.

"There is a way," he reported to the others as darkness fell. "It's direct, but it's risky. If we take it, we're heading right into the heart of the place. It will be dreadful, I'm warning you. But beyond I saw a ravine that leads north by west. You might be able to follow that."

"Let's go," said Selaks, as Tok fluttered onto her back. "As we must do it, the sooner the better."

"Follow us," Durnál told the young wolves as Karah flapped onto his shoulders. "And stay in line — no roaming!"

The pack moved off at a brisk trot, following a hard path that Tok had said would lead toward the broader way into the heart of the many-roosts. Spaced along the path were tall tree-like objects that cast bright pools of light on the ground. The wolves, half-dazzled, shrank toward the edge of the path. But danger lay there, too. For lights were flashing on in the dwellings of the Two-Legs, and *grawls* were arriving at some of them. They could hear the barking of dogs as they passed. One large beast caught their scent and rushed after them, baying at the top of its voice. But one snarl from Rekshana stopped it in its tracks.

At last the main way lay before them.

"Do we have to go on that?" whined Vikka, gazing in terror at the *grawls* that whizzed along it.

"Not *on* it," said Tok. "The *grawls* are too dangerous. But beside it, as much in the shadow as possible."

Durnál growled his agreement, and led the way. The wolves filed down to the edge of the hard path, and moved off trembling, their fur blasted by whirlwinds of air from the passing *grawls*. The roar was terrifying, and the wolves ran in panic, ears laid back. Only the discipline of the pack kept them from scattering and running into the path of the *grawls*. On and on they ran, deeper into the terrible dwelling place of the Two-Legs, with Tok and Brekka winging ahead of them.

Pale faces stared out of some of the grawls as they passed, then one *grawl* gave a hideous blast of sound, and the thing swerved toward the edge of the hard path. There was a piercing squeal, and then the *grawl* hit the barrier at the edge of the hard path and screeched to a stop. Peering back as the wolves fled, Tok saw a Two-Legs struggle out of the *grawl*. It started yelling into a silvery thing it held to the side of its head.

Soon a new sound was heard in the distance, a terrible howl, rising and falling.

"Lanna! What kind of beast howls like that?" panted Barator.

Whatever it was, it was coming closer, and Tok could see lights flashing ahead, red and white. "We must get off," he screamed over the uproar. "Over the side!"

Durnál vaulted the barrier with Selaks on his heels, and the rest of the pack streamed after them. Down into a gully at the side of the path they rushed, and flattened themselves to the ground among low bushes and clumps of dead grass. Above them, on the path, the terrible howling went on, and more and more lights flashed. Two-Legs came to the edge of the barrier and peered down into the gully, sweeping the grass with lights they held up. Tok held his breath. Surely they would be seen, or someone would pursue them. If the Two-Legs had firesticks it would be all over for the wolves.

Instead, the Two-Legs turned back to the path after a few moments.

"Perhaps they didn't want to find us," growled Durnál. "Perhaps they were frightened."

"Frightened of *us*?" Tulik's voice was bright with interest.

"Don't count on it," muttered Selaks. "Anyway, now what?"

Under cover of the darkness, the wolves crept away through the grass, returning nearer to the hard path only when the terrifying lights and sounds were far behind them. Tok flew up onto one of the light-trees along the path and stared ahead. They had covered much of the distance to the heart of the many-roosts, and the tallest structures loomed only a short distance away now. They glowed with light in the darkness. There were other lights too, coloured and flashing. He stared, half-dazzled, listening to the roar of many *grawls* still rolling along the hard paths. His keen eyes could pick out the moving figures of many Two-Legs as well.

"We can try to get through the centre tonight," he told the wolves. "But we must wait. The Two-Legs are still about and there's too much light."

"It is risky," said Selaks. "If things don't quiet down tonight we'll be caught here in the open in daylight."

"We must wait and see," growled Durnál.

The pack curled up and the younger ones soon dozed. But the ravens and older wolves remained alert, their heads turning now and then toward the path as a *grawl* rushed by, and their eyes glowing with its reflected light.

"Have you ever been in one of these places, my *vór?*" asked Barator.

"Never, praise the Lanna," replied Durnál. "But Tok has, and has nothing good to say about them."

110

"This one stinks," complained Rekshana. "Cold nasty smells that sicken me."

Time passed, and overhead the moon rose higher and higher in the sky. Little by little, the noise of the place of the Two-Legs grew less, though an occasional *grawl* still rushed by them. Lights in many of the tall structures winked out, but a sickly glow still washed the sky above them.

At last, Durnál got to his feet. "I say we go. It may not get better than this."

"What do you say, Tok?" asked Selaks.

"I agree with Durnál."

"Follow me, then!" said Selaks, rising.

Tok and Brekka took wing, while Karah dug her claws deeper into the *vór*'s mane. Selaks leaped over the barrier and headed for the looming structures ahead. Soon the wolves were among them, skulking along close to their strange cold substance that was not-stone, not-wood, trying to keep out of the light. With the ravens gliding ahead of them, they moved at a swift, tireless lope, their toenails clicking on the hard path beneath their feet. Now and then they saw *grawls* or groups of Two-Legs in the distance, and slipped deeper into the shadows.

"The whole place *thrums*," muttered Kimmik, as they paused a moment where one broad path crossed another. "I can even feel it under my feet."

"And such strange scents!" said Vikka. "My nose is numb!"

Tulik, seeing movement in a shiny surface beside him, reared up on his hind legs and pressed his front paws and nose against it. "Look!" he yelped. "There's a wolf in there!" The other young wolves crowded around, gazing enchanted as their images, too, appeared.

"The shiny stuff must be like still water," said Fornál. "We're seeing our own reflections."

"Quiet, all of you!" commanded Selaks. "We must run!"

On and on they coursed, following the wide empty path. Tok, flying ahead with Brekka, saw that it seemed to cut the many-roosts in two. If they kept to it, and made good time, they could reach the ravine by first light, he thought. He wheeled back to bring the news to Durnál, then noticed that the line of wolves had grown shorter during his absence.

"Where are Tulik and Vikka?" he called, swooping over Durnál's head.

The *vór* and *vóra* skidded to a halt, the next wolves in line tumbling into them.

"Kimmik, you were ahead of them. Where did they go?" demanded Selaks as they picked themselves up.

"I don't know, my *vóra*," panted Kimmik. "I thought they were right behind me!"

"Mark my words, there will be food at the bottom of it," said Fornál, and Barator gave a bark of laughter.

"This is serious!" growled Durnál. "If they delay us long, we all may pay for their folly!"

"We'll find them," said Tok, flapping away. Gaining height, he and Brekka cruised back the way they had come, scanning all the broad side paths they had crossed. But there was no sign of the wayward wolves.

"What about all the small side paths?" asked Brekka. "The ones that aren't lit up?"

"If they've gone into one of those, it may take much time to find them," said Tok.

They turned north again, flying low this time, and peering into the dark side paths that ran east and west of the main path. To the north, they could see the rest of the pack coming back, casting this way and that, hoping to pick up the scent of the missing wolves.

Crossing a dark side passage between two structures, Tok heard a dull thud, and thought he saw a flicker of movement. Calling Brekka, he dove down it to investigate. And there in the half-light he made out the shapes of Tulik and Vikka. They had ripped open a large soft blackish object and tugged out its contents, spilling chunks of something on the ground. Tok could hear the wolves crunching bones, and then he smelled what they were eating. Something so rich and delicious that saliva began to drip from his beak.

"What is it?" he asked Brekka as they circled down.

"I know such things well," she replied. "It is food cast away by the Two-Legs. I ate such fare all the time on the Hills of Shame."

The two wolves looked up from their meal as Tok and Brekka lit beside them. "Help yourselves," said

Tulik. "It's a feast. And there's so much of it!"

"You must leave it. You're endangering the rest of the pack!" warned Tok.

"Just a few bites more," said Vikka. "We were so hungry, and when we caught a whiff of this we just couldn't help ourselves."

"Leave it!" thundered a voice from behind them. And there stood Durnál with the rest of the pack behind him. "How dare you!" he snarled, his green eyes blazing, as the two young wolves cowered before him.

Suddenly part of the structure behind them opened outward, and they all cringed. Light streamed out from inside, and in the middle of it stood a Two-Legs holding another of the big soft objects. It stared at the wolves, then its mouth opened wide and it began to scream.

Chapter 13

Always do the unexpected.

— Lore of the Lanna

The Two-Legs threw what it was holding at them and closed the opening with a bang.

"Run!" barked Durnál, and the pack fell over each other trying to get out of the narrow passage. They fled north again, running flat out. But after a few moments, they began to hear a terrible howling in the distance.

Tok and Brekka scrambled into the air and circled, scanning the scene below them. "There's one of those *grawls* with the red and white lights again," cried Brekka. "And more — oh, many of them!"

Tok's heart sank. "Those things are closing in on the wolves from all directions," he said. "They're trapped!"

Angling their wings, the ravens plunged downward.

"That Two-Legs who saw us must have warned others," Tok shouted, as he landed on Selaks's back. "*Grawls* are coming — many of them. You're surrounded!"

"What can we do, Tok?"

"We've got to get off this broad path — they'll surely see us here. And we must get to the ravine. We should be safe there."

But even as they spoke, a *grawl* with its red and white lights and dreadful howling voice turned onto the path ahead of them. They turned to flee, but another screeched to a halt some distance behind them.

"There's a side passage!" cried Durnál, and the wolves dashed toward it. But as they reached the mouth of it, they could see lights flashing at the far end. Then some Two-Legs appeared with firesticks in their hands. So the wolves doubled back again.

"We're trapped!" Selaks's voice was sharp with despair.

"We have to break through them. There's no other way," replied Durnál. "I'll go first."

"No!" protested Selaks. "They'll kill you!"

Tok looked around desperately. Not far away, under a round white light, was another opening. "Over here!" he cried, zooming toward it. "It may be a way out!"

The pack sprang forward, with Brekka and Karah flapping behind them. They plunged through the opening, and tumbled down a jagged slope. Picking themselves up, they dashed past a kind of cage from which a lone Two-Legs gaped at them open-mouthed, vaulted a barrier and raced down a dimly-lit passage that stretched ahead of them. The shouts of their pursuers faded in the distance.

On they fled, down another steep slope. Beyond loomed yet another passage, which led to a broad ledge that dropped off abruptly. Below, three narrow silvery tracks emerged from the mouth of a huge tunnel, only to vanish again into another tunnel beyond the ledge.

Tok felt the hairs in Selaks's mane bristle under his claws as she sniffed the stale air. "There is something deadly here. I feel it."

"I do, too," said Tok. "A kind of thrumming in the air. It seems to come from that third track. But the tunnel is our only way out. The one to the right leads roughly north, I think."

The wolves hung back for a moment, then one by one they sprang down from the ledge. The path on which the silvery tracks lay was strangely made, of flat pieces of wood resting crosswise on bits of stone. The round shape of the dark tunnel loomed ahead of them like a gaping hungry mouth.

As they hesitated, shouts echoed from the passage behind the ledge.

"Run!" yelped Selaks, as she plunged ahead into the darkness of the northern tunnel.

The wolves loped onward, keeping as far away as

possible from the perilous third track. The footing was strange, and the pebbles skittered away under their paws. But they kept up a steady pace, coursing deeper and deeper into the dark.

At last pale light gleamed ahead of them, and they strained toward it eagerly. Slowly it increased, revealing the arch of the tunnel they were running through. To one side were three round lights in a row, one above the other. The bottom one glowed red, like a glaring eye. At last they emerged from the tunnel and found themselves below another broad ledge like the one they had just left.

"Maybe we can get up again here," panted Selaks. "I hate the feel of this place."

"Better to go farther," said Durnál. "The Two-Legs know where we went, and may come after us."

They plunged into the dark again. But just as they did, Tok noticed something. There were lights beside the entrance to this tunnel too, and as he watched the red light went out. Now the top light glowed green. It must mean something, he told himself. But what?

The wolves coursed on through the tunnel, their legs eating distance with every bound.

"Surely we have gone far enough," panted Selaks. "The Two-Legs are slow runners. We must have left them far behind. We can get up at the next ledge and be done with this terrible hole!"

But then, "Do you feel something?" asked Durnál.

"What?" said Tok.

"The ground," said Selaks. "I can feel it trembling under my paws." The wolves laid back their ears as a distant rumble behind them grew rapidly into a menacing roar.

"Faster!" yelped Durnál.

But it was too late. A blast of warmer air hit them from behind, almost knocking them off their feet, then a monster with glaring eyes swept around a curve and bore down on them with a great blare of sound.

"Stay against the wall! Don't try to outrun it — it will crush you!" shrieked Tok, digging his claws deeper into Selaks's mane.

The terrified wolves pressed themselves against the side of the tunnel while the thing thundered past and vanished ahead of them into the blackness.

"Karah! Brekka! Are you all right?" Tok called into the quivering silence.

"I am," came his mother's voice from close by.

"Me, too." Brekka's voice came from farther away.

"What about the rest of you?" barked Durnál

"Here!" said Selaks, though her voice trembled.

"And I!" chorused other voices. Tok named them off to himself as they replied. Rekshana, Barator, Fornál, Kimmik, Vikka . . .

"Tulik?" cried Selaks, when there were no more voices. Then, louder, "TULIK!"

Then, "Here he is, my *vóra*," called Barator out of the dark behind them.

They rushed toward the sound of his voice. In the dim light they could barely see his shaggy shape as he stood, head drooping, over a huddled bundle of fur between the tracks.

"I can smell no blood, no wound," Barator moaned as they gathered around him. "I fear he must have been thrown against the track-that-thrums."

"NO!" Selaks's wail of anguish echoed off the walls around them. "No, he cannot be dead!"

Durnál nosed at the still body, blew into Tulik's nostrils, laid his head against his chest. "I can hear a heartbeat!" he said. "But it's faint."

"We must get him out of here!" cried Selaks.

"Whatever we do we'd better hurry," barked Rekshana, glancing over her shoulder. "Another of those terrible things may come down on us at any moment!"

"I'll drag him," said Durnál. "The rest of you go on ahead." As Karah fluttered from his back, the *vór* seized the unconscious Tulik by the scruff of his neck and began to tug him along the passage.

"May I?" asked Karah, landing on Fornál's shoulders.

"I'm honoured, ravenlady," the grey wolf replied, his teeth a flash in the darkness.

The rest of the wolves moved on, glancing back into the dark where Durnál struggled with his burden. Their ears were pricked for the dreaded thrumming of the thing-that-ran-on-tracks. When the *vór* tired, Barator turned back to help him.

Taking wing, Tok flew ahead of them through the dark. The air blew strangely in his feathers, and he hated the closed-in feeling of the place. But he flapped onward until again a gleam of light began to show ahead of them. Perhaps it was another of the places where the passage opened out to a ledge, he thought. But the wolves would never be able to lift Tulik up from the tracks.

As he went farther, he realized the light ahead of him was different from before, greyer, and then with a joyous quork he shot out of the passage into open air and the faint light of dawn. He found himself at the bottom of a ravine. Ahead of him, the tracks curved away into the distance, and wooded slopes rose steeply on either side. He could see roosts of the Two-Legs along the top, but here were earth and trees at last after the long horror of the not-world.

"The Lanna be thanked," breathed Selaks, when Tok thumped down on her back and gave her the news. Rekshana and Fornál now dashed ahead, each vying to be the first to reach the ravine. "There's shelter, and we smelled small game!" they chorused, dashing back to meet the others, who had nearly reached the open end of the passage.

"Hurry!" urged Selaks, for behind them now came a familiar low rumble. Selaks and Kimmik burst from the end of the passage, the ravens tumbling free into the sky overhead. With a mighty heave, Fornál and Durnál yanked Tulik from the passage and rolled him down a slope away from the tracks, just as the monster roared out of the opening and rushed away along the ravine.

Trembling, the wolves slunk under the cover of some bushes below the tracks and threw themselves on the ground. Durnál and Fornál panted from their long struggle with the dead weight of Tulik, who still lay unconscious.

Time passed, and the sun rose high in the sky.

"What will we do if Tulik doesn't wake up?" asked Rekshana.

"I think he will," said Tok, who was perched on a bush near Selaks. He had been thinking hard, remembering his own suffering long ago in a many-roosts of the Two-Legs. "I once lit on one of the Two-Legs' not-trees. It thrummed with the same force as that deadly rail. I, too, fell unconscious, yet I survived."

"Go, run about, forage," Durnál said to the young wolves. "We seem safe enough here for now."

Not long afterward, Tulik moaned and began to stir.

"He's awake!" cried Selaks. Eagerly she nuzzled the little wolf and licked his face, until at last he lifted his head.

"You have been hurt. Try to get up," said Durnál, standing over him. Trembling, Tulik managed to drag himself upright.

Tulik's shaggy head swung first toward one of them,

then toward the other. "My *vór*, my *vóra*," he whimpered, "I hear you, but I cannot see you!"

"He is blind!" growled Durnál.

"Better he were dead." Rekshana's voice came from behind them, where the young wolves had appeared out of the underbrush. "A blind wolf is a threat to the pack. We really must leave him behind now."

Selaks whirled around. "*We* give the orders in this pack," she snarled, moving stiff-legged toward the silver-white wolf. "Do you need me to teach you that?"

"I only thought — " Rekshana's words were cut off as Selaks sprang at her. With a savage growl, the *vóra* threw her to the ground and pinned her there.

At once Rekshana rolled onto her back, exposing her furry belly. "I meant no harm, my *vóra*," she begged, ears flattened, lips pulled back in a submissive grin.

"See that you don't." Selaks let her up and stalked away.

"About Tulik's eyes," said Tok. "Long ago when I was injured as he is now, my sight suffered too. At first I could only see light and dark, then just a blur. But my sight returned."

"May the Lanna grant that Tulik too will recover," said Durnál. "But for now, someone must help him. For we must move on."

"I will," said Kimmik. Then, "Come, my brother," she said to Tulik. " Follow my scent and my voice, and I'll watch over you."

The wolves moved off, Tulik wobbling along at Kimmik's side. For some time they moved along the bottom of the ravine, diving for cover among the bushes whenever one of the things roared by on the rails. The sun was low when Durnál stopped and pricked up his ears.

"Listen!" he said, turning back toward the direction from which they had come.

Tok's hearing was less keen, but at last he too heard it. A distant yelping, broken by baying sounds.

"Dogs!" muttered Durnál. "The Two-Legs know we followed the tracks. They must have guessed we'd come out here. Now they have put dogs on our trail!"

The wolves fled along the ravine, running as much as they dared on the more level ground near the tracks to make better speed. Tulik pressed himself close against Kimmik's flank and matched his stride to hers, running in blind terror.

Tok and Brekka took wing.

"Wait for me!" cried Karah. With clumsy flaps, she heaved herself into the air.

"Come on then," called Tok. "Let's spy on the Two-Legs."

They turned back along the ravine, following its course until they reached the opening of the tunnel. There they saw a group of Two-Legs armed with fire-sticks. Before them went a large pack of dogs, noses to the ground, giving voice when they picked up scent.

When they told him the news, Durnál said, "Quick

— fly ahead and find us a stream. Even a trickle might do. Running through water might put the dogs off our scent long enough for us to get away."

Tok and Brekka zoomed off ahead of the wolves, sweeping far down the ravine and circling the sides.

"Not a glimmer of water," Tok reported when they returned. "Not even a puddle."

Durnál stamped his feet in frustration. Then, "Have another look at the Two-Legs, will you? I don't hear the dogs anymore."

The sun had set and it was beginning to get dark. Tok and Brekka found the Two-Legs gathered in a knot, with the pack of dogs gathered around them. As they watched, the trackers and dogs turned and headed back in the direction they had come.

"They've given up!" Tok reported gleefully when they caught up to the wolves again.

"For now," replied Durnál. "Perhaps the thought of catching wolves in the dark didn't appeal to them," he added, with a savage grin. "But they'll be after us again at dawn. I'm sure of it. And there's something else . . . " His words trailed off, as though he was unwilling to speak the thought.

"At least we can rest a while, as it's safe for the moment," said Selaks, casting herself down on the ground. Tok noticed that the *vóra's* sides were heaving, as if the run had left her short of breath. The others threw themselves down to rest too.

Tok hopped over to Tulik, who lay with his head on

his paws. "How are your eyes?" he asked.

Tulik raised his head. "It's as you said it would be, Tok. I can tell light from dark now, and see blurred shapes. But not much more."

The wolves dozed well past the middle of the night. Then Tok, roosting near Selaks and Durnál, roused as the young wolves fanned out along the ravine in search of something to eat. He saw Tulik following close behind Kimmik as she and the others disappeared into the underbrush. Some time passed, then suddenly there was the sound of a scuffle in the bushes. He heard the snap of teeth, and a startled yelp. Selaks and Durnál were on their feet in an instant, noses quivering.

"What . . . " began Tok. Then even his nostrils, less keen than theirs, caught an unmistakable stench drifting on the night air.

Selaks gave a bark of laughter. "Somebody," she said, "has caught a skunk!"

Chapter 14

It isn't a nest, nor yet a lair,
But a home to the creature that shelters there.
It isn't a cave, or a lodge or a den.
What sort of dwelling is it, then?
An abode of the Two-Legs.

— Wolf riddle

"I couldn't see what it was!" wailed Tulik, as he rubbed his muzzle on the ground trying to get rid of the awful scent. "Kimmik startled something in the underbrush and it dashed right at me. So I snapped at it!"

"Well, you know now," observed Rekshana. "Phew!"

"Poor Tulik. It caught you full in the face," said Barator. But even Tulik's grave elder brother could not keep from grinning. The rest of the young wolves rolled about with yelps and yips of laughter.

"What next?" sighed Selaks. Then, "Quiet, all of

you!" she said. "Do you want to bring the Two-Legs down upon us?"

But Durnál's eyes lit up. "Skunk! Why didn't I think of it? Tulik, you've probably just saved all our lives!"

"I have?" Tulik squinted up at the *vór*, suspecting a joke.

"Didn't I say I was looking for a way to disguise our scent and fool the dogs? This will do it." Durnál stalked into the bushes and rolled about where the skunk had sprayed. Then he dragged the stinking carcass out and raked his paws, front and back, on it.

"Your turn, my *vóra*," he said to Selaks.

"Must I?" she asked, curling her lip in disgust.

"You must," he ordered.

Meekly, she did as he said, and the rest of the pack followed her.

"I think you smell lovely, *vóra*," teased Tok as she shook herself from nose to tail. "I quite like the odour of skunk."

"If the wretched beast was three days dead it would smell even better, I suppose," she snapped, glaring up at him.

"Of course."

"Let's get away from here as fast as we can," said Durnál. "What has been worrying me all night is that the Two-Legs will send firesticks and dogs from the far end of the ravine as well as from behind us. They think we will not dare to break cover. So we must fool them."

"You mean to run among the dwellings of the Two-Legs?" asked Tok.

"I mean to head due north across country, wherever that takes us. With this scent on us, dogs will never be able to smell wolf. But I'm trusting you, Tok, to find us a safe place to hide once the sun comes up."

The *vór* bounded away up the slope of the ravine, and the pack flowed after him. The three ravens fluttered from tree to tree, dodging branches. At the top of the ravine, the wolves encountered a wooden barrier too tall to leap. They padded along beside it, looking for a way around. After a time there was a lower barrier, and this they jumped easily, one after the other. They found themselves in a grassy area behind one of the dwellings of the Two-Legs. All was silent, and they could see no light. Then from inside came the sound of a dog barking.

"The Two-Legs' beast knows we're here," said Durnál. "Let's go before it wakes its masters."

Like shadows, they slunk around the structure and out onto a hard path that ran before it. The light from the not-trees blotted out the stars, but Tok sensed the direction in which they needed to go.

"The ravine took us north by west," he told Durnál in a low voice. "So we must take that into account. North lies *that* way," he added "Toward those structures."

Durnál swung his shaggy head in that direction. "Let's run," he growled.

They covered as much ground as they could while the dark lasted. Down narrow passages, over barriers, across open spaces, using the hard paths only when there was no other way. Once, just as they were crossing one of them, a *grawl* swept down on them, lights blazing. It screeched to a halt as wolves bounded right in front of it and flowed on into the darkness.

Crossing a space behind one of the Two-Legs' dwellings, they leaped a barrier, only to come crashing down among strange objects that rolled and clanged along, spilling their rich-smelling contents on the ground. Lights sprang on in the windows of the dwelling, as the wolves fled onward.

The sky began to grow pale above them, and the lights on the not-trees started to wink out. "Fly, Tok," urged Durnál. "We must soon seek cover."

Tok sprang into the air. There was enough light for him to see by, so he circled, gaining height, until the great dwelling place of the Two-Legs lay spread out beneath him. Well behind and to the west lay the line of the ravine. Farther back still was the great, towering heart of the place that they had passed through. Below, he could see the wolves running in their tireless lope, tiny figures in the hostile world around them. He had to find shelter for them before the Two-Legs sighted them and took up the hunt again.

Wheeling, he gazed eastward. The crust of structures covered the earth for many hundreds of wing-beats. But ahead lay an open space fringed with trees, and in its centre, the eye of a small pond reflected grey light as the sky above grew brighter. It was not much of a refuge, but it would have to do.

The wolves reached it just as the sun rose, and plunged into the undergrowth among the trees, not far from the pond.

Selaks scanned the open space. "This place is so small," she said. "Two-Legs could stumble over us at any moment!"

"We'd better hope they don't," replied Durnál. "Meanwhile, stay still, all of you. Not a whimper, not a yelp out of any of you!"

As the sun climbed the sky, the wolves dozed undisturbed. A few Two-Legs appeared, but they kept to the paths that crisscrossed the grassy space. One of them, huffing and puffing, lumbered right past their hiding place.

"Not much of a runner," muttered Selaks.

"It would run faster if it knew you were here," said Tok, and she flicked an ear in amusement.

As the sun rose higher, more and more Two-Legs arrived. The wolves peered out of the underbrush, frightened to be so close to the dangerous creatures, yet fascinated to see what they were doing. Some of them were leading dogs, fastened to them by long ties.

"Imagine letting yourself be led around like that!" snorted Rekshana.

Then a small, fat dog stopped on the path near them, nostrils twitching. It took a step toward them, off the path, but the Two-Legs that led it jerked it back, and it waddled on.

"That was close. That dog scented us, skunk and all," said Fornál. "Still, it might have made a tasty snack," he added wistfully.

More time passed, and the wolves stirred restlessly. The rumble of *grawls* on the hard paths nearby made them nervous, and even when the open space was empty of Two-Legs again they dared not leave their refuge, not even for a mouthful of water from the pond.

Tok too began to grow restless. "I want to take a look at what lies ahead of us," he said, flapping off.

"Wait for me!" cried Brekka, and Karah followed too.

From the air, the wolves' hiding place vanished amid the grey-brown crust of the Two-Legs' structures. But to the north the number of structures grew fewer, and beyond them, Tok could see a range of low hills. Open country.

"I can see the end of it," he told Durnál when they got back. "But there's at least another night's running."

Tulik, who had been dozing, opened his eyes and gazed up at him. "My eyes are much better!" he said. "I can see you clearly, Tok, even perched up there where you are." Turning his head, he added, "And I can see a Two-Legs over there. What's it doing?"

The other wolves lifted their heads, instantly alert.

A pair of Two-Legs had wandered into the open space. One of them was very short, hardly taller than a large dog, and it moved in an odd, wobbly manner. It had a round red thing that it tossed into the air and tried to catch again. When it missed, the small creature ran after it, making a kind of gurgling sound. Not far away, a taller Two-Legs stood watching near the pond.

Selaks's eyes narrowed, and her nostrils twitched as the short creature stumbled closer, chasing its round thing, which rolled toward them across the grass. "It has a kind of milky smell," she mused. "It must be a Two-Legs pup!"

As she spoke, the round object rolled down a little slope and under the bushes, coming to rest right between Fornál's front paws. Durnál and Selaks exchanged anguished glances as the Two-Legs tottered closer. With the tip of his nose, Fornál gave the round object a push, rolling it back out again. The Two-Legs picked it up. Then it got down on all fours and peered under the bush. The wolves froze as it and Fornál stared straight into each other's eyes.

Then the Two-Legs' mouth turned up at the corners. Putting its forepaw inside the strange covering it wore, it pulled out a flat brown object and held it out. Fornál's nose quivered, and a trail of saliva dripped from his jaws. Reaching forward, he took the morsel delicately in his front teeth. Then he swallowed it in a single gulp. The Two-Legs got up and wobbled back across the grass, where the taller one was waiting. They could hear it making sounds and it pointed toward the bushes. But the bigger one took it by the forepaw and led it off, leaving the open space empty again. The little one looked back over its shoulder all the way.

Tok settled his feathers, which had been standing on end, and the wolves let out their breath in a collective *whoosh*.

"A near thing," said the *vór*. "Luckily you kept your head, Fornál."

"What did the Two-Legs feed you?" Tulik wanted to know.

"Always thinking of food!" jeered Rekshana.

Fornál licked his chops reflectively. "Whatever it was, it tasted delicious," he replied.

The endless day passed at last, and that night the wolves ran as never before, the hope of reaching open country lending strength to their legs. Daylight found them still among the last dwellings of the Two-Legs, but they fled onward toward a scrubby wasteland Tok and Brekka had scouted out. It lay beneath a line of giant not-trees the Two-Legs had planted across the countryside.

"Keep away from those not-trees," Tok cautioned Karah and Brekka as they circled in. "Those vine-things strung between them carry the same prickly force as the death track that injured Tulik. I know — I lit on one once and nearly died of it."

No Two-Legs appeared in the wasteland, and the wolves dozed during most of the day. As dusk fell they began to forage.

"I can hardly even remember the taste of deer," mourned Vikka, between bites of a rabbit she and Kimmik had run down.

"Small game is a lot better than nothing," mumbled Tulik, who was crunching a field mouse.

The wolves moved on again, following the swath of open ground under the not-trees. From the air, Tok could see that this led roughly north, and that few Two-Legs seemed to go near it. By dawn they had left the dwellings of the Two-Legs behind, and were climbing among low hills lightly wooded with poplar and aspen. There was no snow, and the air felt like spring.

Tok, Brekka and Karah mounted into the air, swooping among the brown hills, then circling higher and higher as thermals began to build with the warmth of the sun. Tok felt the weight of fear melt from his feathers. The wolves were safe for the moment, the terrible risk they had taken had proved worthwhile. They had not lost much time, and were heading north again. Surely it could not be far to the fringes of the Cold Forest.

Then, "Look!" cried Brekka, and in a moment Tok had seen it too. A small band of shaggy shapes flapping toward them.

"It's Gloran and the others," Karah said as they came closer.

"Rokah! Gloran!" cried Tok. Then he gave a kark of laughter as Barek swooped impertinently close and did a half-roll right over him.

They came together and began to dance, tumbling joyously in the air. His heart lifting, Tok scanned the blue vault of the sky, which was free at last of the murk and stench of the place of the Two-Legs. But then his wings faltered. Above them, passing like a shadow across the sun, was one of the hated flights of the Overlord.

Part 3

The Skeleton Forest

Chapter 15

Skiffet *never lies*.

— Lore of the Lanna

"Our enemies watch us always now," said Gloran, following the direction of Tok's gaze. "They found us soon after we crossed the city, and have never left us for long."

"But they don't attack," Rokah pointed out.

"Waiting," mused Tok. "But for what?"

Later that day the wolves killed a deer. Tulik and Vikka, last at the carcass, lost many tasty morsels to ravens made bold by hunger. Then, bellies bulging with meat, the wolves lay dozing in the lacy shade of the budding trees. Selaks and Durnál slept side by side, he with a protective leg thrown across her back.

"It's warm for the Moon of Fledglings," said Tok, stretching his wings to the warmth of the sun. "Look how little snow there is, even this far north."

"Winter is over," agreed Rokah.

"How much farther is it to the Cold Forest?" asked Gloran.

"I don't know," admitted Tok. "I have never been even this far north."

Below them, Durnál opened a lazy eye. "I have," he said. "Though the land I knew lies farther to the west. We are at least two weeks' running from the Cold Forest."

The wolves fed again during the night and moved on at dawn. Looking back as the pack crossed a ridge and began to descend the other side, Tok saw a dark horde swooping down to scavenge the last of the carcass.

Selaks, too, had glanced back. "They'll find slim pickings," she said, grinning. "Perhaps they'll grow hungry enough to move on."

But Tok did not think so. And if the Overlord's followers grew hungry enough, what then?

On they journeyed. Sometimes winter returned, with gales that frosted wolf coat and raven wing, and blanketed the land in wet snow. But the days were too long now for the power of the sun to be denied. After each storm the snow melted more quickly. Buds swelled and burst into new leaves, and fresh growth sprang up in the dead grass. The country around them was changing too. The wooded hills had given way to rolling land dotted with small clumps of trees and half-thawed bogs surrounded by dense willow thickets. The wolves and ravens, accustomed to the shelter of the forest, grew uneasy.

"I don't like this country," muttered Gloran, balancing awkwardly on a bush near the spot where the wolves had thrown themselves down to rest.

"It's too open," agreed Selaks. "Not enough cover. And deer are harder to come by."

"Perhaps that is why there are no wolves," mused Durnál. "I have been wondering about that. We have found *skiffet*, but none that is fresh."

But despite their fears, they seemed safe enough, and they saw no sign of the Two-Legs.

Late one afternoon they reached the edge of a large wetland. Most of the ravens flew directly across it, while the wolves floundered around the marshy shore. Durnál stopped suddenly as the wind shifted, his nose quivering at a wave of scent from a clump of willows ahead of them.

"Wait!" he warned, and then they all saw it. An enormous shaggy beast with a hump on its shoulders and short black curving horns was thrashing its way out of the thicket. Catching sight of the wolves, it lowered its massive head and snorted, stamping its forefeet in the squashy earth.

"What is it?" breathed Selaks. "I have never seen anything like it."

"Whatever it is, it's food," said Barator. "And plenty of it."

"It's a wood bison," said Durnál. "I saw one long ago, in the Cold Forest. I don't know what this one is doing this far south. An old bull, by the look of it. Maybe driven off from a herd."

Tok lifted off Selaks's back, and perched with Karah and Brekka on a stunted tree nearby, as the young wolves turned their fierce eyes on their *vór*, eager to spring on this unexpected new prey.

"Be careful," Durnál warned them. "It can break your bones by kicking or trampling you, rip your bellies with its horns. We need to move it farther from the thicket, so we can all attack at once."

Acting as he spoke, he sprang forward. Running right around the bison, he nipped at its heels before darting away to a safe distance. Then the other wolves moved in. Selaks and Rekshana made short rushes at the bison, trying to draw it into a charge, while the others nipped at it from behind. The great beast swung its head angrily from side to side, then at last it charged, while the wolves danced nimbly out of range.

The ravens quorked eagerly, sure that the wolves would make short work of even so big a beast. But the old bull was no easy prey. Swinging its head with its deadly horns, it turned in a circle, driving the wolves off for a moment. Then it backed into the shallow water, where it stood awaiting the wolves' next attack. Tulik, Vikka and Kimmik floundered eagerly into the water and tried to get at it, but it drove them off easily with sharp kicks. One horn toss sent Vikka tumbling end over end. She landed with a splash, then hobbled ashore.

"Now what?" demanded Selaks.

"We wait," said Durnál grimly. "We keep testing it. If it weakens, or comes out of the water, we will have it. If not . . ."

The wolves lay down in a semicircle on the shore. From time to time one of them would make a rush at the old bull, but each time it drove the attacker off with horns and hooves.

Light was fading when Durnál called the pack off. "Let's move away some distance, keeping downwind. Then we'll see what it does."

The wolves faded away among the willow shrubs. The ravens, keeping watch from their perch, could see the old bull standing stubbornly in the water. The wolves tested it again toward the middle of the night. But it was still alert and full of fight. They waited until dawn and tried again. Then Durnál called off the hunt.

"It's a tough old beast," he said. "And it knows where it's safe. We could wait it out, for it has to come ashore sometime. But we need to move on." Wheeling, he headed off along the edge of the marsh, the defeated pack trailing behind him.

"Too bad," said Tok, from his perch on Selaks's shoulders. "I was looking forward to a good meal."

"*Numon* is *numon*, Tok," she replied. "It was not the

old bull's time to die, nor ours to kill. There will be other prey."

Beyond the wetland they found drier country. It was rich in small game, which pleased both wolves and ravens. The sun shone, and for days no flights of raiders could be seen. But as they were about to set out one morning, the *vór* paused, listening.

"I hear something," he said. "Do you, Tok?"

Then Tok thought he heard it too, a low buzzing in the far distance. "It might be a *grawl* of some kind." Taking to the air with Brekka and Karah, he scanned the countryside, but could see nothing.

The wolves moved off, cautiously at first, then more confidently as nothing threatened them. The distant buzz remained in the background, but grew no louder. In late morning, Durnál found fresh *skiffet* in a patch of woods beside a small lake. "Wolves at last," he muttered. "The *skiffet* tells me they were here not many days ago. At least four of them. Maybe six."

"Will they attack if we meet them?" asked Tok.

"They may. But some packs tolerate strangers who are crossing their territories."

The wolves moved ahead more slowly now, casting about widely for traces of the other pack. Tok and the rest of the ravens flew ahead over a stretch of open country between two patches of woods.

"Look!" said Gloran after a few moments' flying. "What's that?"

Below them, a line of still shapes lay strewn across

the meadow. Tok swooped down for a closer look, then shot upward again. "It's the other wolves," he called. "We must warn Durnál!"

But the pack had already left the shelter of the woods, and was running toward them across the meadow.

"The wolves are dead, Durnál. Up ahead there!" cried Tok, circling over the *vór's* head.

"*Dead!* But how?"

"I don't know. They lie in a line, as though they died running."

In moments the pack had reached the place where the other wolves lay. They paused, sniffing each stiff body, while the ravens landed and cautiously hopped closer. There were six dead wolves, each with several bloody holes in its rough fur. The last two were smaller than the rest.

"Last year's pups," mourned Selaks, nosing them gently.

"They've been dead for some days," said Durnál. Then, "Their *vór* died trying to protect them." For the shaggy grey wolf at the head of the line lay twisted around, his fangs bared, as if snarling defiance at some enemy. Between his glazed eyes was a round hole crusted with blood.

"Firesticks have done this," said Selaks. "It's the work of the Two-Legs. But how did they manage to kill them all?"

Suddenly Durnál's eyes grew black with horror.

"That buzzing noise — it must be an air-*grawl!*" he cried. "Run! Run for the woods!"

Even as he spoke, the distant buzz began to grow louder. Taking wing, Tok saw a dot in the sky turn and swoop toward the meadow with a deepening roar. The wolves had been sighted.

The other ravens took off, scattering in panic as the wolves fled toward the shelter of the trees. From the air, Tok could see a Two-Legs leaning from an opening in the *grawl*, its firestick sending a deadly hail into the ground around the fleeing wolves, who dodged as they ran.

As the *grawl* bore down on them, Durnál turned and snarled defiance, prepared to die as the other *vór* had.

They can't make it! thought Tok in anguish. Unless . . . Diving, he swooped low over the wolves' heads. "Drop down! Play dead!" he shrieked above the roar of the *grawl* and the boom of the firestick. "Then run when that thing turns around to make another pass."

Instantly Durnál tumbled to the ground in a heap. Selaks and Barator skidded into him and lay still, and the others dropped in their tracks.

Tok held his breath. Would it work? The wolves were an easy target now. Another blast of that deadly hail . . . But the *grawl* was ahead of the wolves now, pulling up and gaining height to make a turn.

"Run!" screamed Tok.

The wolves sprang to their feet and dashed for the shelter of the woods. They reached the trees only just in time, as the Two-Legs in the *grawl* sent a burst from the firestick rattling among the branches. They cowered in an evergreen thicket as it made two more passes over the woods, then droned away into the distance.

"That pack died the way my first mate and family died long ago," Durnál said sombrely. "We too were caught in the open by an air-*grawl*. That buzz — I should have recognized the danger sooner. But it was so far away."

"We owe you our lives, Tok," said Selaks. "If it hadn't been for you we would be lying dead out there too."

"Why are the Two-Legs killing wolves?" asked Barator. "There are none of their beasts here. We did them no harm. We don't even live in this place."

"I don't know," said Tok wearily.

As he stretched his wings, Karah gave a sharp cry. "Tok! Your right wing — two of your flight feathers have been sheared off!"

"A close call," he said.

"Too close!" muttered Brekka, with a shiver.

Suddenly there was a chorus of karks and quorks from the meadow, and Durnál pricked up his ears. "What's going on out there?" he asked.

Clumsily Tok made his way upward from branch to branch until he had a clear view. But he did not answer the *vór*. For out in the meadow, the bodies of the fallen wolves were black with ravens. The followers of the Overlord had settled in to feast.

Chapter 16

The obvious may be the greatest secret.

— Wisdom of the Tellers

"You risked your life out there." Rokah cocked his head and gazed at Tok through narrowed eyes. "The rest of us took cover in the woods, but you stayed with the wolves. Why?"

Tok stared back at his son, puzzled. "The wolves are my friends," he replied. "We have shared many dangers. How could I save myself and not try to help them? It would be *unkora*."

"But you say you are *unkora* already. Like the rest of these former ravenlords. So why take such a chance?"

Tok flicked his whitelids impatiently. "If you can't understand the obvious, I don't know how I can explain it to you," he snapped.

"Perhaps friendship is not an idea familiar to

Rokah," said Gloran. His tone was neutral, but his eyes were cold as he stared at Tok's son.

Rokah threw his head back, spreading his shoulders and raising his hackles. "Nonsense! I have friends aplenty."

"None that I've seen," replied Gloran, raising his hackles in turn.

"Rokah? Gloran? What is this about?" demanded Tok, his own annoyance fading. "Has something happened between you that I don't know about?"

The two big ravens glared at one another, then Rokah said, "Of course not."

Gloran said nothing.

Rokah shook his feathers into place. "I'll go and round up the rest of our ravens," he said. "We had better be on our guard until the raiders move on." He flapped off among the trees.

"Have you and Rokah quarrelled, Gloran?" asked Tok.

"Not exactly," replied Gloran, "though there is no friendship between us."

"I think Rokah has not much use for ravenlords," put in Brekka, who was perched nearby. "He spends a lot of time with the ravenets. Haven't you noticed?"

"Brekka's right," agreed Gloran. "He's always croaking away with them, but when one of us older ones goes near, they all fall silent."

"Well, there's nothing wrong with that, is there?" replied Tok. But his heart was heavy. It was bad enough that the followers of the Overlord seemed to be able to find them wherever they went. But this discord between Gloran and Rokah was worse. He depended on both of them, and distrust between them meant danger for all.

And Gloran had another trouble, for Kordah, his mate, grew more nervous and unhappy the farther they went. Noticing Gloran's constant attentiveness to her, Tok felt a fresh pang of sorrow. He would have watched over Tarkah like that too. Though she would have faced all hardship with her bright courage.

The wolves waited out the day in the depths of the wood, afraid that the air-*grawl* might return. Meanwhile, Tok kept an eye on the raiders. Late in the afternoon they suddenly broke off feeding and lifted off from the meadow, each bird taking wing at the same moment, as if on command. They climbed high into the air and regrouped, then flew off to the north.

"Gloran, you had better lead the ravens north before the light fails," said Tok. "We do not know how far we have to go, so use your best judgment how far you can travel safely before roosting. And you, Rokah, would you fly ahead and then return to tell us the lie of the land we have to cross?"

At least the two of them will be apart for a while, he thought as they took off.

At dusk, the wolves were eager to leave. "We must run this night," Durnál told the pack as Karah flapped onto his shoulders, "and by day tomorrow too, if there are no more *grawls*. We must reach the Cold Forest soon."

"Very soon," said Selaks, getting to her feet and shaking herself. Tok fluttered down and dug his claws into her mane.

"I would ride too, if Barator will put up with me," hinted Brekka, who had stayed behind with Tok.

"Gladly," said the big wolf, grinning.

The wolves set out at moonrise. The sky was clear and starry, and the temperature had dropped sharply.

"Thank the Lanna for decent cold," Selaks muttered. "It makes running easier. I want to put this horrible wolf-killing country far behind us."

They sped across open ground covered in grass and dense willow scrub. The landscape was dotted with great wetlands, mostly thawed now and shining under the moon, and the wolves lost time going around them.

By dawn they found a thicket and threw themselves down to rest. After sleeping for several hours, they ventured out and stood scenting the air and listening. The sky had become overcast, and feathers of snow floated in the air. Tok and Brekka took off and circled, but they saw no danger. Then a solitary black figure appeared in the north and flew quickly toward them.

"Rokah!" said Tok. "Tell us what you have found."

They circled down, and the wolves gathered around. "I flew far to the north, ahead of the others," Rokah reported. "There are more and more trees ahead, though many seem dead. And beyond, a forest dense and black that runs farther than even my eyes can see. I flew over it for a time and saw no end to it. The others reached it just as I returned. They are now foraging along the southern edge."

"The Cold Forest!" said Durnál, his green eyes glowing. "The greatest wood of all. It stretches all the way to the Barren Lands. Surely we will find a safe home there."

"What about the raiders?" Tok asked Rokah.

"None in sight. No need to worry about them."

The one does not necessarily mean the other, Tok thought. But he said no more.

"You are welcome to ride with us," Durnál said to Rokah.

"I prefer to fly ahead," Rokah replied, lifting off. "I will tell the others you are coming."

"Run, my wolves!" urged Durnál.

And they ran, a tireless ground-eating lope that left the country of the wolf-killers far behind. That day the landscape was dotted with more trees. The next day there were yet more. And the next Tok, Karah and Brekka sighted dense forest in the far distance, and ravens dancing in the skies above it. The wolves yipped with joy when they heard of it.

But as the ravens flew closer, their joy faded, for they saw that the close-packed ranks of deep green spruce and tamarack were dotted with reddish, blighted trees, and there were broad stands of dead ones, silvery-dry as skeletons.

"What's wrong with the trees?" gasped Brekka.

"Rokah said he saw many dead ones," Tok reminded her. "Perhaps Durnál will know about it. He has lived in the Cold Forest."

"I don't like it," Brekka said, with a shudder. "It feels . . . sick."

But when Durnál and the other wolves reached the forest, he too was puzzled by the condition of many of the trees. "It's not like anything I've ever seen," he growled. "Of course trees die. But not like this, not in great swaths. Something is killing them."

"Well, never mind," said Selaks briskly. "Half dead or not, this forest will have to do. Let's hurry up and hunt."

Luckily, deer did not seem to mind the skeleton forest. Bushes and thickets had sprung up among the dead trees, providing plenty of browse. The wolves soon flushed a small herd from a thicket, and managed to bring down two of them.

The pack fed hungrily, while the ravens watched from above, salivating. Then they zoomed in to claim a share.

As usual, the pack dozed after feeding while the ravens quarrelled over scraps and preened themselves. But Tok noticed that Selaks seemed restless. She soon got up and began exploring, scrambling over deadfalls and poking her head into thickets. Then she climbed a large rock and stood gazing around.

"Not here. Not right," she muttered. Then she

bounded down from the rock and disappeared into the underbrush.

Durnál, who had been keeping a lazy eye on Selaks, now got up and followed. But Tok noticed that he kept a respectful distance behind her. Curious, Tok flew ahead and perched above a glade where Selaks was sniffing around again.

"What are you doing?" he asked.

Her ears flicked, but she didn't glance up at him. "Don't bother me," she snapped. "I'm busy."

"Best to leave her alone just now," said Durnál, who had come up behind his mate. He sat down, watching her, his brushy tail moving slowly to and fro.

Selaks moved off among the trees again. She found a spot where bare earth lay exposed, and clawed a scrape in it. "Too heavy," she said, and trotted on.

Gradually, she was moving farther and farther away from the place of the kill. The other wolves now woke up and joined Durnál in following the *vóra*. Rekshana and Kimmik bounded ahead and began exploring too. They both found spots that seemed right to them, and summoned Selaks with a yelp. But each time she turned away disappointed, and at last they gave up. Deeper and deeper they moved into the forest. At last they reached an old beaver meadow, where a silver thread of water made its way through the abandoned dam. On the north side of the meadow was a sandy hillock, now warmed by the afternoon sun.

Suddenly Selaks was all attention. Her ears pricked

up and her head swung from side to side as she scanned the meadow and the little stream. Then she bounded over to the hillock, and scraped eagerly at it with her forepaws. She began to dig furiously, throwing sandy soil in all directions. In a short while she had worked some way in, dirt now flying out in clouds between her hind legs.

Durnál merely sat watching, as did the rest of the pack. But Tok, who had lit among them, could see from the way they pranced with their forepaws that they too were excited.

"She's going after something. Aren't you going to help her?" he asked.

The *vór* ran out his tongue, laughing. "I think none of us is brave enough to try," he said, and the others yipped their agreement.

Selaks emerged from the hole she was digging, and Tok fluttered over to her. The *vóra's* face was a mask of dirt, but her restlessness had vanished and her golden eyes gleamed.

"This is it!" she announced, shaking soil out of her fur. "The perfect place."

Tok gave a quork of annoyance. "Perfect for what?" he demanded.

"For a den."

"A den?" Tok asked, astonished. "Why do you need a den?"

Selaks grinned, showing all her teeth. "For the pups, of course!"

Chapter 17

Nothing braver than a desperate she-wolf.

— Lore of the Lanna

Tok stared at the *vóra* in shock. "Pups! When? Why didn't you tell me?"

"Soon. And I thought you might have guessed," she replied. "After all, you teased me about being fatter than I used to be."

Everything made sense now, all the odd things he had noticed about her along the way, thought Tok. "But . . . *pups!*" he said. "How can we travel?"

"We can't," said Selaks. "Not until they are old enough. Here we must stay until late summer."

There will be trouble when the ravens hear that, thought Tok. And sure enough, when he told them that the wolves would go no farther, there were croaks of anger, especially from the ravenets. But older ravens protested too.

"We can't stay here. This forest is half dead!" complained Kordah.

"Why did we ever leave the Raven Mountains?" wailed another ravenlady.

Tok tried to soothe their ruffled feelings. "We need only stay here a few weeks," he told them. "And remember the Terror, remember the Death. *They* are why you left the Raven Mountains."

"For all we know, the Death may strike us down here too once the weather gets hot," a ravenlord said sullenly. "And as to the Terror, our enemies still follow us."

All the ravenets except Barek clattered their beaks in agreement against the branches they sat on.

"What you say is true," Tok admitted when the noise died down. "Though our enemies have not attacked us lately. But you are not bound to stay here, though I will miss you sorely if you go. For myself, I must remain, for I have promised the wolves that I will guide them."

The next morning all the ravenets except Barek were gone. The remaining lords and ladies eyed him glumly, and Tok's heart sank when he realized that Rokah had disappeared too.

"I suspected he was up to something," said Brekka. "So when I saw him go to roost with the ravenets yesterday, I followed him. He has been turning them against you, Tok, saying you care only about traditions and Korts, not the lives of ordinary ravens."

Tok glared at her. "You spied on him! I don't believe Rokah said such a thing. Why would he?"

"Jealousy, perhaps," said Gloran. "I believe Brekka."

"Thank you, Gloran," huffed Brekka, smoothing her untidy feathers with her beak. "Tok's problem is that he doesn't know who his true friends are."

Tok turned his back on them. In the days that followed, he avoided both when he could and kept more and more to himself.

Meanwhile, even though the forest around them was ugly and blighted, the wolves were full of joy. Selaks dug furiously at her den, while the others hunted and then brought hunks of meat back to her. The pack played boisterous games and paid court to their *vór* and *vóra*, and the younger wolves took to exploring the forest on their own.

After several days, the den was finished. Selaks sunned herself a while, and Durnál helped her groom the dirt out of her fur. Then she got up and disappeared into the tunnel she had dug. The wolves hunted that night and left meat at the entrance to the den for her. She came out and ate it and vanished inside again.

The next day, the wolves lay about in the beaver meadow, keeping a watchful eye on the den. Tok hopped to the mouth of the tunnel and peered in. He could see only a short distance, then all was blackness.

"Selaks?" he croaked.

"Go away!" came her voice in a low growl.

"It's best leave her alone just now, Tok," advised Durnál, who was lying nearby.

After a time, the *vór's* ears pricked up. "Listen!" he said. Tok cocked his head, and then he heard something too. A faint whine, then a yip. The wolves got to their feet, tails waving slowly to and fro. More time passed, and more sounds were heard. At last Durnál went over and stuck his head into the mouth of the tunnel. Tok heard Selaks bark, then the *vór* went all the way in. A while later, he came out again.

"Selaks has something to show you, Tok," he said. "You should be proud, for never has a wolf done a raven such honour."

Tok hopped cautiously into the tunnel. Though there was plenty of space, he felt uncomfortable underground. The passage ran straight for some distance, then curved upward. At last it opened into a larger chamber under a dense mass of tree roots. Only a little light filtered down among them, and at first all Tok could see was the white of Selaks's fur. Then, as his eyes adjusted, he could make out five small dark shapes curled up at her side They had snub noses and round ears, and their eyes were still closed.

"They don't look anything like wolves!" he blurted out.

"They do so!" snapped Selaks. "They're beautiful!"

The pack mobbed Tok when he emerged from the den.

"Well?" demanded Barator. "What do you think of them? Our *vór* says there are five."

"Yes, five fine pups," said Tok. "At least, I think so. I've never seen wolves so young before."

"I don't see why the *vóra* lets him in but not us," complained Rekshana.

"Well, she has known him a very long time," Kimmik pointed out.

"But he's a raven. It's none of his business!"

"It'll be days and days before the pups come out," lamented Vikka. "How can we wait so long?"

Selaks now spent many days nursing the pups inside the den, while the pack brought her all the food she needed. But Tok noticed something different in the way this was done. They would gorge themselves at a kill, then return to the den site. Selaks would emerge from the tunnel, then nip and lick the muzzle of Durnál or one of the others. At this signal, the hunter's belly would heave and he or she would disgorge a pile of fresh meat, red and juicy, which Selaks would gulp down. Then she would quickly return to her pups again.

"I wish I could get a wolf to deliver food to me," he teased, watching her eat one day.

"Have pups, wolf bird, and maybe one will," she replied, running out her tongue and laughing.

Meanwhile, though the ravens ate well from the wolves' kills, many of them carped and bickered among themselves, ill at ease in the skeleton forest.

To escape them, Karah, Gloran and Brekka had taken to spending time with the wolves. Karah often visited with the *vór*, while Brekka sought out Barator. Gloran, who was wary at first, made friends with Kimmik. Kordah, his mate, perched on a branch overhead and looked on jealously.

Tok felt annoyed with all of them, and was short with them when they tried to talk to him.

"Why are you so angry, Tok?" asked Karah.

"I'm tired of raven bickering and quarrelling!" he snapped.

She cocked her head, peering at him. "Is that all? It seems to me that you resent some of us growing closer to the wolves."

"Why should I?" Tok replied. He gave his wings a flip, ending the conversation. He was glad that his mother had taken to Durnál. But Brekka and Gloran didn't deserve the friendship of wolves. Not after what they had said about Rokah. They never mentioned his son's defection now, but it lay like a shadow between him and them. They had made it plain that they believed Rokah guilty of treachery, and by disappearing he seemed to have proved them right. That was the real root of his anger, Tok told himself ruefully.

Then, on a blue, breezy day near the end of the Moon of Fledglings, Rokah reappeared as suddenly as he had left. Circling in over the beaver meadow, he lit beside Tok. Folding his wings with a jaunty flip, he asked what had happened since he had been gone.

"Where have you been?" demanded Tok, half delighted to see him, half angry at his confident manner. "Why didn't you say you were going?"

"I was with the ravenets, of course," replied Rokah, who had set about preening his flight feathers. "They were discontented and determined to leave, so I thought it best to fly ahead with them and help them find better territory. There was no time to tell you, Tok."

"And you did find better territory, of course?" asked Brekka, who had perched nearby.

Rokah gave her a cold stare. "Yes, although there is much of this tree death throughout the forest," he said. "But we found better territory well to the north. The foraging is good, and the ravenets will wait for us there until autumn."

No more was said. But that night Rokah roosted beside Tok. As the other ravens drowsed, he edged closer along the branch. "Tell me," he said, "have you seen the white raven again?"

"No," said Tok. "Not since she taught me how to mend Karah's wing."

"Why doesn't she come, do you think?" asked Rokah.

"She said that the journey was ours to make now. But she promised that if we win through she will meet me at the Gates of the North," replied Tok. "Wherever that may be."

"Can't you summon her when we need her?"

"No! Never!" replied Tok. "She just . . . appears."

"She cannot be a true friend, to abandon us among so many dangers," Rokah said thoughtfully. "After all, you say she told you to make this journey. I think she is not to be trusted."

"I don't believe that," said Tok. And he tucked his head beneath his wing, ending the conversation. But his son's words troubled him. Why was Rokah so interested in the white raven?

Not many days afterward, Selaks proudly led the pups out of the den for the first time. Tok was surprised at how much bigger they were. Their ears stood up now, and their bright eyes looked eagerly about.

"Very pretty," he told her. "They actually look a bit like wolves now."

At this, the *vóra* showed him her teeth in a mock snarl.

The pack gathered around, tails waving. Durnál lowered his shaggy head and gently nosed the largest one. At once it nipped and licked at his muzzle, demanding to be fed.

"I see we had better go hunting," said the *vór*, grinning.

The pack set off, with all the ravens except Tok following them.

Selaks stood patiently while the pups nursed. But she soon stepped away. "Time for them to start learning about the world," she said to Tok. She trotted down to the little stream and drank deeply, while the pups tumbled after her, exploring the beaver meadow.

It was a warm afternoon, much warmer than usual even for the Moon of New Leaves, thought Tok. And there were few new leaves in the skeleton forest. Only the tamaracks wore fresh green needles. The air buzzed with newly-hatched flies, which attacked the tender ears and noses of the pups, making them squeak in annoyance. Tok was glad of his stiff cloak of feathers, but he had to blink his whitelids often to keep the stinging pests out of his eyes.

Selaks returned from the stream and stretched in front of the den for a sun bath. As the pups play-wrestled nearby, Tok noticed that one of them, slightly bigger than the rest, had already established mastery over the others. Now and then he would pounce on the back of one of his brothers and sisters, who would quickly roll over in submission.

"Is that one a *vór* in training?" he asked. "He's starting early."

Selaks opened a lazy eyelid. "It is always so," she said.

Tiring of their games, the pups wandered down to the little stream and scrambled along its bank, dipping their paws and noses into the water, then jerking back in surprise when they got wet. Suddenly, Selaks sat up, her nose lifted to the wind. Then she leaped to her feet, hackles rising. She gave a sharp bark that sent the pups scampering back toward the den.

Tok flew up onto a branch and looked around to see what had alarmed her. Then a huge hump-backed shape, its thick brown fur tipped with silver, moved swiftly out of the underbrush.

"Grizzlies! Three of them," shrieked Tok, launching himself into the air as two big yearling cubs nearly the size of their mother ambled into the meadow after the grizzly sow.

The pups were nearly back to the den, and another urgent bark from Selaks sent them tumbling into it, as their mother turned to face the bear. Selaks uttered a piercing howl, summoning the pack. Then with a snarl she launched herself at the grizzly. The bear rose on its hind legs and batted her aside, then advanced on the den. Selaks threw herself at the bear from the rear, ripping at its haunches with her fangs. Meanwhile, Tok swooped down over the bear's head and slashed at its eyes. He missed, but tore a bloody gash in the fur of its face. He knew there was no way that the two of them could defeat the grizzly. But if they could harry it enough it might break off its attack.

The bear had turned on Selaks again, reaching out with its great forelegs.

"Watch out, it's trying to crush you!" cried Tok. Just as he spoke, Selaks sprang again. Turning, the bear grabbed her in mid-air, but the she-wolf writhed out of its grip and backed away snarling.

Meanwhile, the young bears had been sniffing around the mouth of the den. In horror Tok saw that the boldest wolf pup stood just inside, his baby teeth bared in defiance. With a swift movement of its paw, one of the bears scooped the pup out, tossing it into the air. At once Tok turned his attack on the young bears, wheeling around their heads, screaming and slashing. But while he attacked one of them, the other seized the wolf pup, which was trying to limp back toward the den. The pup shrieked as the bear's jaws closed, then he ceased struggling and hung limp between its fangs.

Hearing his cry, Selaks whirled around. The grizzly seized her, crushing her in its grip, drawing her toward its deadly jaws.

Chapter 18

Every creature fears the righteous rage of wolves.

— Lore of the Lanna

In despair Tok flung himself onto the bear's muzzle, sinking his claws into its flesh. He managed to stab one of its eyes with his beak before it tossed him off. At that moment a chorus of howls split the air as Durnál and the rest of the pack burst from the forest. With a startled "Whuff!" the bear dropped Selaks and ran, the young bears loping after her, while the wolves gathered, raging, around the two still bodies in the meadow.

Selaks lay gasping in pain, her breathing shallow. But the pup, pierced deeply by the bear's teeth, was dead. To Tok, grieving beside the fallen *vóra*, the air seemed to crackle with the wolves' anger.

Durnál's eyes were blazing. "That she-bear and her young attacked our den," he snarled. "They have injured my mate and killed one of our pups. They must never be allowed to do it again, to us or to other wolves. They must die!" There were howls of agreement from the others. With the pack at his heels, he bounded into the forest, hot on the scent of the bears.

They cannot do it, thought Tok. Not even they, fierce and brave as they are, can bring down three grizzlies. He lingered beside Selaks a few moments longer, then he took wing, dodging among the trees, following the direction taken by the wolves. To his surprise, he found them gathered not too far away.

Durnál's first fury had burned down to cold rage, and he had a plan. "The pack must divide," he was saying. "The strongest of us — myself, Barator, Rekshana and Kimmik — will attack the grizzly sow. The rest of you take on the young bears. I'm depending on you, Fornál, to be clever. Get around the bears somehow, staying downwind, then be ready to attack the young ones after we engage the grizzly sow. We must wait until they get into more open space if we hope to kill them."

He looked up at Tok, who had perched above him. "Fly, Tok. Spy out what the bears are doing," he said.

"There's something you should know, *vór*," said Tok. "When Selaks was fighting the grizzly sow, I stabbed one of the beast's eyes with my beak. It will not be able to see as well on that side."

Durnál showed his fangs in a savage grin. "You were ever our friend," he said. Then, turning to the others,

"Let us go now, but cautiously. We don't want the bears to be aware of us too soon."

More slowly now, the pack moved off through the forest. Tok flew above the trees, scanning every open space for a sign of the bears. At last he saw them, crossing a small glade, the grizzly sow stopping now and then to paw its face as if it was in pain. Not too far beyond, he could see a larger open space where dead trees had fallen and new growth was springing up. He zoomed back to tell the wolves.

At once Fornál led his group away from the rest of the pack. From the air, Tok glimpsed him circling far to the north, keeping the scent of his group from drifting to the noses of the bears. Durnál and the others followed the bears' trail, keeping well back.

Meanwhile, the rest of the ravens joined Tok in the air.

"What's going on?" demanded Gloran. "We were all at the wolves' kill, then we heard howling from near the den."

"Come on," cried Tok. "I'll tell you on the wing."

From the air they could see the battle begin to unfold. The grizzlies had moved into the open space. The young bears were foraging, ripping apart rotting logs with their claws and licking up grubs. The grizzly sow lapped water from a stream. Then the beast rubbed the left side of its face in the mud along its bank.

"I did injure her!" Tok gloated. But he did not think

it would really be much help to the wolves.

Beyond the opening in the forest, the ravens could see Fornál, Vikka and Tulik lying in wait in a thicket. Suddenly Durnál and his group burst howling from the edge of the forest. The grizzly sow's head swung around as it caught their scent. Then it charged them. At first the wolves danced away, leading it farther and farther from the young bears. Then they attacked, Durnál throwing himself straight at the bear while the other three moved behind it and tore great gashes in its flanks. The bear reared up, trying to grasp Durnál, who shot under its forelegs and ripped at its underbelly. Now it was Barator's turn to fling himself at the bear, which reared again, still trying for a crushing grip. Seizing the opportunity, Durnál dove under its left foreleg, his fangs slashing deeper wounds in the bear's belly. The great beast was now bleeding heavily, and roaring in pain and fury.

Meanwhile, Fornál and the others had broken cover. He attacked one of the young bears, slashing its flanks and then leaping away out of its reach. When it went down on all fours, he leaped onto its back for a moment, gouging great wounds through its fur before bounding off again. Bleeding heavily, the bear turned and ran into the underbrush, and Fornál turned to help Vikka and Tulik, who had gone after the other young bear. Time after time, it batted them off, tumbling them tail over nose. But each time they hit the ground running and attacked again, inflicting so many bloody wounds that the bear began to waver on its feet.

With fierce cries, Tok, Rokah, Gloran and Barek swooped down to join the battle. To Tok's annoyance, Brekka followed too. "Go back!" he yelled at her. "It's too dangerous!"

But she ignored him, and flew straight into the fight, joining Fornál's group in their battle against the remaining young bear. She and Barek dove at its head, pecking at its face. As Tok attacked the grizzly sow, he saw a blow of the young bear's paw knock Brekka tumbling in the air, but she recovered and launched herself at it again. Slowly the young bear weakened. It stumbled and went down, with the wolves tearing at it. In a few moments it lay still. At once the three young wolves joined the attack on the she-bear.

Seven wolves now threw themselves at the big grizzly in relays, the main attacker dashing in from the bear's left to take advantage of its damaged vision, while the others worried at its haunches. Their fangs tore great gouges in its back and flanks, and the deep wounds Durnál had made in its belly spouted blood. Tok and the other ravens zoomed around its head, slashing at it with their claws. The woods echoed with snarls, roars and the hoarse screams of the ravens.

Rekshana sprang to the attack, but missed her grip and the bear sent her flying with one blow of its great paw. The silver-white wolf hit the ground hard, but she staggered to her feet and limped back to the fight. Snarling, Kimmik threw herself at the bear, laying open its side with her fangs, while the bear's claws raked red gashes down the black wolf's side. Then at last the bear began to tire. It went down on all fours, and the wolves closed in. They slashed at it, tearing at its entrails until its blood drenched the ground and it lay still. Then they tore it to pieces and scattered its remains across the glade.

The wolves were battered and bloody, but their eyes flamed with victory. Throwing back their heads, they howled a song of savage triumph that echoed away among the trees.

"Shall we hunt down the other bear?" asked Fornál. "It's wounded, and should be easy to kill."

"No," growled Durnál. "We have taken vengeance enough." Turning their backs on the blood-soaked glade, the wolves bounded back in the direction of the den.

Chapter 19

The hardest thing to do is nothing.

— Raven proverb

Tok found Selaks struggling to get up. She was surrounded by the surviving pups, who were bunting her with their noses, trying to nurse. With a short bark, the injured *vóra* sent them back to the den. Moments later, the pack arrived.

"We are avenged," Durnál told her. "The grizzly and one of her young are dead. They will not trouble us again."

"Good," wheezed Selaks. "But that does not bring our little one back." She staggered to her feet and limped over to the still body of the pup. Picking it up gently in her mouth, she carried it down to the streamlet where the ground was soft. Laying it down, she scraped a hole in the ground with her forepaws. Then she placed the small body in it and nosed mossy earth over it.

All afternoon she lay outside the den with her head on her paws, while the rest of the pack inspected each other's wounds and licked them clean.

"Are you badly hurt, *vóra?*" Tok asked, dropping down beside her.

"I don't know," she replied. "As you can see, I escaped with few wounds. But it hurts when I breathe."

Brekka, too, had been injured, and when the rest of the ravens returned to the wolves' kill, she remained behind.

"My left wing is sore," she confessed to Tok when he landed beside her.

"I warned you to stay out of the fight," he reminded her.

Brekka's eyes flashed. "You fought," she shot back. "So why shouldn't I?"

Tok sighed. "I suppose I should be grateful that Karah had the sense to keep out of it!"

As they spoke, a low buzzing sound was heard in the distance, growing louder, and both of them raised their heads. High above, the late sunlight gleamed on the wings of an air-*grawl*. At once the wolves moved out of the meadow, seeking the shelter of the trees. The *grawl* droned away to the west, then returned somewhat farther north.

"It seems to be looking for something," said Durnál.

"Us?" asked Tok, who was perched above him.

"I don't think so. The Two-Legs who shot at us

before don't know we're here, after all. No, it must be doing something else. But what?"

As the light faded, the air-*grawl* disappeared to the south and did not return. But the next day and the next they heard it in the distance again, annoying as the drone of a wasp.

Tok noticed that Selaks had grown restless, and at first thought it was because of her injury. But Durnál seemed uneasy too.

"We must move," Selaks said at last. "Though the pups are still too young for it."

"But you are safe here now," Tok pointed out. "That young grizzly would not dare to come back."

"No, Tok, we are not safe," she replied.

"Selaks is right," said Durnál. "If a male grizzly comes across the scent of that female, it will lead him straight here. And against a full-grown male we would have no chance at all."

"But what about the pups?"

"I will carry them," said Selaks.

"But you can't!"

"I can and I will," she said grimly. And none of the wolves tried to argue her out of it.

First, though, they had to find a new den site. "It need not be so deep a den as this one," Selaks pointed out. "The pups will be spending more and more time outside now."

Karah, Gloran and Brekka offered to help Tok search out possible den sites. But Rokah and the other ravens, who had been gorging on the remains of the grizzlies, preferred to go on with their feasting. So Tok and the others veered off in different directions, looking for open spaces with water nearby that were not too far away. The wolves inspected the sites they found, rejecting most. But at last one glade was accepted. There the pack discovered an old fox burrow high in a grassy bank, and Rekshana and Kimmik dug it wider and deeper while Selaks kept a watchful eye on their work.

"Phew!" she said, sniffing disgustedly. "Make sure you get all the old earth out. Foxes do stink!"

"All of you still smell pretty strongly of skunk yourselves," Tok joked.

"Do we?" she asked, giving her hind leg a sniff. "I suppose my nose has grown accustomed to it."

Then slowly, stopping often to catch her breath, the *vóra* moved each pup to the new den, carrying it gently by the scruff of its neck. She refused all offers of aid, even from Durnál. By the time the last pup was safely delivered, her breathing sounded laboured, and she had to lie down and rest.

Spring advanced, and the weather grew much warmer. Though it was only the Moon of New Leaves, it was already hotter than most of the summers Tok remembered. In some places open water was beginning to dry up, the mud along the banks cracked and dry. Luckily, a spring bubbled up from the ground not far from where the den was located, and this source of water did not fail. But all around them the forest became drier and drier. The air was thick with insects, and Tok noticed that the few surviving spruce trees were infested with hordes of caterpillars.

"The pests seem to thrive in this heat," he reported to Durnál and Selaks. "They are eating the buds of the spruce trees. Can that be what is killing the forest?"

The *vór* shook his ears, trying to drive off the biting flies. "I only know that this forest is dying. As soon as the pups are old enough to travel, we must head farther north."

But that was still a long time away, Tok discovered. The pups could not leave the den area until midsummer, and even then they would not be able to travel very far. Meanwhile, the wolves roamed more and more widely, sometimes hunting together, sometimes alone. But they always returned to disgorge food for Selaks and the pups. Tok and Gloran, Karah and Brekka also took turns bringing morsels to them, while the other ravens feasted at the wolves' kills.

The pups grew bigger and stronger, with large heads and big feet they kept tripping over. They played together boisterously, wrestling with each other or struggling over pieces of deer hide brought back for them to chew. In time a new pup established dominance and his brother and sisters had to yield to him. Sometimes Selaks now joined the hunt, leaving Kimmik, Vikka or Tulik to mind the pups. But it seemed to Tok that the *vóra* was not as she had been before the bear's attack. Though as fleet as ever, she quickly became short of breath, and would fall behind the others, panting with pain.

Meanwhile, Tok kept a wary eye on the sky. The air-*grawl* came and went in the distance, but whatever the Two-Legs were doing it didn't seem to concern them. Twice he glimpsed raiders high overhead, but they too passed over harmlessly. Tok began to hope that the Overlord had lost sight of them.

But one day when the wolves had killed again, the sky suddenly darkened above them and the enemy poured down out of the sky.

"Raiders!" Tok yelled, but the horde was already on them. Beaks slashing and claws tearing, the attackers drove Tok and his companions off the carcass by main force.

"It's no use!" cried Gloran, trying in vain to shield his mate from the storm of beaks and claws. "There are too many. We must retreat to the woods!"

Bursting with rage, Tok watched the attackers settle down to enjoy the carcass. Some even harried the wolves who had been resting at the edge of the clearing, pecking at their eyes, nipping their rumps and tweaking their tails. The furious wolves leaped and snapped at them, crushing those they caught in their jaws and throwing them to the ground. But at last they too were driven from the clearing.

"Ravens driving wolves from their kills?" said Selaks, her eyes blazing. "Who ever heard of that?"

"The Overlord has changed many things," said Rokah.

"You sound as if you admire him!" said Brekka.

Rokah spread his shoulders and glared at her. "I didn't say that," he insisted.

The horde stripped every shred of flesh from the carcass, then lifted off with mocking quorks and flew away northward. The next morning, Tok awoke to find that the rest of the ravenlords and ladies had departed. Only Gloran and Kordah, Rokah, Karah, Brekka and Barek remained.

"I tried to talk the others out of going," said Rokah.

"*Did* you?" Gloran asked mockingly, while Brekka stared long and hard at Rokah.

Tok could not blame the others for going. It was their choice, after all, and with him they had found nothing but misery. But why, then, did he feel such an ache in his heart? At least Rokah had remained, and this comforted him.

It was in the Moon of Flowers that the storms began, more violent than anything either wolves or ravens had ever seen. Each afternoon, great towers of cloud built up in the stifling heat, casting deep shadows across the land. Fierce winds gusted through the skeleton trees, sending many crashing to the ground. Then lightning stalked in zigzag strides across the forest, and peals of thunder split the air. Sudden downpours followed sometimes, but more often there was no more than a mocking sprinkle that evaporated as it reached the ground. The thirst of the trees went unquenched.

"I do not like this heat. I fear it," growled Durnál, as the ravens and wolves waited out yet another storm in the shelter of the trees at the edge of the glade. "The Cold Forest is cold no longer." As he spoke, thunder cracked directly overhead and they all flinched.

"It must all be part of the Change," said Tok. "Storms, drought and last winter's scant snowfall — it's as the white raven told me, the world we know is ending."

"She said *that?*" Rokah turned his bright gaze on him. "You have seen her, then, and not told us!"

"Not so," countered Tok. "She said it long ago, the first time I saw her."

Through storm after storm they waited. And with each one Selaks grew more fretful. "There is a strange dread in my heart," she told Durnál. "If the pups could travel safely I would have us leave now, today. But they can't — I know it. I have already lost one of them. I can't bear to lose any more."

Late one afternoon the pack lay panting in the shade, while the ravens drowsed overhead. Having left Kimmik in charge of the pups, they had gone hunting, and had killed a deer some distance away. A fitful breeze sprang up, soughing through the dry needles of the trees, and at once every wolf head turned upwind.

"Another grizzly?" Tok called down to Durnál, for

he could see and smell nothing.

"No," said the *vór*, who was staring fixedly into the depths of the forest.

Then, out of the deep shadows under a spruce tree stepped a tall brindled wolf. It was worn and gaunt, its skin hanging loose on its bony frame. But its dark eyes were keen and bright. Ears pricked, head high, it stared at the other wolves.

Durnál raised his hackles, ready to defend his pack.

Then Selaks cried, "Is it Adanax? Oh, Father, I believed you maimed and dead in the Lost Hills!"

The newcomer looked puzzled. "Adanax?" it said. "No. I am Taxin!"

Chapter 20

Ran he then as no wolf before.
Faster than smoke, sister!
Faster than fire, brother!
Brave heart, never failing.

— from "Song of Vór Durnál,"
Songs of the Lanna

"Taxin? Can it be?" Selaks stepped closer to the strange wolf, her nose sifting his scent. Then she hurled herself on him, nuzzling his neck and throwing a foreleg across his shoulders. A moment later the newcomer vanished under an eager wave of wolves, as the rest of the pack welcomed Timmax's big son.

"What are you doing here, cousin?" demanded Fornál.

"And how did you find us?" asked Kimmik.

"Wait," said Durnál. "There is plenty of time for him to tell his story. Right now, though, he looks like he needs a good meal. Help yourself to our kill, Taxin," he added.

"My thanks," said Taxin, grinning. "It was the scent of it that brought me to this spot, though I've long been searching for you."

While Taxin was feeding, the sky darkened, and the gusts of wind grew stronger, blowing first from one direction, then from another.

"Another storm," said Selaks. "We had better head back to the den. The pups fear the thunder."

But even as she spoke there was a blinding flash, followed by a deafening crack of thunder. Tok, high in a spruce tree, happened to be gazing north when the lightning struck. Its jagged image seared itself into his eyes, and his feathers prickled. When his vision cleared he saw a tall column of smoke and heard the crackle of flames. "Fire!" he yelled.

The wolves were already on their feet, but now lightning was striking all around them. To the south, another column of smoke and flame roared up toward the sky, and Tok could see it spreading with deadly speed through the bone-dry forest. Moments later a third bolt struck to the north again, kindling yet another blaze. Then the wind shifted again, veering into the south, and the fire rolled swiftly toward them.

Taking to the air, Tok and the other ravens could see that the wolves were caught between two advancing fires. "Save yourselves!" he called to the others, as he banked on the wind. Then, when he saw Brekka coming after him, "No! If you want to help, make sure Karah is safe!" She turned back, and he dove down to warn the pack, which was running north.

"I see fires to the north and south of you. But there's a swamp to the northeast," he screamed over the roar of the flames. "That's your only chance."

"Durnál, I must get to the pups!" cried Selaks. "They will be terrified."

"I forbid you," he growled. "You cannot run fast and far enough, injured as you are. It would be certain death. As far as we know they are safe enough, and Kimmik will look after them."

The wolves headed for the swamp. As they got closer they were overrun by a herd of deer dashing in panic through the forest. A black bear shambled out of a thicket, and stood on its hind legs sniffing the acrid smell of smoke. It stared as the wolves raced past, then broke into a clumsy gallop, following them.

At the edge of the swamp, the wolves stopped, dismayed. Drought had shrunk it to no more than a dark eye of water surrounded by a wide space of damp mud and dry cattails. Yet it seemed that every creature of the forest had sought shelter there, prey and predator alike huddled together in a temporary truce.

"Into the water!" Durnál ordered the pack. "Soak yourselves, then roll in the mud. Stay as wet as you can."

The wolves forced their way toward the open water, stepping on snakes and toads, shouldering aside a young deer too terrified of the fire to be afraid of them. Then, dripping wet and caked with mud, they cowered among the other creatures as the fires closed in around them. The smell of smoke grew stronger, and birds unable to fly high enough to escape began to drop dead to the ground, overcome by the heat and fumes.

The *vór's* head swung around, testing the wind, and Tok guessed that he was more worried about the safety of the pups than he had admitted. The fire to the south would soon roll past them, driven by the gusty south wind. If the other fires were driven north too, then the pups might indeed be in danger.

"Is there a way through to the north, Tok?" asked Durnál.

"I saw lightning strike there twice, *vór*, both times kindling fires. But they had not joined up yet."

"Then I will try to find a way between them and get to the pups," said the *vór*.

"No!" cried Selaks. "You said it was death to try."

"Death for you, my *vóra*," he replied, "and for some of the others who are still stiff or lame from our battle with the bear. But I am fit to run fast." Then he turned to Barator. "I place my pack in your charge. Keep wet and hope the fire rolls quickly over you, or veers aside. When you can, make rendezvous with me at the beaver pond northwest of the den. The pups can run that far. And there is still water there in case the fire turns that way."

The *vór* soaked himself once more in the wet mud, then bounded away through the roiling clouds of smoke.

"Help him, Tok!" cried Selaks.

So Tok struggled aloft, buffeted by hot winds, half choked with smoke. Though the forest was now completely ablaze to the south, there still a gap between the two northern fires. But even as he watched he could see them creeping closer together, driven onward by the fierce south wind.

"You will have to be quick," he gasped, fluttering over Durnál's head as he raced forward. "The gap between the fires is closing."

"I will run as wolf never ran before," vowed Durnál. "May the Lanna be with me."

Over the ash-sprinkled ground he sped, leaping fallen logs and crashing through thickets, with the crackling roar of the main fire behind him. Sparks and coils of smoke blew around him from other blazes on both sides. Tok zoomed ahead, hoping to spy out a faster way among the trees, but the ground was dense with underbrush. The forest on both sides was alight now, flames crackling along the dead branches of the skeleton trees. The very ground beneath Durnál's flying feet was beginning to burn. Thunder still cracked overhead, scarcely heard over the roar of the inferno, but only a few drops of rain pattered down, hissing on the flames.

With a roar, the two fires converged, just as Durnál

hurled himself out of the gap. There was a pause as the wind backed and the walls of flame collided and faltered, and the fire turned upon itself. The *vór* began to gain ground. He's going to make it! Tok exulted. For the den clearing lay only a short distance ahead now, and there was no fire to the north of it. They could lead the pups to the beaver pond if only the wind did not shift again!

But just as the *vór* reached the clearing, a screaming gust from the south caught the edge of the fire and hurled it far forward. Long tongues of flame leaped among the crowns of the trees, licking greedily at dead branches, and showering the ground with sparks and burning brands that set the grass and underbrush ablaze.

They found Kimmik digging frantically at a mound of sandy soil where the den had been. "The pups are underneath," she panted. "They panicked when they heard the roar of the fire and saw the flames, and tried to dig deeper into the den. But that only made the roof cave in!"

Durnál joined her, and their digging sent showers of soil in all directions. At last one furry head appeared, then another and another. As the last pup struggled out of the earth, Tok took wing, sparks swirling around him. Peering through the smoke, he saw a tall spruce, livid with flame, toppling toward the den.

"Run!" he shrieked.

But the burning tree crashed down, crushing the

wolves beneath it. Carried aloft on a blazing updraft, Tok felt the edges of his feathers singe as, gasping, he forced himself higher, seeking purer air. Just as he rose above the smoke, there was another clap of thunder. Then came a great downpour, and the air filled with steam from the burning forest. The mocking, longed-for rain had come at last.

Catching his breath, Tok dove down through the smoke. The rain was quenching the fire, though some of the trees around the clearing still flamed defiantly in the downpour.

"Durnál?" called Tok, hopping along the length of the fallen tree. "Kimmik?" But there was no answer. At last, among the thinner branches toward the top of the tree, he saw a movement. Kimmik, charred and scorched, was disentangling herself from the half-burnt branches. Whimpering with fear and pain, she dragged herself out.

His heart sinking, Tok turned back, croaking the *vór's* name.

Then he heard a voice, scarcely more than a whisper. "Tok!" Peering among the charred branches of the heavy trunk, Tok found Durnál. The *vór* was burned almost beyond recognition, only his deep green eyes showing who he was. Crushed beside him lay the bodies of the pups he had tried to protect.

Then, "Kimmik?" gasped Durnál.

She crept nearer. "Here, my *vór!*" she cried.

"Tell . . . Selaks. No blame . . . no bitterness. *Nu-*

mon . . . " The green eyes closed, and Durnál gave a shuddering sigh.

"He has joined the Lanna," said Kimmik. Raising her muzzle, she uttered a long wail of mourning.

Chapter 21

There are no equals in a wolf pack.

— Lore of the Lanna

For days Selaks lay, head on paws, beside the charred tree that was the final resting place of her mate and pups. The leaderless wolves hunted and brought food back to her, but she would not touch it. Gaunt, with lacklustre fur and a great burn mark across her nose where a flaming branch had struck her, the *vóra* was soon no more than a shadow of the wolf she had been.

In vain, Tok tried to comfort her. "Durnál spoke of you at the last," he told her. "He said, 'No blame, no bitterness.' He said his death was *numon*."

Selaks gave a deep sigh that wracked her body. "He would say that! He was ever loving, ever brave. Yet there is blame, and it is all mine."

As Tok watched the wolves, sorrowing, he began to understand for the first time how the will of *Vór*

Durnál had bound them into a unit. For they were a true pack no longer. Before, each wolf had known its place in the order of *karlán*, and they had worked easily together. But now they began to test each other, eyes keen with ambition. Barator and Fornál, who had always been friendly, now fought viciously, contesting the leadership of the hunt and their positions at the kill. Between fights, they both bullied and humiliated Tulik, whose back soon bore many half-healed wounds from the bites of his brothers.

But the change in Rekshana was the greatest of all. She too nipped and tormented Tulik. And every time she met Vikka she attacked her, growling and biting until the brown wolf rolled over on her back and whined in submission. Soon Vikka would lie down and roll over if Rekshana so much as glanced her way. The white wolf then turned her attention to Kimmik, who was still recovering from the injuries she had suffered from the grizzly and the fire. Challenged, Kimmik would snarl and back away, but she was careful not to provoke her pale-eyed sister, who stalked about stiff-legged, daring anyone to get in her way.

The other ravens, attending the wolves at their kills, noticed the change in them, too.

"They can't go on like this," Brekka said one scorching afternoon, as the wolves drowsed in the shade. "Sooner or later they will have to decide on a *vór*. My guess is that my friend Barator will come out on top. He's the biggest."

Kordah fluffed her feathers. "Might isn't always the most important thing," she replied. "I think *my* wolf, Fornál, is far cleverer than Barator."

"What do you say, Tok?" asked Karah. "You know more of wolves than the rest of us."

"I have known four *vórs*," said Tok slowly. "Malik, Selaks's brother, was brave and clever, but he lacked heart. He nearly brought his pack to disaster. Timmax I cannot speak about, for he grew up and became a *vór* after I left the Raven Mountains. Adanax and Durnál were great leaders who always put the pack first. It seems to me that neither Barator nor Fornál is the stuff of which such *vórs* are made."

Rokah cocked his head and gazed at him. "You expect trouble, then?"

"I do," said Tok. "Wolves are unruly and passionate by nature. Without a *vór*, the pack will fall apart."

"Surely Selaks will not let that happen," protested Brekka.

"She doesn't seem to care. And that frightens me more than anything else," replied Tok soberly.

He went on brooding about the wolves, and *karlán*. He was curious to know how Taxin would fit in, and made a point of watching him. He soon saw that the newcomer was careful to avoid both Barator and Fornál when he could, merely following whichever of them led the hunt. When they fought, he stepped aside, favouring neither.

At last Tok decided to seek him out. He spied Taxin

curled up some distance from the rest of the pack and flapped over to light on a branch above him.

"Greetings, Taxin," he said.

"You're Tok, aren't you?" the big wolf replied. "The one the others call 'wolf bird.'"

"I'm still wondering why you left the Raven Mountains and how you found us," said Tok. "You've never said."

Taxin met his gaze. "The pack has more important things to think about."

"Why *did* you leave?"

The eyes of the big brindled wolf grew dark with emotion. "My father, Timmax, was shot by the Two-Legs not long after you left. I can't bring myself to tell Selaks. Not after what has just happened."

Tok's wings drooped in sorrow. "I grieve with you, Taxin. I was very fond of your father."

"I know it," replied the young wolf. "For he often told tales of the great journey he and my mother and Selaks made with you many seasons ago. He called you a hero among ravens and a true wolf friend."

"But why, if your father was dead . . . "

"Did I not become *vór?*" finished Taxin. "That was because of Adánik. You remember, Selaks's son who chose to join the Black Ridge pack, rather than journey with you?"

Tok nodded. "His sister did, too."

"Araxa. Yes. Well, when we found *Vór* Timmax dead, Adánik was ready. He had already been working to gain the favour of my mother and sister. And Araxa, of course, backed him too. Then he told me he would fight me to the death for the *vór*ship. Or I could leave the pack. The choice was mine, but there would be no place for me in his pack."

"And you chose to leave."

The big wolf flinched, as if expecting a reproach. "Yes. Adánik is a year older than I am. He is bigger and heavier. I knew I would surely lose. And so I chose to leave." He put his head down on his paws. "It is not pleasant to discover that you are a coward."

Tok clacked his beak angrily. "It doesn't sound like cowardice to me. It sounds like you made a sensible decision. And another thing. I know something of wolves, thanks to Selaks and Durnál. It seems to me that Adánik behaved badly in forcing you out of the pack. What if something happens to him? There is no other male wolf nearby now. The pack may die out."

Taxin lifted his head. "I begin to see why my father liked the company of ravens. Thank you, Tok."

There was silence between them for a moment, then Tok went on. "But how did you find us, once you decided to leave?"

"Not easily." Taxin grinned. "The trail was old and cold when I set out. I knew you were headed north by the most direct route so I made my way over the pass from the Raven Mountains and down into the valley where the Two-Legs dwell. But from there I could not find a pass to the north."

Tok shuddered, remembering. "Just as well," he said. "It was nearly a deathtrap for us."

"So I turned east," Taxin went on, "and found my way out among the mountains there. Then I turned north again, and circled the great stinking place of the Two-Legs. I found old *skiffet* in the northern hills, and more in the wooded lands beyond. After that, I ran due north until I reached the forest. And so I found you."

"I'm glad," said Tok. "I think the pack needs you."

The brindled wolf gazed at him quizzically. "If so, it is the first pack that does," he said at last, lowering his head onto his paws again.

It was not long afterward that Rekshana made her move. The pack had hunted and had brought food to Selaks again, which she rejected. She lay as before beside the place where Durnál's body rested, only getting up occasionally to lap a little water from the spring.

Rekshana stalked over and stood gazing down at her. "Enough!" she growled. "We all loved our *vór*. And the pups too. You are not the only one who suffers. But we must leave this place. There is nothing to stop us now."

"I cannot leave," mourned Selaks. "I cannot!"

Rekshana's pale eyes flashed. "You can and you will," she growled, "or we will leave you behind. At first I thought we had only lost our *vór*. But now it's clear we have lost our *vóra* too! You have failed us."

For a moment, Selaks's eyes flashed with their old fire. Slowly she got to her feet, and Rekshana backed away a step. Then Selaks's head drooped and she laid back her ears. "You are right. I have failed you all. It was my Seeing that brought us here from the Raven Mountains. The Seeing was true, for everything happened exactly as I Saw it. But I led you toward the danger, not away from it. You might all have died."

Rekshana advanced and stood over her, ears pricked. "At least you admit your failure. Your folly cost the lives of our *vór* and your own pups. You are not fit to rule the pack." She swung around sharply to face the others. "*I* claim Selaks's place. I am the most fit to be *vóra*. Does anyone deny me?"

The male wolves exchanged astonished glances, but none of them said anything.

Vikka rushed eagerly forward and nuzzled the white wolf's face, then rolled over on her back. Rekshana ignored her. Her eyes were fixed on her other sister. "You, Kimmik? You have ever been quick to put yourself forward. Try that now and I will kill you."

Kimmik turned to gaze at Selaks for a long moment.

"You must choose you own trail now, daughter," the sorrowing she-wolf said. "For I am finished."

Tok, who had been watching it all from above, could no longer contain himself. He hurled himself off the branch and landed in front of her. "You cannot give up, *vóra*," he pleaded, spreading his wings. "You must not!"

"It is *numon*," Selaks replied.

Rekshana's eyes gleamed with triumph, and she turned to Kimmik. "Well?" she said, prancing impatiently with her front paws. "I am waiting. Yield or fight."

It seemed to Tok that the air crackled as the two young she-wolves locked eyes. Then, "I yield, sister," said Kimmik. "You are *vóra*." Pacing forward, she nuzzled Rekshana's chin and neck. Then she too rolled over on her back in submission.

Rekshana's silvery eyes flicked to Selaks. "And you?" she challenged.

Slowly, step by step, Selaks approached until the two of them stood nose to nose. For a moment Selaks hesitated, and a shiver rippled along her creamy coat from nose to tail. Then she gently mouthed Rekshana's muzzle and lay down at her feet.

Chapter 22

*Change can mean life or death. Only the wise
know which.*

— Wisdom of the Tellers

Now Barator and Fornál moved forward, tails waving. With nose nudges and shoulder bunts the senior males acknowledged their sister's change of *karlán*. Tulik skulked behind them, too timid to approach the new *vóra*.

Rekshana stared at him and he dropped his eyes. "Remember, nothing has changed for you, *karlás*," she growled, showing all her teeth. Then she turned to Taxin, who had not approached her either. "And you?" she asked in a gentler tone. "Have you no word to say?"

"Congratulations, *vóra*," he replied. "I thought it better not to put myself forward, newcomer that I am."

"He's right," said Barator. "Taxin is not a member of this pack." Fornál growled his agreement.

"His *karlán* is something the three of you must settle," returned Rekshana. "But I may as well tell you that Taxin will always be part of *my* pack."

Fornál's eyes narrowed. "So that's the way of it," he said, staring first at his sister and then at the brindled wolf. Barator gave him a puzzled glance.

Ears pricked, head held high, Rekshana faced the pack. "We must decide what we will do," she said. "As we have no *vór* — yet — I will lead the pack with Barator, who is the eldest-born. Agreed?"

The others signalled their acceptance with a chorus of barks.

"For myself," the *vóra* went on, "I will not dwell in this forest. It is a place of danger and death. We have found no other wolves here, and that means this is not a good place for wolves to be. So the question is, do we try to go back to the Raven Mountains, or do we go forward?"

"May I speak?" asked Taxin.

"Of course."

"The Raven Mountains are no better than here. In fact, it is worse there — the land was bone-dry by early spring. There will surely be forest fires there too. As my father *Vór* Timmax told *Vór* Durnál, the Black Ridge, where my pack lived, was partly burned last summer."

The pack exchanged glances.

"Also, the Two-Legs are stripping more of the forest every day, cutting down the trees and dragging them away," Taxin went on. "They started in a new place this spring, right on our territory. And they set leg traps and began hunting us down. That's how my father was killed."

At this, Selaks's head jerked up. "No!" she cried. "Not Timmax! He can't be dead too!"

"Forgive me for not telling you sooner," said Taxin. "I did not want to add to your sorrow."

Selaks stared at him a moment, her eyes dark with grief. Then she laid her head on her paws again.

"It seems, then," said Rekshana, "that we should not return to the Raven Mountains. And, speaking for myself, I wish to live in none of the lands we have crossed to get here."

"Nor I! Nor I!" The protest of the pack came loud and clear.

Then Fornál spoke up. "Other lands lie to the east and west of us. But they are likely as hot and parched as this one. That leaves only the far north, though we do not know what kind of country lies that way."

"Let us go north then," said Rekshana, and there were yelps of agreement. She glanced up at Tok, who was perched overhead. "I hope that as our former *vór* and *vóra* did, we can trust in Tok's help," she added.

"I have promised to help the pack find a new home — *vóra*," he said, faltering as he gave Rekshana her title for the first time. "I will do it if I can."

"Good," she said. "You are welcome to ride with me as you have done with Selaks."

Tok bowed on his branch. "I thank you. But I must remain with Selaks."

Rekshana tossed her head. "As you will," she replied coldly.

"I will ride with the new *vóra*, if she will have me." Rokah spread his wings and floated to the ground in front of Rekshana. "After all, I am Tok's son."

It was not often, Tok thought, that he acknowledged the relationship.

The white she-wolf eyed the glossy raven while he cocked his head and stared back at her. Then Rekshana replied, with a wave of her tail, "True. And I am Selaks's daughter. Yes, it is fitting."

With a flip of his wings, Rokah launched himself onto her shoulders. Then the new *vóra* proudly led the pack out of the clearing, while the rest of the ravens took to the air, heading north.

Only Tok remained behind. For Selaks had returned to the spot beside the fallen tree, and lay as before with her head on her paws.

He fluttered over and looked her in the eye. "Will you lie here and die of grief, then?" he asked her.

"I had thought to," she said. "So farewell, Tok. For you have a promise to keep to the pack."

"So have you."

"I? The pack has a new *vóra*. I am nothing now. Not even *karlás*," she added. "It is easier to die."

Tok quorked angrily. "What has *easier* to do with it?" he demanded. "You and Durnál undertook to lead your pack to a safe home. They have not found one yet. You must go with them and do what you can to help. What of that wonderful valley you Saw during the ice storm? The one with the cloven mountain and the winding river. You made me see it so clearly that my heart yearns for it still."

"But I don't know where it is, Tok," protested Selaks. "I sense only that it is north and far. And even if I wished to seek it, how can I leave Durnál and our pups?" she added, with a mournful glance at the fallen tree.

"They are not here, Selaks, as you well know. They have joined the Lanna." When she still lay with her head on her paws, he went on. "Think! I faced the very same choice you face now. When you summoned me, how do you think I brought myself to leave the place where Tarkah died? Only because I knew that she was not truly there. She is closer to me in the sky when I dance."

Selaks lifted her head. "Ah, Tok," she said, her golden eyes luminous in her scarred face. "It is true that you have suffered as I do now. And how seldom in these many days have I thought of your loss. Only you can truly understand what I am feeling." She heaved herself to her feet. "My spirit feels dead. I cannot sense my *numon*. But if you say my duty is to go, I will go. For you are *lóran* — the friend of my heart."

Tok fluttered onto her back as she set off. "*Vóra* you will always be to me," he said, leaning close to her ear. But from then on his heart bore a double burden, for his broken *kora* and for Selaks's loss of *karlán*.

For many days and nights, the pack moved north through the skeleton forest. Storms still raged, and they often smelled smoke on the wind. But none of the fires threatened them. Rekshana and Barator moved swiftly, pausing only to hunt and rest before forging on. Most of the time Selaks could not keep up the pace and lagged far behind, arriving only in time to join the ravens in picking the last scraps from a carcass. When they rested, Tok noticed that she kept her distance from the other wolves, most of whom ignored her presence. Only Kimmik bedded down near her sometimes, though Taxin often appeared with a gift of small game.

Barator and Fornál continued to eye each other uneasily, but Tok could see that both of them now watched Taxin closely as well. The young wolf had filled out during the time he had been with the pack. He was tall and deep-chested, and his brindled coat glistened with health. He had turned out to be a skilled hunter, well able to bring down a deer unaided. Thanks largely to him, the pack fed often.

Rekshana made no attempt to hide her fondness for him, often wandering over to lie down near him, and Tok noticed that Kimmik's eyes often rested on the young wolf too. Yet Taxin remained aloof, only seeking out Tulik sometimes, giving him a friendly shoulder slam, then play-bowing to invite him to a game of tag.

"Taxin is very like both Adanax and my brother Timmax," said Selaks, watching them play one day. "He has his father's merry heart. And my father's noble one."

"And so?" Tok hinted, giving her a meaningful look. But Selaks only flicked her ears and turned her gaze away.

One morning, Tok opened his eyes and scanned the sky, still pale with the first light of dawn. Not a cloud was to be seen. It will be hot again, he thought, and the forest will go on burning. And his heart yearned for clean cold and deep winter snows.

Beneath the branch he perched on, Selaks yawned and stretched and began to lick her feet, cleaning the fur between her toes and picking out small twigs and bits of bark that clung there. She nibbled and gnawed at one paw, then shook it.

"What is it?" he asked, fluttering down beside her.

"A thorn, I think. I can't get it out," she replied.

"Let me have a look," he offered, hopping closer. He peered at the crevices in the damp fur and at last saw a small brown thorn embedded between two pads of her paw. Clamping his beak around it, he jerked it free.

"That's better," she said, licking the spot. "Thank you, *lóran*. Paws matter, for we wolves must be able to run. We feed ourselves with our feet."

Tok glanced around. Other wolves were similarly tending their paws or chewing bones or play-wrestling. Looking on and preening themselves were their raven companions. Rokah, of course, was with Rekshana, and Brekka had long ridden with Barator. After Durnál's death, Karah had befriended Taxin, and Tok often saw the two of them speaking gravely together. Gloran had bonded with Kimmik, and his mate, Kordah, who at first had been darkly suspicious of the wolves, now spent much time with Fornál. He treated her with marked courtesy, and the ravenlady appeared more content now than she had since the journey began. Even young Barek had taken up with Vikka. Only Tulik of all the wolves had no raven rider. But then, the dejected young *karlás* did not have much of anything else, either, Tok reflected.

"Have you noticed how all the ravens have chosen wolf companions?" he asked Selaks.

She snorted, with a show of her old spirit. "How do you know it is not the wolves who have chosen them?" she asked. "*Lóran*ship is a way of wolves. Though not all of these may become *lórans*. It is more than companionship. It runs much deeper. Some go all their lives without finding a *lóran*."

"A kind of *numon?*" asked Tok.

She nodded. "Indeed, though I had never thought of it like that. And I had never before thought a creature of a different kind could be *lóran* to me. Until you proved it, Tok."

"We all come from the One," he said, remembering the myth of the Tellers.

It was a beautiful morning, the sky by now bright blue above the feathery treetops. No rain had fallen since the last storm, and down on the forest floor the air was perfectly still. Rekshana and Barator soon set off, and the ravens rose into the air to stretch their wings. The sun already felt warm on Tok's back. Soon enough it would become stiflingly hot. Already, thermals were building as the air heated, and he and the others rode them, rising higher and higher with easy movements of their wings. The forest, dark spruce sprinkled with the lighter greens of tamarack and fir, stretched beneath them to the farthest horizon. But here too great swaths of grey skeleton trees marred the healthy forest.

From far to the south came the drone of one of the air-*grawls* of the Two-Legs. Tok turned his head and saw the silver glint of it heading in their direction. They still saw or heard the air-*grawls* most days, flying their mysterious rounds over the forest. This one was a blight on the peace of the morning, thought Tok. But at least it could do no harm to the wolves, who were well concealed under the boughs of the forest below.

But as the air-*grawl* slowly drew closer, flying low, Tok began to grow anxious.

"Let's get down," he called to the others. "The Two-Legs may have firesticks!"

The ravens dove for the treetops. But before they could reach shelter, the air-*grawl* had roared past above them. Suddenly a dense mist of bright red droplets spewed from behind it, drifting down toward the trees and enveloping the ravens as it fell.

"Tok, where are you?" he heard Karah call.

"Here! I can't see you either!" he called back, staring vainly into the red mist that was all around them now.

From the distance he heard Gloran scream, "Blood! The Two-Legs are raining blood on the forest."

Now Brekka, who was flying just ahead of Tok, vanished into the mist, too, and suddenly he heard her cry out in pain. And then the mist was in Tok's nostrils, choking his breath, coating his feathers, burning into his eyes. Blind, he plummeted out of the sky, unable to see the jagged tops of the trees reaching up for him.

Chapter 23

Mysterious as night,
Strange as snow in summer,
Deadly as viper's fang
Are the ways of the Two-Legs.

— Sayings of the Tellers

Tok hit the topmost branches and struck out blindly with his claws, trying to find a hold. He grasped needles, then a bending twig, and swung upside down, unable to right himself. For a moment he dangled, panicked. Then, summoning his courage, he released his hold, allowing himself to drop farther. Righting himself in mid-air, he spread his wings to slow his fall and reached out with his claws again. This time he grasped a thicker branch and clung there, heart pounding. His eyes were burning and he could barely see. He tried rubbing them with one foot, but that made it worse. He could smell and taste the bitter red spray that coated his feathers. Whatever the foul stuff was, it wasn't blood, he thought.

But what had happened to the others? He began to quork loudly, turning his head this way and that, listening for an answer. At last he heard an answering croak from some distance away.

"Brekka?" he shouted. "Are you all right? Keep calling."

Then he heard Karah's voice. "I can hear Gloran!" she shouted. Tok turned his head, listening, and after a moment he heard Gloran too, and then the deeper voice of Rokah a little farther off.

"Can you see?" he called to Rokah.

"A little, though my eyes burn. Not enough to fly."

"Keep calling. The wolves may hear. We need their help."

They set up a deafening racket, which Barek and Kordah picked up. At last, through the din of their calling, he heard a sharp bark from the forest floor below.

"Selaks?" he cried.

"Why are you making such a row?"

"We need help. The Two-Legs sprayed something from an air-*grawl*, and we flew into it. Our eyes are burning and we can't see to fly."

"Curse the Two-Legs!" he heard her growl. Then, "The pack is some distance ahead — I'm behind as usual. But I'll summon them, though I don't know whether Rekshana will come."

A moment later her howl echoed through the forest. There was silence, then a longer answering howl some distance to the north.

"That's Barator," Selaks called up to Tok. "Perhaps they will come after all. Meanwhile, you must try to get down."

"Keep calling, so we can find you!" Tok yelled to the other ravens. Then he launched himself downward again, once more using his half-spread wings to brake his fall. He thumped down onto a lower branch, then another, then another. At last he fluttered down to the ground at Selaks's feet. Moments later, they heard the air-*grawl* roar by overhead.

"Don't look up!" he warned her. "The stuff burns in your eyes."

"There's a kind of mist in the air," she replied, when the air-*grawl* had passed. "Though it's very thin down here." She sniffed at him. "I can smell something nasty on your feathers." She howled again, and this time the answering cry was much closer.

Tok flapped onto her shoulders, and they set off through the woods, heading in the direction of Brekka's voice. By the time she had descended to the forest floor, the pack had found them.

"Ride on me, Brekka," said Barator.

One by one they collected the stranded ravens, though it took a lot of arguing to convince Kordah to abandon her precarious perch high above.

"Find us water," Tok begged the wolves. "If we don't get this stuff out of our eyes it may blind us."

"We had just reached the shore of a lake when we heard Selaks call," said Barator, as the wolves loped off. "You can bathe there."

The ravens plunged eagerly into the shallows at the edge of the lake, dashing water into their eyes and rinsing their feathers. Then they made their way ashore, where they stretched their wings to the sun to dry their plumage. After that they began to preen one another. But their eyes still burned, and they had to return to the water again and again.

"How are your eyes?" Selaks asked Tok, as the light began to fade.

"Better, though they're still sore. Praise Skyah that we're not worse off than we are." There were croaks of agreement from the other ravens.

"Were the Two-Legs trying to kill us?" asked Kordah, in a trembling voice.

"I doubt it," said Tok. "Two-Legs here have not shown interest in us before. Perhaps they were just spraying that stuff on the forest."

"But why?" asked Tulik, who was lying nearby.

"Who knows why the Two-Legs do anything?" growled Rekshana. "But whatever they do it is bad for other creatures."

Because of their repeated soakings, the ravens' feathers remained too wet for them to fly. Growing restless, the wolves set off alone to hunt. They returned at dusk, and threw themselves down, licking blood from their paws and faces. The smell of fresh meat on their fur made saliva drip from the ravens' beaks.

"Carcass to pick tomorrow," Barator promised them. "Prime deer."

"But I'm hungry now," said Kordah plaintively.

Fornál pricked up his ears. "It is not so far, raven-lady," he said. "If you care to ride, I could take you there."

"Wolves carrying ravens to kills? What next?" Rekshana said scornfully, as Kordah hopped onto Fornál's back.

At once Brekka flapped onto Barator's shoulder and gave him a cheeky peck between the ears. "Oh, why not?" the big wolf sighed, heaving himself to his feet.

One by one the other ravens prodded their wolves into action. Even riderless Tulik tagged along. But Rekshana held out to the last

"Come now, vóra," coaxed Rokah. "I promise that in exchange I'll give you the most exquisite ear scratch you have ever had."

The vóra snorted, but she let him mount.

Tok and Selaks watched it all. "Never did I think, when I first let you ride on me long ago during that blizzard, that it would come to this," she said, as they followed the others.

The next day the wolves moved off around the shore of the lake, while the ravens took to the air. Although their eyes were still sore, they could see well enough to make out the extent of the lake. It was huge.

"Many days' journey around it. Too wide to swim across," Rokah reported to Rekshana. "There's a big many-roosts of the Two-Legs on the shore ahead of us, and another strange place farther inland. We saw smoke rising from there."

"We will try to run around them," the *vóra* replied. "I have no stomach for visiting another stinking abode of the Two-Legs."

The pack loped off while the ravens circled overhead. It seemed easy enough for the wolves to get around the many-roosts located on the shore. From it a path of the kind the Two-Legs used for their *grawls* led inland, though it was not nearly as wide as the ones they had seen in the great many-roosts to the south. Though Tok could see many *grawls* moving back and forth along it, raising clouds of dust, he thought it should be easy enough for the wolves to dash across. The path ended at a great raw wound in the earth where all the trees had been cleared away and an ugly pit gaped up at the sky. Swooping over it, they could see huge *grawls* at work, some digging furiously in the ground, others loading loose earth into other *grawls*. Nearby was a large structure that belched dark smoke that spread like a stain across the sky.

"What under Skyah are the Two-Legs doing there?" called Barek.

"Who knows? Maybe there is something they want

in the earth," said Tok. "Anyway, the wolves need not come this far. Once past the many-roosts, they can easily run across the path, and after that they should be out of danger."

The ravens turned back to seek the wolves. To the northwest, Tok could now see what he first took to be more black smoke coiling up from the forest.

Then, "Do you see them?" called Gloran, who was flying off Tok's right wing. Tok narrowed his eyes and gazed again. His heart tightened as he realized the black mass was not smoke but ravens. Even as he watched, the mass separated, forming itself into several angled flights.

"Every raven in this forest must belong to the Overlord," muttered Rokah from behind him.

"And where are our own ravenets, Rokah?" demanded Gloran. "You said they would be waiting ahead for us, but we have seen none of them."

"True," replied Rokah. "And we have already passed the place where I left them. I did not like to say so, but they must have got tired of waiting for us and gone on ahead."

"Perhaps," said Tok. And perhaps they are over there in that mob that obeys the Overlord, he added to himself. "Anyway, let's get down," he said to the others. "The wolves may need us to help them avoid those *grawls*."

Through the trees they glimpsed the line of wolves loping along. The pack reached the path of the Two-

Legs, but instead of bounding across it, they spread out, hesitating. Then they backed away. The ravens circled lower, as a chorus of howls split the air.

"What is it? What's wrong?" Tok cried to Selaks, who for once had managed to keep up with the others.

"It is death! It is death!" she wailed, her voice blending into the anguished lament of the pack.

"Why are you afraid? It's only a path," he said, landing beside her. "There are *grawls*, but not too many. We'll watch from the air and call down when it's safe to cross."

"No! No! It is death, death, death!" wailed the wolves. Trembling, eyes dark with fear, they cowered among the bushes at the side of the path. Then a *grawl* approached and they dashed back under the shelter of the trees as it thundered past them.

Tok hopped to the side of the path and peered at it, trying to understand what had terrified the pack. It was not hard and black like the paths of the great many-roosts. It seemed rather to be made of sharp bits of stone mixed with pieces of something whitish. He looked closer at a pale object protruding from the side of the path, then jumped backward with a croak of horror. He was looking at the jawbone of a wolf, its fangs exposed in a ghastly grin. A little farther away he could see cracked ribs, then the fragments of a skull.

The Two-Legs had mixed the crushed bones of wolves into their stony path.

Chapter 24

Then, sisters, danced he;
Under the antlers and hooves of death
He danced, brothers,
Danced with joy.

— from "The Dancing Wolf," Songs of the Lanna

"They must have killed every wolf in the Cold Forest," said Rekshana, as the pack stared back at the path from under the trees. "No wonder we found no *skiffet*."

"But how could they kill so many?" whimpered Vikka.

"Firesticks, traps," said Selaks, when none of the others spoke. "Worst of all is poison bait at carcasses, for that way many unwary wolves die. And when we are dead they cut off our skins and hang them up to dry. I saw it all long ago in the Lost Hills." She shuddered.

"But why do they hate wolves so?" asked Tok, from

his perch over their heads. He was remembering the great massacre of the crows he had witnessed long ago. But there, at least, the crows had done some harm. They had eaten the Two-Legs' corn.

"Who can understand the Two-Legs?" replied Selaks. "I think they must be proud of their killing. This path of bones is surely meant to tell any passing wolf not to linger here."

"Nor will we," growled Barator. "But we will not cross the path of bones. It is an insult to our Lanna!" Howls of rage burst from the rest of the pack.

The wolves faded deep into the woods, heading eastward to circle around the place of the smoke and the great digging. All that day and through the night they ran, but they could not outrun the memory of the horror they had seen. The mood of the pack was sombre, and when at last they stopped to rest, they cast themselves down in gloomy silence.

Perched above them, the ravens murmured among themselves, trying to think of a way to ease the suffering of their companions.

At last Karah spoke up. "Barator, Rekshana," she said, "I know a story that explains why such things happen. Though I know not whether it will ease your hearts."

"Tell us," said Barator, and the pack pricked up their ears.

Karah smoothed her feathers tight against her body, and took the formal Teller's stance, head high, shoulders back and wingtips crossed on her back. "This is the Legend of the Three," she began. "It happened long ago, in the days of the Later Time, the time of many animals. Among them, the wisest and most powerful creatures were the Three, who were Wolf, Raven — and Two-Legs."

Cries of anguish burst from the wolves when she spoke the hated name of their enemy.

"Wolf and Two-Legs were great hunters who killed only what they needed, as Skyah intended," Karah went on. "And Raven hunted with both."

Now the ravens quorked their anger and disbelief.

"It was so, in those long-ago days," Karah assured them. "But at last Two-Legs grew greedy. 'The Earth is mine alone,' he said, and he began to cut down forests and grow crops and raise tame beasts. Many wild creatures did he kill. And he warned his old companions, Wolf and Raven, to stay away from what was his. But Wolf would not agree. 'You have killed the game I need to survive,' he said. 'And so, in need, I will hunt what is yours.' And he did, and Raven feasted with him. After that war began between Two-Legs and Wolf. Wolf preyed upon the animals of the Two-Legs in order to live. Two-Legs killed Wolf in revenge. At last, Wolf and Raven were driven away into far places that Two-Legs did not want. And the war continues to this very day."

Karah looked down and bowed. "My Telling is done," she finished.

"We thank you," said Rekshana, as the pack curled up to sleep. "It is best to try to understand, though we will never accept the cruelty of the Two-Legs."

After running far to the east, the wolves circled back to the north and west, until they came again to the shore of the great lake, far from the places of the dreaded Two-Legs. There they rested a while. But they had not killed for several days, so they set out to hunt in the failing light while the ravens settled in to roost.

The pack made no kill that night, but by dawn the ravens could tell that they had picked up a teasing scent, for they set off again, ears pricked, tails wagging. Hungry and hopeful, Tok and the others followed. From the air, they soon saw what had attracted the wolves' attention. Browsing in the reedy shallows at the edge of the lake stood a huge blackish creature with humped shoulders and broad spreading antlers. As they watched, it dipped its bulbous nose into the water, and yanked up a dripping mass of water weed.

"Moose!" cried Tok. "A big one."

"Can the wolves really kill that?" asked Brekka, awed.

"Let's hope so," said Gloran. "Look at all that meat."

Just then the moose raised its head, turning into the wind. Then it splashed out of the shallows and moved off at an ungainly trot, disappearing into the dense underbrush.

"It must have scented them," said Rokah, as the

wolves paused at the edge of the forest.

The ravens flew among the trees, trying to find the moose. At last they discovered it, half hidden in a thicket, its back to a rocky outcropping. At once they set up a racket, and it was not long before they glimpsed the wolves, spread out in a line, slipping like shadows among the trees.

"The moose scented you back by the lake," Tok warned Barator, thumping down on Selaks's back. "It's no use trying to sneak up on it."

The wolves crept closer, but the moose snorted and tossed its head. It was clearly aware of the danger it faced.

"At least it's not in the lake," said Fornál. "We must get it to move away from the thicket. If it runs into the open we may have a chance. Let's test it."

He, Barator and Taxin bounded into the open to confront the moose, which snorted and pawed the ground, tossing its heavy antlers. Rekshana, Kimmik and Selaks, staying under cover, attempted to work their way around behind the animal. But the moose had chosen its spot well. The thicket around it was prickly and dense, and the rock face too close to allow the pack to manoeuvre behind it. Suddenly the wolves in front charged straight at the moose, while Rekshana and Kimmik darted in and attacked its flanks. With a sideways sweep of its antlers, the moose caught Fornál and tossed him through the air, at the same time lashing out against Barator and Taxin with its front hooves. Taxin managed to dodge, but Barator gave a yelp of pain as he darted away. Meanwhile Rekshana and Kimmik tried to sink their teeth into the moose's flanks. But it shook them off, then kicked with its hind feet, tumbling them tail over nose. Eyes rolling, nostrils flared, the great beast faced its attackers.

Taxin ran out his tongue, laughing. "Well, Fornál, we tested it," he said. "Though I'd say it tested *us* more."

"We'll wait a while," growled Barator, "then try again."

The wolves lay down at a safe distance, and began licking their sore spots. The moose stood its ground, never taking its eyes off them. Whenever one of the wolves moved, it tossed its head and pawed the earth with its front hooves. Some time later, the wolves tried rushing it again, with the same result. Then they slipped out of sight among the trees, hoping the moose would emerge from its refuge. But the beast continued to stand its ground. After some time had passed with no movement, they tried a third attack. It gained them nothing but more injuries to lick.

Barator had had enough. "It's not ready to die," he said. "We're wasting our time."

"I agree with Barator," said Rekshana. "Though I hate to admit it, there's nothing more we can do."

"No!" protested Fornál. "We mustn't give up. We can't allow ourselves to be humiliated by that beast!"

"He's right," Tok said quietly to Karah, who was perched beside him.

"Yes," she agreed. "After the horrors they have gone through, the pack needs the victory even more than they need the meat."

Below them, his ears pricked, Taxin stood listening. He glanced up at them, then went to join the rest of the pack as they got to their feet. Tails down, ears lowered, the defeated wolves gathered around Barator and their *vóra*.

Then Taxin spoke up. "I have an idea," he said. "If you'll let me try it."

All heads turned toward him. "We have nothing to lose," rumbled Barator. "Go ahead. What do you want us to do?"

"Wait until I get the beast to move away from the thicket," said Taxin. "Then attack it from the front and back at once. You'll know when to move."

"You'll never get it out of that thicket," mocked Fornál.

"Won't I?" Taxin grinned, showing gleaming fangs. "Wait and see."

This time Tulik and Vikka joined Selaks, Rekshana and Kimmik. The five of them faded into the woods, then circled around toward the thicket. The wind had shifted and now blew straight toward the moose.

"You two stay hidden until the last moment," Taxin warned Barator and Fornál. The two big wolves moved in, staying hidden behind the trees in which the ravens perched.

Now Taxin strolled forward toward the moose,

which snorted and pawed the ground, ready for combat. But the brindled wolf did not attack. He made a little rush at the moose, which swept its antlers to and fro menacingly. Taxin leaped lightly sideways, then made another brief rush. The moose turned its head that way, but did not stir a step. Back leaped Taxin, and back turned the moose. Another leap, another rush. Another toss of the head.

"What's he doing?" grumbled Fornál. "Dancing with the beast?"

But Tok noticed that each rush, each leap, brought Taxin just a little closer to the moose.

The strange dance went on for some time. At last the moose stopped moving, merely following the wolf's movements with its eyes. Closer and closer Taxin danced, this way and that. Then, with a mighty leap, he sprang forward and seized the bulbous nose of the moose in his fangs. The moose reared, slashing at him with its front hooves, but Taxin kicked out with his hind legs, still hanging on. His swinging weight made the moose stumble forward, as it threw its head from side to side, trying to smash Taxin against the ground. A gap opened between it and the thicket.

"Now!" cried Barator. He and Fornál leaped forward to attack the moose's shoulders, as the rest of the pack sprang from cover to attack its flanks and rump, opening great gashes in its body. Quorking with excitement, the ravens circled over the battle.

The enraged moose thrashed Taxin back and forth

against the ground, but he hung on stubbornly. Scrabbling with his feet, he braced himself and backed away, stretching out the animal's head and neck. Seeing the opening, Barator leaped upward, his fangs slicing the beast's throat, and blood sprayed into the air. Swarmed by the wolves, bleeding from many wounds, the moose sank to its knees. But it struggled up again, trying to kick its way free of its attackers. Still holding on, Taxin backed away once again, as Barator and Fornál slashed again at the beast's underbelly, opening it. The moose went down in a welter of blood as the wolves closed in again. At last, with a final heave, it died.

The wolves, their faces masked with gore, stared at each other in astonishment, while the ravens swooped gleefully overhead. Then all eyes turned toward Taxin.

"We did it!" cried Rekshana.

"It was thanks to you, Taxin," said Barator, a new note of respect in his voice. "We could not have done it without you." Even Fornál growled his agreement.

Selaks too was staring at the young wolf, her golden eyes glowing. "The story of the dancing wolf will be told among the Lanna forever!" she said softly.

Then the pack raised their muzzles and, voices intertwining, sang a wild song of triumph, pride and joy.

Chapter 25

Knowing your enemy, sometimes, is easier
than knowing your friends.

— Raven proverb

The famished wolves fell upon the moose, while the ravens swooped among them seizing gobbets of rich red flesh. Tok noticed that Taxin stepped up to feed alongside Barator and Rekshana at the best part of the carcass, while the rest of the pack hung back respectfully, darting in when they dared, to snatch a mouthful. Fornál's eyes narrowed when he saw the young wolf take this place of honour, but he said nothing.

Before the wolves and ravens had nearly satisfied their hunger, they heard a loud cry from Rokah, who had offered to stand sentry at the top of a tree. "Raiders to the north!" he shouted. "Two flights!"

"This carcass they will not steal from us," vowed

Rekshana, baring her teeth as the raiders descended on them like a black cloud.

But though the wolves fought valiantly, the raiders had learned that by striking at their eyes they could eventually force them to retreat. Even so, many of the attackers died trying to mob the wolves, snatched in mid-air and crushed in the fangs of the pack. Tok noticed that most of those who died were ravenets who flung themselves blindly, almost eagerly, into the jaws of death. Tok and the other ravens fought fiercely alongside the wolves, but sheer numbers beat them to the ground. Battered and bleeding from many pecks, the pack and their raven companions were at last driven back into the woods. The raiders made no attempt to follow them, but instead settled down to feed greedily on the moose.

The wolves' eyes blazed as they watched the attackers steal their kill. Tok, too, felt a great rage building in his heart, and his mind buzzed with questions. Why did the attackers do this? Was it just because it was easier than finding their own kills? How did they always seem to know where to find the wolves? Who was this Overlord the raiders served? There was only one way to find out, he told himself.

The sun was swinging toward the west when suddenly a call rang down from high above. With a great beating of wings, the raven horde at once began to lift off. They moved as one, as if controlled by a single mind, a single thought, gathering in the air and forming up their flights before heading north. At once the wolves and ravens rushed out of the forest to reclaim what was left of the carcass.

Tok hesitated. If he followed the enemy, they might lead him to the Overlord. Here was his chance to keep his vow to find the Overlord, and his heart yearned to do it. But it would mean leaving the wolves, breaking his promise to them. Break your vow or break your promise? he asked himself bitterly. Either was *unkora*. But Rokah and Gloran could guide the wolves, perhaps even better than he could. They were both able leaders. It was up to him to find the Overlord and try to stop him.

He slipped away through the trees, keeping low and out of sight. Then, circling higher, he sped swiftly after the departing raiders. It did not take him long to catch up with one of the flights. Slipping in at the end of the line, he flew along behind the others.

The raven ahead of him glanced back curiously. "I don't remember you, brother," he said.

"Nor I you, brother," Tok replied boldly. "I came in with another flight."

High above the silver-blue expanse of the great lake they flew, veering northwest now, toward the far shore furred with dark forest. In the distance Tok could see other flights heading toward them. All seeming to be converging on a single spot.

"There will be a Great Roost tonight," the raven ahead exulted. "We will hear many tales of bold deeds done. The Overlord will be proud of us."

Tok's heart beat faster. "The Overlord! Will he be there?" he asked, as they wheeled toward other converging flights.

"Who can tell? He ranges far and wide among his raven hordes and is not always with us. But all his followers live in the hope of seeing him."

"Indeed," muttered Tok.

And then they were swirling down in a vortex of beating wings. The sky was black with ravens funnelling toward a clearing in the forest. Below, the boughs of the trees were already weighed down with them. The gathering was greater by far than any Kort he had ever seen. Yet there was total silence, total order, as the raven horde settled among the trees. It was unnerving, thought Tok. Where were the cheerful greetings and good-natured bickering that went with going to roost? These ravens were orderly and quiet, hardly like ravens at all.

The last flights descended, filling the trees around the sides of a large clearing where many trees had died. There was no spacious central roost like the noble Kort Tree on the slopes of Mount Storm, just a tall dead spruce with only a few stubs of branches left near the top of it. Then, from the north, the figure of a single raven appeared, growing rapidly larger as it zoomed toward them.

Excited whispers ran through the assembled host.

"Is it he?"

"Perhaps! It is a mighty bird."

"No, it is not the Master," said another bird. "It is Parok, one of his most trusted Horde Leaders."

"We are still honoured, then. Parok stands high in the favour of the Overlord."

The great raven wheeled insolently over the clearing and lit on a branch stub near the top of the skeleton tree. "In the name of the Overlord," he cried, staring around him with fierce amber eyes. Tok noticed that he had positioned himself so the descending sun shone around him like a glory.

"IN HIS NAME!" came a thundering chorus from hundreds of raven throats.

"The Overlord knows of your many exploits in this country. He is pleased."

"ALL HONOUR IS DUE HIM!"

"Yet his heart is also saddened," Parok went on, his voice breaking as if he too felt sorrow.

At this, a tremor went through the ranks of birds, who exchanged nervous glances.

"There are traitors among us," the Overlord's lieutenant shouted, spreading his wings dramatically. "Traitors who wish to betray our Master."

"WE SHALL FIND THEM!" roared the host.

"And when we do?" asked Parok, sweeping his gaze around the clearing.

"WE WILL KILL THEM! KILL THEM! KILL THEM!" The forest echoed with the fierce cries of the raven horde.

"I do not hear your voice, brother," said one of the ravens next to Tok, as the echoes died away. "Are you one of the traitors Parok spoke of?"

"No more than you, brother," snapped Tok.

Then a sudden movement drew all eyes downward. Two rumpled and bedraggled ravenets fluttered into the air, as if making a desperate effort to escape. But they were beaten to the ground by six burly guard ravens. They cowered at the foot of the stub where Parok perched.

"*Here* are traitors," he said, glaring down at them. Then, raising his head proudly, he swept the clearing with his ferocious gaze.

For a moment his eyes rested on Tok, who felt as though a flash of fire burned through him. His breath caught in his throat. Had he been discovered somehow?

But Parok's gaze moved on. "They have worked against you, brothers, and against our beloved Master," he went on, speaking again in soft, sorrowful tones. "They have pretended to join us. But they really serve the Enemy, he who through lies and deceit tried to destroy our Overlord. Thanks to your vigilance, loyal brothers, they have been found out. They are guilty!"

"GUILTY! GUILTY! GUILTY!" echoed the horde.

Tok clung horrified to his perch. What mockery of a trial was this? No evidence. No vote of the Kort. Just condemnation.

"What then shall their punishment be?" cried Parok.

"DEATH! DEATH! DEATH!"

"So be it," said Parok when the echoes had died again. Then, almost as an afterthought, he glanced down at the guards, who still held the prisoners on the ground. "Let them go," he said coldly.

At once the two prisoners sprang into the air, flapping desperately to gain height. As they did so, the last rays of the sinking sun caught them, and with horror Tok recognized two of the ravenets from the Raven Mountains. He gave a great cry and launched himself toward them. But at the same moment the rest of the horde also took to the air, buffeting each other with their wings in their eagerness to get at the accused birds. Half stunned, Tok was knocked earthward, while around him rained drops of blood and broken feathers as the horde tore the ravenets to pieces in mid-air.

When their murderous frenzy had passed, the horde settled in to roost, chattering to one another as their excitement died away. Parok had vanished as suddenly as he had appeared. Trembling, Tok settled in with the rest.

"That was a good show," said one big bird, stretching a wing and refolding it. "Parok knows how to make a rally exciting."

There was silence for a moment. Then, "A show? You mean . . . they were not truly traitors, Flight

Leader?" asked a female raven timidly.

"What does truth matter?" he replied, giving her a hard stare. "They were expendable. I'll be watching to make sure you fight hard for the Overlord. Or you may become expendable too."

At that, the group fell silent.

Tok shivered in rage and disgust. What the Overlord had done to these birds was worse than anything he had imagined. But he did not know what to do now, for the Overlord was not there. And he had thought it would be easy to find him! Now he knew that his only chance of doing it was to join the enemy and follow them wherever they went. Even then it might be long before he met the Overlord.

And now another thought rose to torment him. Perhaps he had been wrong to leave the wolves in the first place. When he had rushed off after the enemy, he had comforted himself that Gloran and Rokah could replace him. But what of the white raven, and the journey she had foretold? Could he just abandon that? And now the memory of Selaks's scarred face and sorrowful eyes rose to haunt him too. She had only stayed with the pack, living with her dishonour, because of him, her *lóran*. Could he abandon her now?

Make up your mind, you fool! Tok thought bitterly. He brooded long, listening to the night sounds of the roost — sleepy quorks, the scrape of claws on bark, the soft rustle of feathers. At last he decided. He could not keep his vow to find the Overlord. He had to go back.

Gradually he began to shift his perch until he was able to flap to another tree, and then another and another, each time moving deeper into the forest. The night was cloudy dark, and not liking to fly in unknown country in poor light, he decided to stay where he was until daybreak. The first pale light of dawn found him winging his way southeast across the great lake. He thought he heard cries far behind him, but flew on with rapid wingbeats. Just as he reached the far shore, he heard them again, not far behind him now.

"Tok! Wait for me!"

Tok tilted his right wing, banking in a tight circle. There behind him, winging straight from the direction of the Great Roost, was Rokah.

All the anger, fear and horror of the day before rose into Tok's throat, choking him for a moment. Then, "You!" he yelled. "You are one of them, Rokah!" Swooping at his son, he attacked with his claws, and the two of them plunged headlong into the forest below.

Chapter 26

Numon reveals all, like dawn after darkness.

— Wolf proverb

They hit the treetops with a crash. Forced apart by the impact, they plunged among the branches, finally coming to rest opposite each other. Fanning their wings for balance, the two of them glared at each other.

Tok's feathery hackles bristled with fury. "You are worse than any traitor!" he shouted. "Gloran and Brekka are right — you are *unkora*. You have been working for the Overlord all along!" His thoughts were spinning, as he tried to remember Rokah's every suspicious action. There had been so many!

Rokah's eyes flashed, and he too raised his hackles. "Noble Tok!" he jeered. "Who are *you* to talk of *kora*? You told me yourself that you have none. Yet you are eager to condemn me unjustly, with no evidence. You are no better than Parok!"

It took Tok a moment to understand him, so great was his rage. "No evidence? Did I not see you with my own eyes following me from the Great Roost of the Overlord? You were there!"

"Of course I was there!" snapped Rokah. "I followed you yesterday when you slipped away after the fight. I guessed what you were up to and I was afraid for you. Yes, *afraid for you!*" he repeated, when Tok tried to interrupt.

Tok lowered his hackles and gazed at his son. Was he telling the truth, or was this just another lie?

"So I followed you all the way to the Great Roost," Rokah went on.

"I did not see you there."

"Among so many? How could you? I purposely kept out of sight, so as to be able to rush in and help you if you were discovered. Then I lost you in the dark. This morning I watched for you and followed again, fearful you might be seen and attacked by the enemy. Have Gloran or any of your other so-called friends ever done as much for you? They were too busy gorging themselves at the carcass yesterday to even notice you were gone!"

Tok's heart went cold within him. "Rokah, if I am wrong, if I have misjudged you — " he began.

But Rokah cut him off. "You have!" he insisted.

"Then I humbly beg you to forgive me," said Tok. "What I saw yesterday has poisoned my heart. I was wrong to believe you capable of such evil."

"Well said," replied Rokah. "You are good at feigned humility. But no, I will never forgive you. You have insulted me in a way that neither of us can forget." Spreading his wings, he wheeled away down the lakeshore.

He is right, thought Tok grimly, as he followed, heavy-winged. This is something neither of us will ever forget.

The wolves had already moved on from the moose kill. From the air, Tok could glimpse them coursing among the trees, heading north again, away from the shores of the great lake. Rokah angled down to join them, but Tok, still heartsick over their quarrel, flew on for a time. He needed to be alone. Soon, though, he saw Gloran and Brekka circling up to join him.

"Where have you been?" yelled Brekka.

"Didn't Rokah explain?"

"Need you ask?" said Gloran. "He never speaks to us if he can help it. He dropped down onto Rekshana's back like a thunderbolt just now, and hasn't said a word to anyone."

"I went with the raiders," said Tok. "To see if I could find the Overlord."

Brekka turned on him and gave him a great buffet with her wing. "With the raiders? Alone? You had no right!" she cried.

"No right?" Tok was astonished.

"Oh, you are selfish, *selfish!*" she cried. "Always thinking of no one but yourself!" With that she wheeled away, banking down toward the forest.

"What under Skyah is wrong with her?" demanded Tok. "Do you blame me too, Gloran?"

Gloran gave him a sidelong glance. "I do," he replied. "Brekka is right. You keep saying you are not our leader, yet our journey depends on you. The wolves depend on you too."

"Ravens act as they please. And you can guide the wolves as well as I can," Tok protested.

But Gloran shook his head angrily. "No! Can't you understand that it is you who holds us together, gives us all hope? As for the wolves, they do not trust me as they do you. And what about Selaks?"

"She is why I came back," replied Tok. And the white raven, he added to himself.

"But what if the raiders had killed you?" Gloran went on.

"Well, they didn't," snapped Tok. "And, as it turned out, I wasn't alone. Rokah followed me because he was worried I might get into trouble. We returned together." He said nothing about his quarrel with Rokah, for his heart was too sore. After all, it was the suspicions of Gloran and Brekka that had made him distrust his son in the first place.

The two of them flew on for a while. Then, "So, did you learn anything worth the risk you took?" asked Gloran.

"I saw how the Overlord and his followers control the ravens. It is horrible, as if they have stopped thinking for themselves. They are overawed, and say and do what they are told. Two of our ravenets who had joined them were put to death for no reason, and I couldn't stop it. But of the Overlord himself I saw nothing."

They flapped on in gloomy silence.

By evening the wolves were deep into a less-damaged part of the forest, where the trees grew thick and straight. Still well-fed from their moose feast, they did not bother to hunt, but lay about resting and grooming themselves. Their raven companions gossiped and preened overhead.

Tok briefly recounted to the others what had happened at the Great Roost. But only to Selaks did he reveal the encounter between himself and Rokah. He could not bring himself to tell Karah.

"Don't blame yourself too much, Tok," Selaks said gravely. "And don't blame your friends, either. They only spoke their suspicions out of their care for you."

"But I allowed myself to be turned against him. And now he will never forgive me."

"Give him time," she replied. "He is, I think, much like Rekshana. Both are proud, willful, ambitious, but also very brave. Who knows? They may become true *lórans*," she added, glancing at the silver-white *vóra* and her big raven companion.

As she spoke, Taxin got to his feet and ambled toward Kimmik. At once the ears of the pack pricked and every eye was on him. Selaks's head too turned to follow his steps, though Tok noticed that she also glanced at Barator and Fornál.

"You are all on edge," said Tok. "And it's to do with Taxin."

"I think, I hope, a *vór* is emerging," she replied. "Only Fornál stands between Taxin and the *vór*ship."

"But . . . Barator?"

Selaks flicked an ear. "Barator does not have the stuff from which *vór*s are made, though he was a capable *anvór* when Durnál was alive. For pride's sake he will challenge Fornál, I think, if he claims the *vór*ship. But he will not challenge Taxin."

"What about Fornál?"

She sighed. "Fornál is as stubborn as he is clever. He will not give up the *vór*ship without a fight."

"I doubt Taxin will challenge him for it," said Tok. "He considers himself a coward."

Selaks gave a short bark of laughter. "Pulling that monster moose by the nose was hardly the act of a coward! We all know it, and I think in his heart Taxin does too."

Later that night, they moved on, each raven riding on the back of its companion. Tok noticed that Rekshana was never far from Taxin's side, interposing herself between him and Kimmik whenever she could. That young wolf has more than one problem to solve, he thought.

The burning summer died as they ran. The terrible storms had ceased, and the nights were growing cooler and the days shorter. The sombre fir and spruce showed no sign of the changing season, but the slender needles of the tamaracks had begun to change to shining gold.

And not only the weather had changed. The attacks of the enemy ceased, and days often passed without their seeing the raiders. Tok brooded much on this. The attacks were not random, that much he was sure of. They were meant to harass, but not to kill . . . yet. His group was watched by the followers of the Overlord. But why? Through many sleepless nights he pondered the question, but could never find an answer. What could the Overlord know of any of them, after all?

Meanwhile, the tension within the pack grew by the day. The wolves still worked together during the hunt, but furious fights now broke out over each kill, and all their coats showed wounds and scars from their combats.

Only Selaks stood apart from it all, with the pack but not of it. "*Karlán* has broken down," she told Tok. "We must have a *vór*, and soon."

Yet despite all the watching and waiting and fighting, the crisis, when it came, caught them all by surprise. One morning midway through the Moon of Flocks, they were resting near a marsh after a long night's run. The water near the centre was still unfrozen, but a thin crust of ice had formed near the shore overnight. The open water was crowded with hundreds of migrating waterfowl, and Tulik, hungry and restless, was creeping on his belly among the cattails that lined the shore, trying to sneak up on a large goose that was dabbling in the shallows. Suddenly he broke through the ice, hitting the water with a loud splash and seizing the goose by its long neck. A mighty thrashing of wings and agonized honking brought the pack to its feet, and sent every other bird in the marsh winging into the air with a sound like thunder. The goose buffeted Tulik fiercely with its wings, plunging him underwater, but he struggled to the surface still stubbornly clutching his prize.

Rekshana ran out her tongue, laughing. "Poor Tulik. It looks like that goose is going to drown him," she said.

"Maybe I should help him out," said Taxin. He moved toward the shore, brushing past Fornál, who turned and without warning sprang for his throat. Knocked off balance, Taxin went down with Fornál on top of him. But the grey wolf's hold was not secure, and the two of them rolled over and over, biting and snarling. At last, Taxin flipped his attacker off and backed away a few steps. The two of them stood glaring at each other, while the rest of the pack moved apart, leaving space for the combat.

"You want this now?" asked Taxin.

"Now!" snarled Fornál, and leaped at him again.

This time Taxin dodged sideways, moving under

Fornál's body as he sprang. Hitting the ground hard with all four paws, he bounded upward, knocking the wind out of his opponent and flipping him onto his back. In a flash Taxin turned and bit deep into the fur of Fornál's neck, pinning him to the ground.

For long moments the pack stood frozen, with every eye fixed on Taxin. In the silence Tok heard his own heart beating wildly. Then Fornál laid his ears back and whined. Taxin bit deeper, shaking him furiously, and Fornál whined again. At last Taxin released his grip, but still stood over his defeated opponent, ears pricked, tail high.

"Well?" he growled.

"I submit," wheezed Fornál.

Taxin stepped away from him. "Louder," he commanded. "So all the pack can hear you."

"I submit!" Fornál rolled over and crept on his belly to Taxin's feet.

There were joyous barks from the pack, but Taxin silenced them with a stern glance. Turning again to Fornál, he asked, "And will you obey me, or will you follow your own trail?"

Fornál got to his feet. "I will serve you, my *vór*, if you will have me. For I know now that of the two of us you are the better." Reaching up, he mouthed Fornál's muzzle.

"Good!" said Taxin. "You are clever, and the pack would be worse off without you. For I have much to learn." Then he swung his shaggy head toward Barator. "And you?" he demanded, baring his teeth. "Yield now, or fight."

The big brown wolf bounded forward. But his ears were laid back, and his jaws spread in a submissive grin. "I will serve you loyally," he said, bunting Taxin under the chin with his nose. "I know in my heart that it is not my *numon* to be a *vór*."

The rest of the wolves now rushed forward, capering around the new *vór* and vying to demonstrate their loyalty.

At that moment, Tulik, whom everyone had forgotten, emerged dripping from the cattails with the limp goose in his jaws. When he saw the celebration, he dropped it and stared wide-eyed at the pack. "What's happened? Did I miss something?" he asked.

"As usual, brother," laughed Kimmik. "Come and greet your new *vór*."

Picking up the goose, Tulik trotted forward and proudly laid it at Taxin's feet. Then the wolves raised their voices in a song of celebration, while the ravens danced swoops and rolls above the trees.

Part 4

The Wanderers

Chapter 27

Fearless, on wings unwearied
Sped Tok Wolf Bird to the Gates of the North.

— from "The Saga of Tok Wolf Rider,"
Tales of the Tellers

On they journeyed through the turning time of the year. One after another the great flocks passed by overhead, disappearing to the south. Tok noticed that Selaks had begun to coat up for winter, darker guard hairs growing through her creamy fur, and a woolly undercoat coming in underneath it. His own autumn moult made his feathers prickle, and he often chose to ride while new ones grew in.

Now the weather became stormy again, with great gales that roared among the boughs of the trees. They had left the skeleton forest behind at last, and the trees grew straight and healthy, with only the occasional deadfall.

"This is the Cold Forest as Durnál so often described it to me," Selaks told Tok. "Before the Change made it begin to sicken and die."

But after many days, the evergreens began to thin out, standing farther and farther apart. Among them grew a dense cover of willow and birch, more like tall bushes than trees. Between them grew a springy cover of moss and lichen. It was a country of marshes and swamps, though these were frozen over now.

One night Rekshana called a council. "Why do we journey on and on?" she demanded, gazing around the circle of wolves and ravens. "The part of the Cold Forest we passed through recently was healthy, and there were plenty of deer too. Why not go back? For I do not care as much for this land of bush and swamp."

At once every head turned toward Taxin. "As a newcomer I will not speak. This is something the rest of you must decide," he said. "As Rekshana says, the Cold Forest can sustain us. There was water there and much game. We could go back. And yet, I think some of you at least are travelling for other reasons."

"I fear the Overlord," said Tok. "His raiders have driven you from your kills at will. If we go no farther they will surely find us again. They will take what they want and leave us only scraps. And for us ravens, it will be like the Raven Mountains all over again. If we settle down, they will try to destroy us. I, at least, wish to go on."

The other ravens karked and quorked their agreement, though Tok noticed that Rokah said nothing.

"But we've come so far! We can't just run on to the end of the world," said Vikka. "I agree with our *vóra*. We should return to the forest."

"That forest is not the great valley among the mountains that I Saw," said Selaks from outside the circle. As always, she had arrived after the rest.

Rekshana turned to glare at her. "Why should we listen to you?" she snapped. "You admitted yourself that your Seeing about the fire was wrong."

"I did not say that!" cried Selaks. "The Seeing is never wrong. I was wrong about where the fire that I Saw would happen. But I know the valley of the cloven mountain exists somewhere, and my heart longs for it."

Rekshana stamped impatiently with her front paws. "What *you* want no longer matters," she said. "Kimmik?"

"I would go on to find that valley," her sister replied. "If only we knew where it was!"

"But we don't," Fornál pointed out. "And if we leave this place, may we not be going toward something worse even than here? Another skeleton forest? A place with no large game?"

"So you are with me," said Rekshana. "Good."

Tok was surprised when Tulik suddenly spoke up. "I am with Kimmik," he said. "I think we should go on."

"You have no say in this, *karlás*," snapped Rekshana.

The little grey wolf laid back his ears. "Maybe not. But that's what I think," he said stubbornly.

"He has a right to say it," growled Barator. "And I agree with him. The Cold Forest was well enough, but it is not the land of my heart. Even if we never find that great valley, I would still go on looking."

Rekshana glowered at her brother. "I thought you had more sense," she said. "But it doesn't matter. Taxin chooses not to speak, and Selaks and Tulik may not. Fornál, Vikka and I are for going back, and only you and Kimmik are against." Her eyes flashed as she glanced around the circle. "Therefore, we go back," she announced.

Then Taxin got to his feet, and all eyes turned to him. "No, *vóra*," he said. "I did say I would not speak, but now I think that is wrong. Newcomer I may be, but I rule this pack now. And I agree with Kimmik and Barator. So the two sides are evenly matched. Therefore, let us go on for a time and then speak again. If we change our minds, we can always return to the Cold Forest before winter closes in. Agreed?"

The pack barked their agreement, and Tok fluttered over to land on Selaks's back. But he noticed that Rekshana's eyes followed Taxin with a troubled expression.

"She frets about him," said Selaks, when he mentioned it.

"I don't understand," said Tok. "He is *vór*, she is

vóra. Doesn't that mean they will become mates in time? Yet they often seem at cross purposes."

"*Vór* usually mates with *vóra,*" replied Selaks. "It was so with my parents, and with Durnál and me. But not always. That is the problem, you see. For Taxin prefers Kimmik, and Rekshana cannot accept that. Ahhh, that's good," she added, as Tok's beak scratched deep behind her ears.

"Too bad you can't return the favour," he joked.

"Wolf fangs are not made for preening ravens. But there is one of your company who would gladly oblige you."

"Karah?" said Tok. "Yes, why not? I must ask her."

Selaks gave a bark of laughter.

That night, the wind shifted again, veering into the north. The stars appeared, glittering like ice crystals overhead. The temperature fell, and Tok's feathers tingled in the crackling frost. The next morning he decided to fly ahead of the wolves to scout. Not wanting Brekka or Gloran to go with him, he told only Selaks what he planned to do, and slipped away. He flew on for many hundreds of wingbeats, keeping a wary eye out for raiders. The country of bush and swamp seemed to stretch on forever. But two days later, when the sun stood well past midday, he saw that the bush was gradually becoming sparse, with open stretches of moss and lichen. And soon, to his astonishment, there were no trees at all. A vast empty-looking land began to unfold beneath his wings, rolling treeless to the horizon.

No trees! Not one! Stunned by what he was seeing, Tok spiralled down to rest. The ground was dotted with blazing yellow clumps of stunted willow bushes, interspersed with tufts of wiry grass, and the crimson leaves of some low-spreading plant. Lichen-crusted rocks poked up here and there. When he landed, the ground beneath his claws seemed crisp and dry, and he stalked about, pecking insects from the carpet of vegetation.

After a while, he flew on, his throat choked with disappointment. There had to be something more ahead, he told himself. There *had* to be. Selaks had been so sure about the great valley, and he had come to believe that it waited for them beyond the Cold Forest, beyond the bush lands. Yet here were no mountains, no winding river. Just an empty land without comfort or shelter.

The sun was already sinking, and Tok realized it was too late to turn back that day. In the distance, he spied two massive rocky outcrops that reared up against the horizon, and flew toward them. It was as if the heart of some great hill had been gnawed away by ice, snow and wind, leaving a pair of cliffs that stood apart, framing the darkening northern sky.

Better than roosting on the ground, he thought, circling down. Then his eyes widened in astonishment. For there, perched on a rocky pinnacle in the failing light, was the white raven.

"Tunavik!" he cried. He lit beside her, half disbelieving his own eyes.

The white raven gazed back at him, and her silvery voice was the voice of his dreams. "I told you that if you lived we would meet again at the Gates of the North," she said. "And so we have. You and the wolves have become what you had to be to survive. For together you are far stronger than either one is separately."

"I left the others two days' flight behind me," said Tok. "Many days' running for the wolves."

"Find them," urged Tunavik. "Bring them here quickly. For soon it will be too late."

"Are there no tall mountains between here and the Frozen Ocean?" asked Tok. "No forests, no great valleys?"

A spark kindled deep in the white raven's eyes. "Due north of here there is only this," she replied, indicating the darkening country around them with a sweep of her wing. "The great Barren Lands. But why do you ask about mountains and valleys?"

So Tok told him of Selaks's Snow Seeing of the land that would be their home. The white raven listened closely, then she said, "Selaks is right. The Valley of the Cloven Mountain indeed exists."

Tok's heart lifted, but he spoke a thought that had long troubled him. "Can it really be a haven for us? For the Change seems to be everywhere. Why would that valley be safer than the Cold Forest?"

Tunavik roused her feathers. "The Change is indeed everywhere. You have seen it in the Raven Mountains and the Cold Forest. I have seen it on the shores of the Frozen Ocean, where the forever-ice is melting. But other places are better off. The Valley of the Cloven Mountain lies among high peaks, far from the warming ocean. It is farther north and colder than the Cold Forest. So the temperature will be warmer in the valley, yes, but not as warm as in other places. There is still ice and snow in winter. The forest is not dying."

Tok thought for a moment. "Do you come from the Valley, Tunavik?"

"I was Sent to seek you out and, if you won through on your journey north, to show you how to find the Valley."

"But why do you want us to go there?"

"Because great wrong was done there long ago, and now there are no wolves or ravens. The Valley is out of balance, and must be put right."

Tok's suspicions were roused. "What wrong? Why are there no wolves or ravens?" he demanded.

Tunavik bowed her head. "The Two-Legs killed them all long ago."

"Two-Legs! Then the Valley is no more than another deathtrap for us!" cried Tok

"Not so!" replied Tunavik. "The Two-Legs do not always do evil. Sometimes they do good."

"I don't believe you!"

"But it is true! The Two-Legs have decided that the Valley of the Cloven Mountain will be a place apart. They will slaughter there no more. They will dig the earth and fell the trees no more. They will leave the land to become again what the Maker intended. You and the wolves will be safe there now."

"But where is the Valley?" asked Tok. "What can I tell the wolves?"

"It lies far away to the west and north."

"How would we find it?" protested Tok. "With winter coming, the wolves will refuse to go on!"

"Entreat them to follow you here to the Gates of the North," said the white raven, spreading her wings. "Tell them that beyond they will find a wonder such as they have never seen. For the Wanderers go to the Valley. You have only to follow them."

"Wanderers?"

But Tunavik had already vanished into the deepening dusk. Tok settled himself as best he could in a rocky crevice, but he found it hard to sleep, for his mind buzzed with questions. What were the Wanderers? How long would it take to reach the Valley? And something more. The white raven said she had been sent to find him. But if she was the Messenger, who was the Sender?

Chapter 28

From the lowlands they turn,
To the mountains and the Valley they go.
In their multitude they go.

— from "The Wanderers," Songs of the Lanna

As Tok had feared, most of the wolves did not want to go on when they learned what lay beyond the country of bush and swamp. Neither did some of the ravens.

"What about the Overlord?" asked Kordah, with a shiver.

"Yes," said Barek. "If there are no trees, how can we hide from the raiders? They will pick us off one by one."

"I saw no enemies on my journey," Tok told them. And it was true. The skies over the Barren Lands had been empty.

"A land with no trees must be a land of no prey,"

said Rekshana grimly. "There can be no place for wolves there."

Even Taxin and Kimmik looked doubtful.

But Selaks's eyes glowed when she heard what the white raven had said. "Though I am no longer your *vóra*, I beg you to do this last thing for me," she pleaded with the pack. "I would see the Wanderers, whatever they may be."

Taxin looked at her long, but at last he said, "Let it be so, Selaks. But if the Barren Lands are as empty as Tok says, we must return."

It took the wolves many days' running to reach the northern fringes of the bush country. The days were much shorter now, and the sun hung low above the horizon. The cover of vegetation grew sparser and sparser, and at last the wolves came to the end of it, skulking from one clump of bushes to the next. But when even those failed, they ventured out into the Barren Lands. A cold wind blew from the north, and they sniffed the strange scents it carried, overawed by the vastness of the land.

"I could not imagine a world without a single tree," said Barator. "Yet it is true."

"It seems like a harsh land," said Kimmik. "Is it all like this, Tok?"

"All that I have seen. The white raven says it is so all the way north to the Frozen Ocean."

"Ah, yes, the white raven again," said Rokah, looking sidelong at the others. "Why should all of us risk our lives on the word of some creature that only you can see?"

Selaks gazed into the distance, the wind ruffling her fur. "Strange this treeless land may be, yet it is beautiful," she said. "But it is not the place of my Seeing."

"Your Seeing is nothing but dreaming," grumbled Rekshana. "It's time you stopped trying to fool yourself — and us!"

"But Tunavik said Selaks was right," Tok reminded them.

"This white raven is a creation of Tok's to make himself important," scoffed Rokah. "She doesn't exist. She never did. Otherwise, why haven't any of us seen her?"

"Liars always look for lies," said Brekka coldly. The two of them glared at each other.

"I think Rokah is right," said Rekshana, staring at Tok. "There is no white raven. If there is, let us see the wonder she has promised us."

"She said you must go beyond the Gates of the North to find the Wanderers," said Tok. "That's no more than another day's running from here. Will you do it?"

"But where is the Valley?" chorused the wolves. "We have come so far already!"

"Tunavik says the Valley of the Cloven Mountain lies far to the west and north, beyond these cold meadows," said Tok.

"What, we must travel so much farther even after we

reach these . . . Gates?" Even Taxin seemed daunted.

"Yes," Tok replied. "But we can follow the Wanderers, once we find them."

"How can we follow anything? There's nothing to eat out here!" moaned Vikka.

"She's right. We cannot eat grass, Tok," said Taxin. "My pack needs game, much game, to survive. How can we find that in lands such as you describe? You say there are no trees anywhere, scarcely even bushes. How can there be any deer?"

"You are right," said Tok. "I have seen no deer in these lands."

A long silence followed. Then there was a sudden sharp squeak and Tulik crunched a hapless vole that had popped out of the grass right at his feet.

"Nothing to eat, Taxin?" joked Tok. "Tulik has already proven you wrong!"

"Small game," snapped Rekshana. "Wolves need more than that."

"Yet we will follow you to the Gates of the North, Tok," said Taxin. "We owe you that much."

Grumbling among themselves, the wolves set off again. All that day they ran, the ravens flying ahead. The wolves paused only to rest and soon got up to run again. Selaks, as always, lagged far behind. They ran most of the night too, and by dawn the rocky profile of the Gates of the North loomed ahead of them. The wolves coursed between its stony cliffs, and Tok flew ahead of them toward a low ridge in the distance, the other ravens streaming behind him.

This was the end, Tok told himself. If there was nothing beyond the ridge, the wolves would surely turn back. Soaring over it, he first saw only the vast dun-coloured land rolling toward the horizon. Then he saw something moving across it, a darker flow that divided sometimes into strands, then wove itself together again, always moving westward. A river? he wondered. Focussing his long sight on it, he looked again and then his heart began to pound. This was no river, but a procession of living creatures winding its way across the Barren Lands. Thousands upon thousands of antlered beasts, bigger than deer, with shaggy dun-coloured coats. They flowed steadily toward the northwest in a narrow living stream as far as even his keen eyes could see.

Seeing them, the other ravens began to quork for joy, tumbling and dancing in the sky. Below them, the wolves surged to the crest of the ridge and stopped short as a wave of scent rushed toward them from the great river of beasts. Then, throwing back their heads, the pack began to sing.

"There, surely, is the wonder you were promised," cried Tok, swooping over Taxin's head. "They are the Wanderers, and they will lead us home."

Chapter 29

For the wolf its fangs,
For the prey its speed,
And the race is numon.

— Lore of the Lanna

The wolves rushed down the hill in pursuit of the nearest animals. So great were the numbers of the Wanderers that only the ones nearby paid heed to the danger, taking to their heels and dashing away in all directions.

"They are faster than deer!" marvelled Tok, as the ravens wheeled above the hunt.

"Look! The wolves have broken off the chase already," said Gloran. "We won't be tasting fresh meat just yet."

"Taxin must have been testing the Wanderers," said Tok. "He wouldn't waste the pack's strength in a hopeless chase."

They found the pack holding a council, tails waving in excitement.

Rekshana turned on Tok. "The beasts are many, but you did not say they were impossible to catch!" she said accusingly.

"Perhaps you need to learn their ways," he replied.

"He's right," said Taxin. "Let's go on, keeping as close to them as we can, until we see a chance."

The wolves picked up their pace, loping alongside the Wanderers, but not trying to attack. Tok, clinging to Selaks's back, could hear and feel her laboured breathing. She had been hard pressed to keep up in the forest, where the pace had been slower. What would happen to her now?

A group of beasts slowed down to browse on the yellow and grey lichen that covered much of the ground. The rest of the river of animals trotted on, filtering among those who had stopped to graze. The wolves slowed their pace too, and when some of the Wanderers stopped, they stopped. As long as the wolves did not charge, they found they could actually move among the animals, whose eyes only shifted warily, keeping them in sight.

"How do they know we're not hunting them now?" asked Tulik, puzzled.

"*Numon* is *numon*," panted Selaks, throwing herself down to rest.

Suddenly Taxin, who had been casting restlessly about, stiffened. His nostrils twitched as scent flowed to him on the wind. Then he moved toward a tussock of dried grass. "*Skiffet*," he said. "Fresh, too. There are wolves here." Lifting his leg, he over-marked the spot.

At once the pack became alert, sifting the breeze for further clues. "And that means the Wanderers can be caught," Taxin went on. "How else could a pack get enough to eat in the Barren Lands?"

That night the Wanderers slowed their pace, but most kept moving. The wolves followed. The ravens clung drowsily to the backs of their companions, lulled by the steady *chuk-chuk-chuk* of many hooves on the frosty grass and a strange clicking sound that seemed to come from the legs of the beasts.

"Work your way in among them. Get as close as they will let you without stampeding," ordered Taxin. "If we can find a calf we may be able to bring it down."

By daybreak, they had found their prey, a big calf that lagged toward the rear of the herd, stopping to look around as if separated from its mother. In the darkness, Taxin had worked his way closer to the Wanderers, his grey and black coat blending with the shadows. The beasts huffed and moved away nervously, but did not stampede. Now he edged closer and closer to the calf, patiently working himself between it and the stream of other animals. Suddenly Rekshana sprang forward, scattering the animals directly in front of her, while Taxin drove the calf away from the main herd. Barator and the rest of the pack were waiting. While the other beasts dashed away, they surrounded the hapless calf. Taxin seized it by the throat, pulling it down. It struggled to its feet, but the wolves dragged it down again, sinking their teeth into its flanks and shoulders. In moments it lay still. Only a short distance away, the Wanderers regrouped and trotted on.

The pack and the ravens made short work of the calf. Soon there was nothing left but a scrap of hide and a few bones. "Not much," said Rekshana, licking blood off her muzzle. "If only we could bring down one of the big ones!"

"Just think of all that meat," sighed Vikka, who was stripping the last shreds of flesh from a rib.

"Enough even for you, greedy one," joked Kimmik. "But, Tok, you say that the Wanderers are going to the Valley of the Cloven Mountain?"

"So Tunavik told me," said Tok.

Taxin's forehead was furrowed. "But they are here now. So they must go to the Valley for the winter, and then come back to the Barren Lands in spring," he said in an awed voice. "No wonder they are called the Wanderers."

Around them the great stream of the Wanderers flowed again on both sides, their breath steaming in the frosty air.

"You have seen the wonder Tunavik promised," said Tok, gazing from one wolf to another. "Have you ever dreamed of such bounty? Will you not follow the Wanderers home to the Valley?"

"Wonder they may be, but the big ones are too fast for us to catch." Rekshana's tone was bitter.

"No!" Taxin suddenly bounded to his feet and shook himself. "We will learn!" he cried. "We know now that there are other wolves here. They must hunt the Wanderers. And what others do, we can do too!" Energy seemed to flow from the young *vór* as he flung the challenge at his pack, ears pricked, tail held high. "Tok is right, my wolves," he went on. "Here is a new world, one that may prove better than any we have known. If all those beasts travel so far to reach the Valley, must it not be worth our seeking?"

Throwing back his head, he howled a long high note that died away across the great empty land. The other wolves crowded around him, and their riders lifted into the air. The pack mobbed Taxin, bunting his muzzle, shouldering him and throwing their forepaws across his back. They too began to sing, while the ravens tumbled and danced overhead. Then, without another word, the wolves set off after the Wanderers.

All that day and the next night they travelled, and everywhere they found fresh *skiffet*. The wolves overmarked it, to show that they had been there.

"Where are they?" muttered Taxin. "Why don't they show themselves?"

Tok and the other ravens circled widely above the great herd, but even their sharp eyes saw no other movement below.

"If they are out there, they are trying not to be seen," he reported to Taxin. "Hugging the shadows of ridges, perhaps."

"Or moving among the Wanderers, as we are learning to do." The *vór's* eyes were thoughtful.

That night the sky cleared and the temperature dropped. Strange lights danced across the heavens, green, red and pink. Awed, the ravens kept vigil, and the wolves were alert too. Toward midnight they heard a long wavering howl from the north, answered after a time by others to the south, east and west.

"All around us," said Rekshana, her pale eyes glinting in the dim light. "Should we howl back?"

"Wait," said Taxin. "I'd rather know how many they are first."

The howling continued most of the night, then faded away toward morning.

The next day they moved on as before. At midday, the Wanderers were following a track that wound below a rocky ridge, while the pack trotted alongside them. Suddenly the figure of a wolf appeared on the top of the ridge. For a long moment it stood outlined against the pale blue sky, and then it disappeared.

"A scout," said Taxin. "They will be waiting for us on the other side."

"I'll take a look," offered Tok.

But the *vór* was wrong. For even as Tok lifted away, gaunt shapes dark as shadows spilled over the crest of the ridge and rushed down upon the pack.

Chapter 30

It is not always easy to recognize a friend
among enemies.

— Wisdom of the Tellers

"They are using the beasts against you!" shrieked Tok, as a mass of the terrified animals stampeded blindly ahead of the charging wolves. But his warning came too late. The flying hooves of the herd caught the pack leaders, bowling Taxin over backward. Rekshana caught a glancing blow in the ribs, and cried out in pain. The other wolves scattered in time, all but Tulik, who disappeared under the thundering hooves of the Wanderers.

"The other pack has been watching us," cried Gloran, as the ravens regrouped overhead. "Their leaders know which of us to attack." For a tall grey wolf had flung himself upon Taxin as the herd scattered, and another large animal and two smaller ones were attacking Rekshana.

Tok shot toward Selaks, who was rolling over and over with an enemy wolf at her throat. She managed to shake it off, but it sprang at her again, laying open her flank with its fangs as she dodged away. Tok flew into its face and slashed open its right eye. Howling, the wounded animal retreated, while Selaks bounded back to the battle.

Meanwhile Kimmik had gone to the aid of Rekshana. The two smaller wolves turned on her, while the *vóra* and the big one rolled snarling on the ground. Barator and Fornál were throwing themselves at a huge whitish wolf. But it held them off easily, snapping now and then at Brekka, who was flying into its face. Vikka was battling another wolf, while Tulik, who had reappeared, limping badly, dashed in to bite and worry her opponent when he could.

The battle between Taxin and the leader of the attacking wolves raged back and forth furiously. They seemed evenly matched, and both were now bleeding from many wounds. Then the young *vór* charged straight for his opponent, ducking at the last moment so that its teeth closed harmlessly in his mane. He hit it full force in the chest, the impact knocking the other wolf off its feet. In a moment, Taxin fixed his fangs in his opponent's throat, and tore it open. Blood gushed onto the ground and the wolf went limp. Eyes flashing, Taxin threw back his head and gave a savage howl of victory.

At the sound, the wolves paused in their struggles. Breaking away from her opponent, Rekshana turned her head toward Taxin. Seeing its chance, her enemy sprang and seized her throat in its jaws, crushing and tearing. In vain Rekshana fought to throw it off, while Rokah battered at the beast's head with his wings and tried to reach its eyes. Selaks too joined the fight, throwing herself on Rekshana's attacker from behind, tearing gaping wounds in its back with her teeth. Still it held on, shaking Rekshana fiercely as it worked its grip deeper. Blood drenched the silver-white fur of the *vóra's* chest, and at last she stopped struggling. Her attacker flung the limp body aside and shook off Selaks. With a fierce bark, it summoned the rest of the attackers, and loped off.

Tails drooping, ears low, the battered wolves gathered around their fallen *vóra*, while Rokah perched grieving beside her.

The silver eyes fluttered open. "Tax . . . in?" she whispered, her voice bubbling painfully in her torn throat.

"I am here, *vóra*," he said, moving closer.

"You . . . won?"

"*We* won, *vóra*. From his size, that was the *anvór* of the other pack you fought. If he had attacked me too, it would have been all over."

A shiver ran through Rekshana's body, then her eyes closed. Around her, the pack raised its voice in a long mournful wail.

"Let us leave this place," said Taxin, after the song died away into silence.

The pack moved slowly away, the ravens winging low over their heads. The great river of the Wanderers had re-formed after their panic, and the wolves followed wearily after them. There was no sign of the other pack.

Selaks lagged behind the rest, and Tok swooped down to land on her back, carefully avoiding the bloody gashes in her fur. "Will they attack again, do you think?" he asked.

"Not without their *vór*. Not for a while, at least." She drew a shaky breath. "I hope not. We need time to recover."

Tok noticed how slowly she moved, head down, and fear gripped his heart. "Your wounds — are you all right?" he asked.

"The wounds are nothing," she replied. "But I am very weary. It is this thing in my chest, from when the bear crushed me. It does not let me breathe easily. And I fear it grows worse."

"You must not give up, my *vóra*."

"I will not, *lóran*," she said, lifting her head a little higher. "For I would see my Valley."

Tok lifted away again, still scanning the landscape for any sign of the rival pack. His eye was drawn by a whitish patch on the slope of a distant hill. Old snow, he thought, then checked himself. There was no old snow here, and despite the deepening cold, no new

269

snow had yet fallen. He angled his wings, skimming across the wind, to take a closer look. But when he saw what the white patch was, his heart sank. There on the hillside, brushy tail curled comfortably around its paws, lay the big whitish wolf that had fought off Barator and Fornál.

Spy! thought Tok. It's watching us! He zoomed low over the wolf's head with a harsh quork, just to let it know it had been seen, then headed back toward the herd. He decided not to report what he had seen to the wolves yet. Exhausted and grieving as they were, they did not need another worry. But he did tell the other ravens.

"Let's take turns keeping an eye on that beast," he told them. "Whatever it does gives us advance warning of another attack."

At dusk the Wanderers slowed to a walk. The wolves, too worn out to try to hunt them, foraged among the low bushes, hoping to unearth a few voles. Then Vikka, who had climbed a little hillock, gave a sharp cry.

"There's a beast lying down," she yelped. "Not moving!"

The pack flowed eagerly around the hillock, the ravens tumbling overhead. There indeed lay one of the Wanderers. They approached cautiously, expecting it to spring up and lash out with its hooves, but it did not move.

Taxin moved closer, his nostrils twitching. "Dead,

but not dead long," he announced.

"The Lanna's gift to deserving wolves," said Fornál, grinning. "It must have died of old age or sickness. There are no wounds on it."

The wolves and ravens fell eagerly upon it. Later, full-fed, the ravens hopped about among the low bushes, trying to find places to roost.

"Could Skyah not have allowed just a few trees here and there?" complained Brekka, trying to make herself comfortable on a grassy hummock.

Meanwhile the wolves had settled down to rest. There was much mutual licking of wounds, but now and then their eyes kept returning to Kimmik. At last she got up and stalked stiff-legged over to where Vikka and Tulik were lying.

At once Vikka rolled over on her back, grinning submissively. "My *vóra*," she whined.

The black wolf stood over her a moment, then allowed Vikka to get up and mouth her muzzle. Then her golden eyes turned to Selaks. "Do you deny me?" she asked. "Will you seek your old place?"

"No," said Selaks. "*Vóra* you are, with my full heart." Getting up painfully, she walked over and nuzzled the black wolf, leaning against her shoulder.

Kimmik's eyes glowed with joy as she turned to Taxin.

"*Vóra*," he greeted her formally, waving his tail. Then, "My *vóra*," he added. He walked over and they stood nose to nose, breathing each other's breath.

The pack went wild, yelping and yipping their delight. Stately Barator and clever Fornál, timid Vikka and clumsy Tulik mobbed their *vór* and *vóra*, rolling about them like pups.

Selaks looked on, laughing. "The Lanna be praised," she said. "We are whole again."

The ravens joined in the celebration of their companions, but Rokah stayed apart. Tok knew he was grieving for Rekshana and yearned to comfort him.

"They scarcely mourned her!" Rokah said bitterly, when Tok landed beside him.

"It is not that they don't mourn," Tok said. "But *karlán* is *karlán*. There must be a *vór* and a *vóra*, or the pack falls apart."

Rokah said no more. But the next morning when the ravens awoke, he was gone.

Karah shot Tok a glance of sympathy, saying nothing.

But Brekka was less discreet. "Of course he would leave!" she said. "He has found out what he wanted to know — where we are going. All he has to do now is follow the Wanderers, as Tunavik told you."

"I am only surprised that he has stayed as long as this," said Gloran.

Tok glared at the two of them. "You are always quick to blame Rokah," he snapped. "He has left us before and returned. He will do the same again."

"Perhaps," said Gloran. But he did not sound convinced.

Gloran and Barek flew off to scout, hoping to catch sight of the spy wolf. "It's still out there," Gloran reported later. "Not far away. But there's no sign of the other pack."

Barek, who had flown south, had seen no wolves at all. "But there was something in the sky," he said. "Far to the south, like a black cloud."

"Raiders?" demanded Tok, his heart tightening.

"No form to it. Just a blackness at the southern horizon. And then it vanished."

The next day, the white wolf was still there, not too far away.

Tok decided it was time to tell the wolves. "We've been keeping a watch on this spy," he told Taxin. "It does nothing, though each day it has come a little closer. When you move, it moves. When you stop to rest, it lies down. There's no sign of the other pack, though."

"They're probably fighting among themselves over the *vórship*," mused Taxin. "Let's hope so. But this spy we must deal with."

The pack and their riders moved out, dividing into two groups. Taxin led one slowly across the rolling ground, heading straight for where the ravens told them the spy was. Kimmik led the other group to outflank the enemy and attack it from behind.

"There it is," said Taxin, as a white spot appeared in the distance. "Be careful. It's dangerous. Or the pack would not have given it this duty."

"You don't have to tell me," growled Fornál. "I have his tooth marks on me to prove it."

Tok lifted away from Selaks's back. From the air he could see Taxin moving forward slowly, with the others following. Then he stopped and waited. The distant wolf moved forward too, then also stopped and waited.

"It doesn't look much like an attack," said Karah, who had followed him aloft.

"Maybe Taxin is waiting for the others to come around. There they are!"

They watched the black dot that was Kimmik leading her group around behind the spy, cutting off his retreat. Then she began to move forward at a swift trot, and at the same moment Taxin moved forward too. This time the white wolf stood awaiting them, doing nothing.

"It's not going to fight! Let's get down," said Tok, diving for the ground.

Taxin and the strange wolf stepped closer and closer until they stood confronting each other. "You are spying on us for our enemies," challenged Taxin. "You must fight."

Looking at it up close, Tok could see that the stranger looked different from the other wolves. He was a male, bigger even than Taxin. His muzzle was shorter and wider, his ears less pointed, and the ruff of fur around his face was thicker and deeper. Now he grinned, wrinkling his muzzle, his narrow eyes almost disappearing in his furry face. "I will not fight you, brother," he said, his voice a deep rumble. "And while it's true that I have been spying, I do it only for myself."

"You were with the pack that attacked us, though," snarled Fornál. "I know, because my brother and I fought you."

"True enough," said the other. "But I did not seek to fight you. You attacked me, and I defended myself. That is all."

Barator wrinkled his forehead. "It's true, Taxin," he said. "I attacked him, and Fornál helped me. He did no more than hold both of us off."

Taxin measured the big white wolf with a cold gaze. "Why do you follow us then? What do you want?"

The eyes of the stranger travelled from wolf to wolf, each with its raven rider, coming to rest finally on Selaks and Tok. "I would like to join you, perhaps. I want to learn more about wolves with raven riders," he said.

"Who are you?" demanded Taxin. "If you do not belong to the other pack, where do you come from?"

"From across the Frozen Ocean," the other said. "My name is Sibirok."

Chapter 31

Half-blind, long seer;
Nose-numb, far finder;
Slow-foot, fast mover.
What is it? A Two-Legs.

— Wolf riddle

Taxin stalked forward, and the two big wolves exchanged greetings, nose to nose, nose to tail. "For my part, you are welcome," said the *vór*. "But the unity of this pack comes first. Some of us still bear the marks of your teeth. So travel with us, hunt with us. Later we shall see if you indeed prove worthy."

"It is all I ask, *vór*," said Sibirok. He paid no homage to Taxin, but stood apart, tail waving, as he surveyed the pack.

The wolves turned back to follow the Wanderers. The animals seemed to be moving faster now, their long legs eating up distance. The pack, too, picked up its pace, and again Tok became aware of Selaks's laboured breathing and her desperate effort to keep up with the others. It seemed that the newcomer had noticed her trouble too, for however far behind she lagged, Sibirok was never far away.

"We must kill again soon," she panted, when they stopped to rest one midday. "It has been days since we found that dead beast."

"Yet here are thousands of prey right before your eyes," said Sibirok, who had curled up nearby. "I have been wondering why you fast."

Selaks turned her golden gaze on him. "We come from a land farther south," she said. "These Wanderers are faster than the deer we used to hunt."

"Yet caribou can be taken," the stranger replied.

"Caribou?" asked Selaks, tasting the strange word. "Is that what you call them? Well, if you know how to catch them, tell Taxin."

"If you think he will not be offended." The big wolf got to his feet and moved toward the *vór*, who was lying some distance away near Kimmik.

"Go with him, Tok," urged Selaks. "I want to know what he says."

Tok flapped after Sibirok and dropped onto his shoulders with a thump. "Ah!" the stranger said, turning his head in surprise. "So that is what it feels like to have a raven rider. Do all the wolves of your country have them?"

"Only these," said Tok. "It is a long story."

"You must tell me some time," said Sibirok.

Taxin looked up questioningly as they approached, and Karah, who was perched a short distance away, flapped closer.

"Sibirok says he knows how to catch the . . . caribou. That's what he calls the Wanderers," said Tok.

"I do not mean to insult you by trying to teach you your business, *vór*," said Sibirok, laying his ears back politely.

"My business is to keep my pack fed," growled Taxin. "Tell me what you know."

The two of them spoke for a long time, and Tok listened intently.

"He says the pack must use the terrain more," he reported later to Selaks. "Taxin is going to try it. He has asked us ravens to fly ahead looking for hills or ridges near the route the caribou are following."

The ravens soon saw a low ridge not far ahead, and the pack moved off. Taxin, Kimmik and Barator loped ahead to lie in ambush, with their ravens flying overhead. Meanwhile the others tested the caribou, trying to find one more vulnerable than the rest.

"That big one, I think," said Fornál, narrowing his eyes in concentration. "See how its gait is a little uneven?"

"Probably something wrong with a leg or hoof," agreed Sibirok. The two of them picked up the pace, dodging in and out of the herd, as they forced the chosen caribou toward the edge of the great stream of beasts. Then they charged, driving it toward the ridge. Tok and the other ravens took flight as Selaks, Vikka and Tulik loped in, cutting the fleeing beast off from open ground.

The great animal bounded forward, its snowy chest heaving and its antler-crowned head held high. Now the wolves spread out into a line behind it, not trying to catch it, just driving it forward. They turned it up the hill, and even then it might have easily outrun them. But now Taxin, Kimmik and Barator burst from behind the rocks that had concealed them. They rushed downhill upon the startled animal, their ravens screaming and flying into its face, while the other wolves put on a burst of speed and sprang upon it from behind. The caribou reared, only its antlered head visible above the mantle of wolves that fastened themselves upon it, their teeth tearing deep into its flesh.

Taxin sprang for the beast's underbelly, slicing it open, and a spray of blood drenched the ground and the nearest attackers. The caribou went down, and though it still heaved and struggled, could not rise again. Soon it lay still, and the wolves raised their bloody muzzles in a song of victory. Among the rest was the deep voice of Sibirok, a dark note that wove itself among their higher ones to make a perfect chord.

The pack feasted long, heedless of the sinking of the sun or the steady onward movement of the great herd below them. When at last, bellies bulging, they had to stop, only the antlers and backbone of the caribou remained.

"Well done, Sibirok. It worked exactly as you said," groaned Taxin, rolling over on his back. Then, fixing his dark eyes on the stranger, "But what happens where there are no hills or ridges?"

Sibirok ran out his tongue, laughing. "Why, then we run in turns, *vór*," he rumbled. "I'll tell you about that another time."

On they journeyed under the overarching sky. Around them, the brief autumn was already turning to winter. The flaming reds and glowing yellows of the low vegetation had dulled to brown. Heavy frost crusted the ground, which was hard as wood under their feet. The only sounds in the vast land were those of the herd, the *thud-thud-thud* of hooves on the ground, the huff of their breaths, the strange clicking of their legs, and the "mah!" of calves seeking their mothers.

One day the sky became overcast, and Tok felt dampness in his feathers. Karah complained that her shoulder felt stiff again.

"Will it snow?" asked Selaks. "I long for it!"

"And I!" "And I!" chorused other wolf voices.

The snow came at dusk, the first feathery flakes drifting down around them, veiling the land in white and frosting the backs of the caribou. The wolves capered with delight, leaping up to catch snowflakes in their mouths, uttering little yelps of joy.

And with the snow and the dark came the white raven, swooping in on silent wings to land near Tok and Selaks.

Before Tok could speak, Selaks lifted her head, staring through the falling snow. Then she stiffened and her mane stood on end.

"What is it?" he asked. Then he realized what was happening. "It's the snow! You're Seeing Tunavik at last!" he cried joyously.

"I See her — and more besides," replied Selaks, and there was a tremor in her voice that Tok had never heard before. The pupils of her eyes expanded until all the gold was gone, leaving black mirrors of terror.

Tunavik's strange dark eyes stared back at the white wolf. Then she bowed, spreading her wings. "You See far, Selaks," she said. "There is no need to be afraid. But I pray you, say no more of this."

Selaks shivered and closed her eyes.

"What has she Seen that frightens her?" Tok demanded of the white raven.

"That I may not tell you — for now," replied Tunavik.

Tok's frustration exploded. "I tire of your mysteries!" he cried.

"I only came to see that you are with the Wanderers, that all is well," she replied.

"Well, you have seen!" he snapped. As he spoke, an eddy of snow swirled around the white raven and she vanished.

Selaks gave a shuddering sigh and laid her head upon her paws.

"Why do you fear Tunavik?" asked Tok. "Tell me!"

"Don't ask," she said. And would say no more, no matter how he pleaded.

The next day the pack moved on. There was an uncomfortable silence between Tok and Selaks, and he left her and flew off to ride a while with Sibirok.

"The ex-*vóra* is unhappy," the lone wolf said.

"How do you know she was a *vóra*?" asked Tok.

"Any wolf would know," Sibirok replied. "It shines through her. She is a noble creature. How came she to lose her pack?"

"Her mate, the former *vór*, was killed. She blamed herself and gave up her rank. And she was badly injured defending her pups against a grizzly. She suffers, Sibirok."

"I can see that. And am sorry for it. I would befriend her, if she would let me."

The sky was overcast, although the snow had stopped, and it was long before Tok became aware of a muffled roar in the distance. Air-*grawl!* he thought, his heart leaping to his throat. But though he scanned the sky he saw nothing. The wolves had heard it too, and had stopped, gazing upward.

"I feared this above all," said Taxin. "For here there is no forest to conceal us. Head for the herd and try to hide among them!" He led the pack forward at a gallop.

The roar grew louder, and at last the air-*grawl* broke through the clouds above them. It made one low pass over the fleeing wolves and caribou, then vanished into the clouds again, the sound of it fading into the distance.

"Curse the Two-Legs," muttered Selaks. "Can we never be free of them?"

"At least this one has gone away," said Tok.

But even as he spoke he heard a different sound, a frightful clatter approaching rapidly from behind them. It thrummed in his ears, blotting out all other sounds. Terrified, he and the other ravens threw themselves into the air.

Then out of the clouds descended a kind of *grawl* he had never seen before. Its body was red and bulbous, and above it, narrow wings whirled fiercely, sending a downdraft of air that dashed the ravens earthward amid a cloud of snow. The awful thing moved onward, following the fleeing wolves. They plunged desperately among the caribou, but the herd scattered in terror. Close, close the *grawl* hovered above the pack, whipping their fur in its wind.

Then Tok, who had scrambled into the air again, saw a Two-Legs lean out with a large firestick. There were two loud bangs heard even over the dreadful roar of the *grawl*, and Tok saw Taxin break stride, then Kimmik. But the other wolves raced on, with Selaks trailing far behind.

The Two-Legs missed! thought Tok. Then came

another loud bang, and this time Selaks faltered. Yet the wolves ran on.

Now the terrible *grawl* rose higher into the air.

"What are they waiting for?" shrieked Gloran, as he, Tok and Karah battled through the fierce cross-winds created by the *grawl,* trying to stay aloft.

A moment later, they knew. Taxin, the first to be hit, suddenly stumbled and rolled tail over nose in the snow. The *vór* raised himself on his forelegs, trying to drag himself forward, but his hind legs refused to obey him and then his forelegs failed too. He struggled briefly, then lay still. Behind him, Kimmik also collapsed, and then Selaks. The rest of the wolves fled in all directions.

Now the terrible *grawl* moved lower and lower, until it came to rest on the ground. The whirling wings on top of it slowed, their heart-stopping clatter dying away to a high whine. Then the side of it opened, and a pair of Two-Legs sprang out and closed in on the three bodies lying still on the snow.

Chapter 32

Hope remains when all else is gone.

— Raven proverb

"Murderers!" shrieked Tok, diving in fury at the Two-Legs, with Gloran, Brekka and Karah behind him.

Shouting and waving their front paws, the Two-Legs beat off the attacking ravens. Then they knelt beside Taxin. To skin him? Tok wondered, heartsick, as he circled back. But instead, one of the pair gently stroked Taxin's cloud-and-shadow fur. Then it pulled out a long narrow strip of some kind and laid it from the tip of the big wolf's nose to the end of his tail. After that it worked a broad band under the wolf's belly and then lifted it, raising Taxin's body off the ground for a moment. That done, the first one jabbed Taxin with something small and sharp. Meanwhile, the other Two-Legs had examined Taxin's teeth and fastened something around the *vór*'s neck. Then the two of them turned to Kimmik.

"What are they doing?" asked Gloran, as the ravens circled, making angry passes at the Two-Legs as they worked.

"I don't know," said Tok. "No hunters I have ever seen behaved like this."

Now the Two-Legs were kneeling beside Selaks. But they did not do the same things to her. Instead, they listened at her chest, and lifted one of her eyelids. One of them ran a hand along her side, and said something sharply to the other. Then, lifting the white wolf by her forelegs and hind legs they carried her toward the *grawl*.

Tok swooped after them, but the deadly turning wings of the *grawl* kept him at a distance. He watched in anguish as the Two-Legs stowed Selaks inside and climbed in after her. The whine of the *grawl* rose to a deafening clatter and the thing lifted off the ground.

Then Karah, who had swooped down to land beside Taxin, gave a great cry of joy. "He is alive!" she called to the others.

The *vór* was trying to lift his head. After a few moments' struggle, he succeeded. "What happened? Where is Kimmik?" he asked, his voice thick and slurred.

"If he's alive the others may be!" shouted Tok, over the noise of the departing *grawl*. "I'm going after Selaks!"

The *grawl* rose slowly into the air, turning toward

the north and gaining speed as it went. Tok flew after it with desperate wingbeats, but it soon disappeared over the horizon ahead of him. On he flew, hoping to catch sight of it again, but the sky was empty now. Clouds were gathering and the day grew darker. Soon the land disappeared in whirling snow. Where had they taken Selaks? he thought desperately. How could he ever find her?

The only way was to struggle head on into the wind. At least that way he would not lose his direction. Tok flew low, not wanting to miss the *grawl* if it had landed, yet fearful of flying into the kind of massive structures the Two-Legs often built. But when shapes loomed at last through the swirling snow, they were not like any he had seen before. This was no many-roosts, but a huddle of small low structures lost in the vastness of the Barren Lands. Tok shot over them almost before he saw them, and had to turn back. On the north side was an open space with *grawls* lined up on the ground, and he zoomed down to investigate. The red *grawl* was not among them, but nearby stood a structure that had one open side, and there at last he found it.

Its terrible whirling wings were now still, and melting snow still dripped from them. Tok landed on the air-*grawl* and peered inside, but it was empty. He gave a cry of disappointment. They had taken Selaks! He shot away into the outer air again

Outside, the clouds were breaking, but the day was

already growing dark. Tok flew toward a low structure nearby. Light streamed out through the clear ice-like substance the Two-Legs used in the sides of their dwellings, and a large snow-*grawl* stood beside it. So some of the Two-Legs must be inside the dwelling, he thought.

Behind the structure was an open enclosure with high sides. Tok had seen such things before, and knew the Two-Legs sometimes kept animals inside them. But there was no sign of Selaks. He landed on the top of the structure, and cocked his head, listening. He heard sounds coming from inside, so fluttering down, he perched on a ledge outside the ice-like opening and peered inside.

To his horror, he saw Selaks stretched out on top of a flat object. She lay limp and still. A group of Two-Legs were bending over her and he could see the flash of silvery objects probing her body. They were killing her, cutting her up!

Sick with despair, he clung to the ledge. At last the Two-Legs moved away from Selaks's body. Leaving her where she was, they disappeared farther inside the structure and the light went out. Moments later Tok heard the snarl of the *grawl* going away into the distance. Desperately, he pecked at the shining barrier between him and Selaks, but it was harder than the hardest ice. Then, lifting into the air, he flew over the structure and found the way the Two-Legs must have gone out. But the opening was closed tight, and there was nothing to grasp but a shiny knob. He could do nothing with it.

Miserably, he perched again on the top of the structure. Selaks seemed dead, yet he could not leave her. It would be like leaving his heart behind, he thought, appalled at the loneliness that lay ahead of him if she had truly joined the Lanna. Who else understood him, cared for him as Selaks did? Not even Karah knew him so well. He had told himself that he chose to stay with the pack because Selaks needed him. How noble he had made himself out to be. And how blind he had been! Only now did he see that he needed her just as much as she needed him, this utterly different creature who was his *lóran*.

Hours passed, as the northern stars wheeled above him. At last he dozed off, only to awaken in the early morning hours. And there, high above him, were the shining colours he had seen once before, wavering in luminous folds of crimson and blue across the sky. In the deep cold and silence, Tok felt his feathers prickle, as if some unseen force was all around him. Somehow it kindled a tiny flame of hope in the depths of his heart. The Two-Legs had not killed Taxin, had they? So why should they kill Selaks? They had examined her closely — had they somehow sensed the deep hurt that stole her breath and caused her so much pain?

"I will not believe her dead!" he told the shining sky. "Not until I see her stiff and cold!"

Fluffing his feathers defiantly against the frost, he watched until the dazzling colours faded from the sky and the stars paled in the east before the coming of the sun.

Chapter 33

*Now fled Tok Wolf Bird and his lóran across
the white wastes.
Heavy was his heart, torn between love and duty.*

— from "The Saga of Tok Wolf Rider,"
Sagas of the Tellers

It was the middle of the morning before the Two-Legs
came back. Tok had already tried to peer through the
ice-sheet again, but the morning light reflected only
his own image and he could not see inside. Frantic
now, he hopped back and forth, listening to the
voices from within. Then he heard a noise from the
side where the enclosure was. Flapping over the top of
the structure, he saw the Two-Legs carrying Selaks,
who lay limp in their grasp. They spread something on
the ground inside the enclosure and laid her gently on
it. One of them brought a flat object with water in it,
and left it near her head. Then they closed the open-

ing in the enclosure and went back inside.

"Selaks! Wake up!" Tok cried, fluttering down beside her. He did not know how he would get her out of this place, but somehow he would.

But the white wolf slept on, her sides rising and falling gently. Tok saw that a long strip of bare skin extended along her side, where the fur had been removed. A narrow wound ran the length of it, its edges held together with a line of little black marks. Tok picked at one gently. It gave a little, and the edge of the wound underneath gaped ever so slightly. Best to leave it alone, he decided. He also noticed that the Two-Legs had fastened around her neck one of the round things they had put on Taxin and Kimmik. Curious, he pecked and tugged at it. It had a hard part and a softer part, and for all his tugging he could not budge it.

Around midday, a Two-Legs brought fresh water. From a safe distance, Tok watched as it bent over Selaks and seemed to listen to her breathing. Then it went inside again. Not long afterward, Selaks began to stir. She tried to lift her head, her tongue lolling from her mouth, and Tok flew down to nudge the water closer so she could reach it easily.

"Selaks!" he cried. "Are you all right?"

The white wolf stared at Tok with glazed eyes, seeming not to recognize him. After taking a few laps of water, she let her head sink to the ground, and slept again.

Tok stalked back and forth, fretting. Twice more that afternoon a Two-Legs brought water and looked closely at the wounded wolf. At dusk, one of them brought a mound of meat, and left it in the enclosure. Soon Tok heard the roar of the snow-*grawl* fading into the distance.

"Wake up, Selaks!" he croaked in her ear. "Now is our chance — the Two-Legs are gone."

At last she roused, and this time she seemed to know him. She rolled onto her belly and tried to get up, but sank back with a whine of pain. "What . . . ? Where am I?" she asked, gazing around dizzily.

"The Two-Legs got you. We must escape now, while they're gone."

"I . . . can't. Not yet. Much pain." Selaks turned her head and tried to lick the wound in her flank. "What have they done to me?"

"I don't know," said Tok, settling down again by her side. It was clear that she could not go anywhere yet. "Are you hungry? They left meat."

She dropped her head onto her paws. "No. But help yourself, if you dare. It's probably poisoned," she added, closing her eyes again.

Tok decided to risk it, and ate heartily. He didn't think the Two-Legs would poison Selaks, not after they had spent so much time on her. The meat was delicious, dark and fatty, and there were cracked caribou bones oozing with rich marrow.

By the next morning, Selaks was much better. Her

eyes were bright, and she eagerly gobbled down the remaining meat. "You're still alive, so it must be safe enough," she said, gnawing the last bone.

Soon the Two-Legs arrived. They seemed pleased by her recovery, and gathered around the enclosure, grinning and talking excitedly. But what would they do with her now? wondered Tok. After a while, the Two-Legs went away, leaving fresh water and more meat.

"Can you travel yet?" asked Tok, as Selaks got to her feet and stretched cautiously.

"I'm sore. Very sore. But, yes, I think so," she replied.

"We go tonight, then, as soon as they leave," promised Tok.

"But how do I get out of here?" demanded Selaks. She paced around the enclosure, judging the height of it. "I certainly can't jump!"

Tok had already been investigating the side of the enclosure the Two-Legs used to go in and out. There was a silver-coloured fastener on it. Long ago he too had been a prisoner of the Two-Legs, and had managed to escape. Now, clinging to the side of the enclosure, he cocked his head this way and that, inspecting the silvery thing. "I think I can open this!" he said to Selaks, who stood gazing up at him. For the fastener was the same sliding kind as the one he had opened before. It had a long slender piece like a twig that slid through two hollow pieces. On one side of it a kind of tooth jutted out, and Tok pecked at it, trying to grasp it in his beak. After a few tries, he managed to shift the slider. Cautiously, he moved it one way, then back the other way.

"As soon as they're gone, we'll leave," he promised.

Her eyes beamed at him, full of their old warmth. "What would I do without you, *lóran?*" she said.

As soon as the Two-Legs had left for the night, Tok pulled the slider back. Selaks pushed against the inside of the enclosure, and it swung open. She took a deep breath, and gazed around. "Which way now?" she asked.

Tok had used the afternoon to do some scouting, and led her out of the dwelling place of the Two-Legs by the shortest route. They flitted among the lighted structures, and only the barking of dogs marked their passing. Soon they emerged into open country.

Selaks had gasped with pain when she first tried to run, but as they went on she became less stiff, and her movements became easier.

"We'll go just far enough to be safe tonight," he promised. "You must rest a while. We'll lie up during the day, and travel by night. That way they won't be able to see us from the *grawl.*"

The next morning they hid among some stunted bushes below a ridge. Selaks slept most of the day, while Tok foraged among the snow-covered tussocks of dried grass. He startled a colony of little squirrel-like animals that darted into their burrows uttering a sharp "*Sik-sik!*" before he could catch any of them. Then he uncovered voles in a snow tunnel, and killed several with sharp blows of his beak. He ate one, then carried the rest back to Selaks. She bolted them down, and soon began to cast about for something more. A big-footed snowshoe hare broke cover and dashed away and she bounded after it. But it turned nimbly, zigzagging this way and that, and at last she gave up. She trotted back to Tok looking puzzled.

"What's the matter?" he asked, landing on her back.

"I'm not sure. I'll tell you when I am," she replied.

On they journeyed across a white and frozen world. They were heading south by west, searching for the great herd of caribou, which would have gone some distance by now. Soon, having seen and heard nothing of the air-*grawls*, they ventured to travel by day as well as by night, with only brief stops to rest and forage. Selaks grew stronger and faster, and soon was able to catch all the hares they needed.

It was a time apart. Tok often rode on Selaks's back for the sheer pleasure of knowing he was no longer a burden. They talked much under the stars or waiting out blizzards, Selaks, warm in her thick fur, curled up with her back to the wind and Tok snug inside the brushy curve of her tail.

"I feel at peace now," she said on one such night. "For the first time since Durnál died. Our journey is not over, but I know we will find the pack and reach the Valley."

"Will you become *vóra* again there?" he asked.

"No, not I. Taxin and Kimmik are worthy pack leaders. I cannot See what lies ahead for me. But there is something. I feel it."

There was a pause while they listened to the dry hiss of the driving snow.

Then Selaks asked, "And you, Tok?"

"I am less content," he confessed. "For one thing, what frightened you when you Saw Tunavik through the snow? You saw something important, I know it. Yet you will not tell me."

There was a silence, then Selaks replied. "Forgive me, *lóran*. For myself I would gladly tell you. But Tunavik asked me not to. And if you have chosen to trust her, how can I do less?"

"Then I suppose I must wait until she tells me herself. If she ever does." Tok brooded a while, then continued, "Something else troubles me too."

Selaks lifted her head and gazed at him through the whirling snow. "Rokah," she said.

"I judged him too harshly, Selaks, and he has never forgiven me!" Tok's voice was sharp with anguish.

"Rekshana's death shook him too. I saw that."

"He blames us all for not mourning her enough."

"He is wrong." The white wolf shook snow from her ears. "We all mourn her still. Even I."

"But she humiliated you!"

"Yes. And I suffered. But Rekshana looked to the future and saw the need to move on when I could not." Selaks sighed. "My brave daughter had the makings of a fine *vóra*. But she could never have what she had set her heart on — Taxin. Her death was bitter, but perhaps in a way the Lanna showed her mercy."

For a moment both were silent, listening to the keening of the wind.

Then, "I also think much about the Overlord," Tok confessed. "My promise to you and the pack will be kept when we find the Valley. But I also vowed to confront the Overlord. What he has done to raven-kind is monstrous. He is still out there somewhere, and I have done nothing to stop him. I just went away and left all that suffering behind. If I had not already been *unkora* at the beginning of our journey, I would be now."

"You are not *unkora*," she replied. "For you have always done your best, and your friends honour you for it. Surely that is *kora* enough for any raven. Even a stiff-necked one like you," she added, with a huff of laughter.

Could she be right? wondered Tok, wishing it were so. But how could she be? For he had broken raven-law in failing to guard his mate and in abandoning his territory. Surely that made him forever *unkora* even had he not broken his promise to find the Overlord.

But Selaks was not done yet. "Have you ever thought, Tok," she went on, "that being *kora* is not what you believe it to be?"

Tok stared into her eyes, shocked. Not understand *kora*? But he understood it all too well. Tradition, law, duty, honour, self-respect — all these were part of it. And he had turned his back on all of them. No, Selaks was wrong.

Yet the warmth of her affection comforted his sore heart. Later, as she slept in the silence after the storm passed, he made another vow. He would see her and the other wolves safely to the Valley. Then he would return to the Cold Forest. And this time he would not give up until he found the Overlord and ended the Terror, or died trying.

Part 5

The Overlord

Chapter 34

I live to greet the sun again, sisters,
Hunt with gleam of fang
Under cold moons, brothers,
Tasting the hot blood black as shadows.

— from "Selaks's Return," *Songs of the Lanna*

The next morning, the wind had died down. Tok and Selaks woke to find themselves enclosed by a layer of ice formed by the warmth of their bodies. She jumped up, shattering it, and glittering shards tinkled onto the hard-packed snow. Tok shook his wings in the brilliant sunshine and began to preen himself, zipping his beak along his flight feathers. Then he paused as he heard a frantic drumming. Selaks had heard it too, and was creeping up on a small mound in the snow. Then she sprang, crashing down on it. Out rocketed a terrified white bird with feathery feet, which had also been made a prisoner by the ice. One snap of

Selaks's jaws put an end to its freedom.

"Ptarmigan," she said, chewing on it thoughtfully, while Tok bolted down the bits she let fall. "Mostly feathers, but at least it's a change from hare."

The sun stayed low all the brief day now, rolling across the sky not far above the horizon, and shadows lay blue and long across the snow as they journeyed. One afternoon, Tok watched from the air as Selaks crossed a series of low ridges, racing effortlessly up one side and down the other. She paused at the crest of one, scenting the wind, as Tok swooped over her.

She glanced up at him, her eyes sparkling and her coat gleaming cream and gold in the sunlight. Only the pink line of the scar along her side showed that she had ever been wounded. Even the mark of the burn across her nose had faded to silver, blending into her fur.

"It is a wonder," he said, as he landed on her back. "You are as you used to be."

"That's what I meant, Tok," she replied. "Days ago, when I said I still wasn't sure. But now I am. Ever since the bear crushed me, I have run with a sharp pain through my chest. It hurt to breathe, and I grew weary unto death. I believed all was over for me. But that's all gone now. Whatever the Two-Legs did, it cured me."

Selaks bounded on, and Tok mounted into the air again. Higher and higher he rose, till the earth lay spread out below him. For the first time since Tarkah died, his wings felt weightless, and the old pain melted from his heart. *Selaks is right,* he thought in wonder. *No matter what I have done, I am not* unkora. *I cannot be, and feel such joy!*

Twirling and diving through the icy air, he danced the sun down. By its last rays he saw the white wolf running free across the land, and far ahead at last, the great winding river of caribou. And beyond even that, at the farthest edge of his vision, there loomed a line of distant mountains purple as wild grapes, their summits frosted with snow.

The next day, long before Tok and Selaks caught up with the herd, Sibirok came bounding to meet them. "I stayed behind, waiting and hoping," he said. "Now I have my reward." His eyes widened as he stared at Selaks. "Can this be the half-dead creature who used to lag behind the pack?" he went on, with a grin that showed his gleaming white teeth.

Selaks gazed back at him, head high, tail waving. "The Two-Legs cured me," she replied.

"So?" said Sibirok, surprised. "But they have left you with something you do not need. That thing around your neck."

"I pecked and pecked at it," said Tok. "But it won't come off."

"We will see about that," replied Sibirok, as they moved on. "Taxin and Kimmik helped each other get rid of theirs long ago." As soon as they stopped to rest he lay down beside Selaks, and chewed patiently at the Two-Legs' thing until at last it came free. With a toss of his head, Sibirok flung it away. Strolling over, he lifted his leg, marking it. Then he kicked snow over it.

Selaks happily scratched the fur around her neck with a hind foot. "Thank you, Sibirok. That thing made me itch," she said.

The pack greeted Selaks joyously when they caught up, jumping on her to play-wrestle and rolling her in the snow, as if she were one of them again. But in Kimmik's eyes there was the shadow of a question.

"Greetings, *vóra*," said Selaks, bunting her fondly under the chin with her nose, and the tension in the black wolf melted away.

"Your pack is looking fit and well-fed, Taxin," Selaks went on, her eyes travelling from one sleek body to another.

"Sibirok has taught us another way to hunt caribou," Tulik broke in excitedly. "It's easy when you know how!"

Karah, Brekka and the other ravens greeted Tok, but Rokah was not among them. Tok looked around, but did not see him.

"Rokah has not returned, Tok," said Gloran, guessing the meaning of his gaze. "I'm sorry. At least for your sake."

"Any sign of enemy flights?" asked Tok.

"I've headed south almost every day there was decent flying," Barek reported. "But I have seen no raiders. And no more of the strange black cloud I saw before. The skies are empty."

The next day, Tok watched as Taxin and Barator cut a big caribou out from the herd and pursued it, turning it back toward where Sibirok and Fornál waited to take up the chase. When they grew tired, Kimmik and Selaks took over, and then Vikka and Tulik. In this way even the magnificent speed of the Wanderers could be worn down at last.

"Meat, glorious meat!" gloated Selaks, her muzzle red with gore. "I've eaten enough small game lately to last me the rest of my life."

Days passed as the great herd of caribou climbed toward higher ground, turning toward the mountains. The Wanderers grew restless, the big bulls charging each other and sparring with their tall antlers, sometimes fighting pitched battles in which one or another of them was driven off. One day the antlers of two of them locked together, and both fought to a standstill. Then the wolves fell upon them and feasted.

The land grew rougher as the mountains closed around them. The caribou picked their way along packed trails among the rocks. The temperature dropped sharply, and their pace quickened, as if they were eager to find safety in the Valley before heavier snows came upon them. They did not stop to eat now, pausing only to kick the snow and snatch a few mouthfuls of lichen before trotting on. Young bulls led groups of yearlings, urging them on when they dallied.

Females shepherded their weary calves, fighting fiercely to defend them from the wolves. Many weak and injured animals lagged farther and farther behind. Yet even these, gasping for breath, limping on injured limbs, plodding along on damaged hooves, struggled after the rest.

"We kill them for our need, and that is right," mused Taxin, as the wolves gazed down at the herd winding below them. "Yet they are the noblest creatures I have ever seen."

"The white raven was right to call them a gift," said Selaks. "How much poorer would our lives have been if we had not come here, experienced this great river of life!"

At last the urge to see what lay ahead overcame Tok. Saying nothing to his companions, he slipped away one morning while the wolves were hunting, and flew deep among the mountains. The way forward narrowed at last to a rocky pass like a great notch between the peaks. Below he could see the first of the Wanderers reach it and begin to file through it, some of them bounding forward with new energy, as if sensing that their destination lay not far ahead. Tok soared, breathing the icy air while the heat of the sun soaked into his black feathers, and his heart began to beat faster. Soon he would see it, any moment now!

Then, out of the pass, a winged black shape shot toward him. A raven, big, black, glossy . . .

Tok gave a great cry of joy. "Rokah! How I hoped

you would be here. You came ahead to wait for us!"

Rokah's eyes flashed, as he turned to fly wingtip to wingtip with Tok. "Indeed," he said. "And I have brought others with me too. We have all been waiting for you, Lord Tok," he added, with mocking emphasis.

For there were other ravens around him now, and many more of them, rising from among the rocks where they had concealed themselves. They swarmed about Tok, cutting off his retreat, urging him forward with the rush of their wings.

"And Gloran and dear Brekka?" Rokah went on, glancing back down the pass. "Have they come too?"

"Yes, all of us," said Tok. "But I flew on ahead. I could not wait to see the Valley."

"And you shall see it." Rokah flew faster, so that Tok had to increase his wingbeats to keep up.

They reached the end of the pass, and shot out into the open air. Puzzled as he was by Rokah's odd manner, Tok's heart still raced when he saw the view that opened below him. There was the Valley, just as Selaks had described it. It lay folded among snow-frosted mountains, with a great river, its shores silvered with ice, winding like a snake along the bottom of it. Dark forest mantled with snow covered the shoulders of the slopes, and in the distance loomed the Cloven Mountain, split from crest to base, showing a pure wedge of achingly blue sky at its heart.

But there above it all . . .

"No!" cried Tok, unable to believe what he was seeing. For in the sky over the Valley wheeled a multitude of the Overlord's raiders. "We must warn the others," he gasped, trying to turn back. But the press of the flock of ravens behind him was too great.

"They will know soon enough," said Rokah. "For the Valley belongs to the Overlord."

"It cannot be! Not after we have come so far!" shouted Tok. "We must fight him somehow, drive him out. Your friends, Rokah, will they help us?"

Rokah uttered a harsh quork of laughter. "I think not, Tok. For they belong to him. As do I. You see, the Overlord is my master."

Chapter 35

Kora cannot understand unkora.

— Wisdom of the Tellers

Before the words had fully sunk into Tok's mind, the mass of ravens began to swirl around him, forming a powerful vortex that swept him downward. As the rocky cliffs of the pass loomed around him, he thought for a moment that the horde would drive him to his death against them. But at the very last moment it swerved, forcing him down among the rocks at the west end of the pass. There the ravens attacked him, buffeting him with their wings, and plucking feathers from his back.

Then Rokah wheeled overhead, alighting on a rocky pinnacle that jutted out from the face of the cliff. "Enough!" he shouted. "The Overlord will deal with this criminal."

"Good," said the burly raven who was holding Tok

down. "But any trouble from you," he said, thrusting his beak close to Tok, "and I'll break your wings."

No use trying to escape, thought Tok. They would beat him down from the sky. Here on the very edge of the valley of hope, everything was at an end. Bewildered, he stared up at Rokah, who glared back with angry amber eyes.

"How long?" said Tok at last. "How long have you been a traitor?"

"To my master, never," said Rokah proudly. "You and your gang I have deceived from the very beginning."

"The Raven Mountains?"

"Even before that." Rokah raised his hackles, which gleamed iridescent purple and green in the sun. "For I am the Chief Horde Leader of the Overlord. It was I who led the flights that searched for you in the eastern mountains. I did not find you, but those who did said you were headed west. So I knew where to look." He gave a mocking quork. "Who has not heard the stories of Tok Skydancer and the Grey Lords? I knew you would return to Mount Storm."

Tok's mind swam. All that time, when he had been so happy to be with his son, Rokah had hated him, had worked against him. It was all so obvious now. Rokah's mysterious disappearances. Barek, on guard, mysteriously attacked so that the prisoner escaped. The way the raiders always seemed to know exactly where to find the wolves and their ravens. Rokah's pursuing him from the Great Roost.

"You *lied* about following me to the Great Roost," Tok spat at Rokah. "You were part of it, just like Parok. Gloran and Brekka were right about you all along. And to think that I turned against them, and blamed myself for accusing you unjustly!"

Rokah gave a kark of laughter. "You are easily fooled," he said.

Tok gazed long at him. "*Why?*" he cried at last. "Why do you serve the Overlord? For position, for power?"

"I have won those for myself. The Overlord knows how to reward loyal service," snapped Rokah. "But I first began to serve him for the truth. He told me the truth about how my mother died. How you abandoned her to a miserable death."

Tok was bewildered. "But I told you myself what happened to your mother. I did leave her, foolishly, to pursue a strange flight of ravens. When I returned the next morning, she had been torn to pieces."

"You know that's a lie. She caught the Death, and suffered greatly. You Shunned her, left her to die in agony without food or water."

Tok shuddered. The Overlord had lied to Rokah, and Rokah had believed the lie, deeming his father *unkora*. "No!" Tok said. "That never happened. Tarkah meant everything to me. Sick, dying — it would not have mattered. I would never have abandoned her. You should have known that, Rokah.

Your Overlord is the one who lies."

He turned his back on his son. Why would anyone tell Rokah such a vicious lie? Tok asked himself. It had to be someone who hated him and wished to destroy him.

Suddenly there was a great karking and croaking from the ravens overhead, as another horde of birds swept in from the east. The Overlord? wondered Tok, bracing himself to face what must come. But moments later the battered forms of Gloran and the others were driven to the ground beside him.

"Not you too!" cried Tok, as Brekka and Karah fluttered to his side. "I tried to get back to warn you, but they captured me. Yet I hoped you would see the raiders and escape in time."

"They poured down on us while we were still at the kill," said Gloran, stretching his wings cautiously as if not quite sure they were still whole. "They beat us, and attacked the wolves too. At first we thought they intended to kill us, but then they forced us into the air and drove us here."

The eyes of all of them turned toward Rokah, who sat preening himself on the stone pinnacle. "Gloran, Brekka, I beg your forgiveness," said Tok. "You were right about Rokah. He has betrayed us from the beginning. I blame myself for not believing you. I fear that my folly will cost all of us our lives."

"You were blind because you are *kora*," said Gloran, and the others quorked their agreement.

Then the ranks of caribou filing through the pass broke and scattered, as Taxin and his wolves bounded among them. The pack charged up the slope toward them, trampling any raven guards that did not take to the air.

"Come, mount!" barked Taxin. "We'll get you out of here somehow!"

But even as he spoke the raven horde came down on them, stabbing with their beaks and slashing with their claws. Tok, trying to fight them away from Selaks, heard Kimmik gave a cry of pain as a claw sliced perilously close to her eye, opening a deep gouge in her face.

"STOP!" Rokah's voice boomed off the cliffs, dying away in echoes. "LEAVE THEM! I COMMAND YOU!"

At once the attackers banked away. Some circled low overhead, while others landed among the rocks.

"Is this what you want?" Rokah demanded, glaring down at Tok. "For the rest of them to die alongside you?"

Tok gazed into the faces of his friends. Bleeding and battered as they were, he knew they would fight to the last for him. "No," he shouted. "Let them go. It is me you want, after all."

"We're not leaving you," growled Taxin. And Sibi-rok, his narrow eyes blazing with the light of battle, rumbled his agreement.

"Keep them well-guarded," ordered Rokah, as yet another enemy flight came in to land. Then, turning to the prisoners, "The Overlord will decide what to do with you," he said coldly. "For now you will stay where you are. If you try to get away, we will put out your eyes." Taking wing, he flew down into the Valley with heavy wingbeats.

The pale winter daylight was already dying, and the temperature was dropping. There was no shelter here on the heights, not even much snow. The wolves curled up, wrapping their riders inside their tails, and as they always did, dropped effortlessly into sleep. The ravens kept vigil, saying nothing, for there was nothing more to say.

The moon rose in the east, drenching the scene with milky light. Tok watched the guard ravens closely, but they never closed their eyes. After a time, others came to relieve them. It would be no use trying to slip away. In the bright moonlight the enemy could see them clearly, and on the barren heights could pursue them at night without fear.

He shifted his position slightly, careful not to rouse Selaks, and gazed down into the Valley they had struggled toward for so long. Dark yet bright, under fiery northern stars, it lay before him more beautiful even than by day. The last of the caribou were flowing down from the pass now, their backs frosted with moonlight. The Wanderers were home.

We nearly reached it, thought Tok. No matter what happened tomorrow, he had kept his promise to the wolves. Surely they at least could still dwell in the

Valley, for the Overlord would have no reason to harm them. Perhaps the other ravens would be spared too, and could share the Valley with their wolf companions. But the thought of brave Gloran and feisty Brekka bowing to the Overlord was a bitter one. There had to be something he could do to win their freedom. For himself, all he wanted now was to come face to face with the Overlord. That would fulfill his vow, and whatever came of it would have to be enough.

"Tok!" said a silvery voice.

He turned his head, and saw the familiar pale figure appear, as though weaving itself from the moonlight.

"Tunavik!" he cried, stepping away from the shelter of Selaks's sleeping body. "Our journey has been in vain. We have been betrayed and the Overlord has won."

"Not yet. But only you can stop him. Raven must defeat raven."

"Stop him? How? He is too strong."

"His strength is his weakness," she replied. "That is what I have come to tell you. Remember it!"

Already the snowy figure was wavering in the moonlight. Only the eyes remained, dark and steady. And then the white raven was gone.

The wolves began to stir long before daybreak, and with their companions they watched the sky grow lighter. The guard ravens were replaced by others, and flights began to form over the Valley.

Then Rokah returned and perched high above the prisoners. "We have had messengers," he announced. "The Overlord will be here at dawn to inspect his new land. And I will have a great surprise for him. You."

Now there was a great bustle and massing of the raven horde along the pass. High overhead, the pale sky darkened with many angled flights.

The blazing rim of the sun appeared above the horizon, and a chant broke from the thousand throats of the raven horde as every head turned toward the east. "MASTER! MASTER! MASTER!"

Then, from out of the rising sun, a dark dot appeared, flying swiftly closer. Behind it, blocking out the sun's glory, winged another dark mass of ravens. Rokah took off and flew swiftly to meet the oncoming horde. Turning in the air, he fell in at the head of the flight that followed the lead raven, who swept in to land on the same pinnacle of rock. Rokah and another raven Tok recognized as Parok took up positions behind him. Rousing his feathers and hackles, the Overlord glared around at the assembled host.

"MASTER! MASTER! MASTER!" The mountains echoed to the terrible chant of the raven horde.

Tok felt the fierce gaze of the Overlord sweep past him and the others, then stop, then dart back. Their eyes locked.

In that moment of shocked recognition, he heard Karah cry out.

"Groh!" she screamed, in a voice that pierced

through the chant and died away down the Valley.

Tok stared into the burning eyes of the Overlord. And suddenly everything became perfectly clear.

Chapter 36

Serpents and liars follow twisted paths.

— Lore of the Lanna

"You, Groh!" he gasped. "It is *you* who created the Terror!"

"Did you never guess? Truly?" the Overlord asked, with a mocking bow. Then, raising his voice, he shouted, "Ravens of the Horde! Here is the Enemy, a prisoner at my feet. This is Tok Skydancer, who unjustly accused me and had me condemned before a corrupt Kort. Because of him I was exiled from the Raven Mountains."

A wordless roar of rage rose from the raven horde.

"He lies!" shouted Tok. "He is no Overlord, no Master. He is Groh, a disgraced ex-lord and my mother's second mate. He killed Rokan, my father, and dishonoured his name. He confessed it himself before the Kort of the Raven Mountains. That is why they drove him away in shame!"

There was a moment of shocked silence. Then karks and rattles of disbelief filled the air.

The Overlord uttered a harsh croak of laughter. "Shout all you like. They will never believe you," he said. "You are going to die, Tok, and slowly."

"You'll have to kill all of us first!" yelled Brekka, her feathers standing on end defiantly. Gloran and the others screamed their support, and the wolves howled their fury.

"Even better," said Groh. Then he turned to Rokah and Parok. "Who has delivered the Enemy into my power?" he asked.

"I, Master," said Rokah, bending his proud neck. "I spied upon him and his friends as you ordered, to discover where they were going. Then I summoned my hordes and Parok's from the Cold Forest to fly here ahead of them."

The Overlord's eyes glinted. "Well done," he said. "It couldn't be better. You have deserved my trust, Rokah." He turned to Parok. "Seize him!" he ordered. "Throw him down with the other prisoners."

Parok stared back at him dumfounded, and loud quorks of alarm burst from the raven horde.

"Not Rokah!" cried a single female voice. "Not our brave leader!"

"I said, 'Seize him!'" screamed the Overlord.

With a sweep of his wing, Parok summoned more guards, who hurled Rokah from his perch and knocked him to the ground beside Tok. There he crouched, beak agape, too stunned to defend himself.

The raven host began to stir and to mutter uneasily among themselves.

"Rokah doesn't deserve this!"

"If *he* falls, who among us is safe?"

Neighbour glanced at neighbour, and all eyes shifted back and forth between the Overlord on his pinnacle and the figure of their disgraced horde leader.

The Overlord leaned forward. "I give you back your son, Tok," he said. "He is as I have made him. A liar. A traitor. He kills on order, and has been as utterly loyal to me as he has been disloyal to you."

To Tok, the world narrowed to a single point, the hateful voice and eyes of his enemy.

"Let me tell you a story," the Overlord went on. "I know you'll find it interesting. It begins in the Raven Mountains, when you had me driven out."

"I have already said that is a lie," shouted Tok. "You were shamed and exiled by the Kort for your *unkora* behaviour."

The Overlord ignored him. "Thanks to you I lost everything — lordship and lady too," he went on, with a menacing glance at Karah.

Karah roused her feathers. "Had you been *kora* I would have followed you anywhere," she said scornfully. "But you are *unkora*, and abused me. And so I left you."

He glared down at her. "You will die along with your

son," he said. "But first you will learn more of my revenge. Bring my mate!" he added, turning to Parok.

Parok winged away, returning almost at once with a female raven flying between two guards. In her prime, she would have been beautiful. But now her feathers were dishevelled and lustreless, and she drooped between her captors as though she feared a beating.

Tok's heart clenched. "Tarkah?" he gasped. But even as he said it, he knew it could not be. Tarkah was long dead, and this raven was smaller than his mate had been.

The female raven's eyes widened at the sight of him. "Father?" she said. "Don't you know me? I'm Parvah, your daughter!"

"Let her join the prisoners," ordered Groh. And the guards forced Parvah to the foot of the pinnacle.

Trembling, she crept to Tok's side. Turning to Rokah she said, "I warned you, my brother. I told you what your precious Overlord is like. But you refused to believe, even when you saw what he did to me."

Rokah stared up frozen-eyed at the master who had betrayed him. "I did not think it could be as bad as you said," he replied. "I did not want to believe it!"

"What a happy family," gloated Groh. "You should thank me for bringing you together again. All except for poor Tarkah, of course. Her I had to kill outright, because she saw me when I was searching for you, and would have warned you."

At that, Rokah gave a great cry of anguish, struggling against the guards who held him down. Tok broke away and shot upward, claws extended, his only wish to tear the killer to pieces. But he was beaten back to the ground by the guards, as the clamour among the raven horde grew louder

"Murderer!" yelled Tok, over the commotion.

"Silence, all of you!" shouted the Overlord, glaring not only at Tok but also at the ranks of his followers. Then as the noise died down he went on, "But I am getting ahead of myself. As I said, the story begins in the Raven Mountains. From there I flew north until I reached the Cold Forest. I had had enough of Korts and *kora*. I wanted a different sort of ravenkind, faithful, fearless, obedient. So I organized my first flights. In time I was strong enough to attack the Raven Mountains. I found Rokah there, and he joined me. Parvah too. And they told me where to find you, Tok. But instead I found Tarkah."

"Why didn't you kill me then, when you killed her?" said Tok bitterly.

"Oh, I tried." The Overlord spread his wings mockingly, then closed them with a snap. "But my searchers could not find you. Then Rokah reported you had returned to the Raven Mountains, but were leaving with the wolves to find a safer home." He cocked his head. "This interested me, for the Change was in my thoughts. I had already seen that much of the Cold Forest was dying, and I wanted to know what haven you were seeking. So I set Rokah to spy on you and report to me while I bided my time, waiting for a more perfect vengeance." He turned to gaze down at the sweeping view of the Valley. "This was worth the wait."

A clamour rose again from the raven horde, each bird repeating to its neighbour what their master had said. The sound rippled outward to the farthest edge of the restless mass of birds.

The Overlord's throat swelled, his gleaming hackles standing out like a ruff around his neck, and Tok knew what would come next would be a death sentence for him and his companions.

"I challenge you, Groh!" he screamed, his voice echoing off the cliffs above them. "You call me the Enemy. But your followers have now heard from you yourself what you have done. I repeat that you are a liar and a murderer! If you are *kora*, you must fight to prove me wrong!"

There was silence for a moment, then a roar burst from the throats of the horde, neighbour shouting down neighbour.

"He's right! Let the Master fight him!"

"No! Don't listen to the Enemy!"

Then, "FIGHT!" shouted one shrill voice above the rest.

"No. Just kill the Enemy now!" cried another.

"Yes! He must die! But let the Overlord do it!"

"FIGHT! FIGHT!" clamoured more voices.

"I have no need to fight," croaked the Overlord,

glowering down at Tok. Then he turned to Parok. "Kill the prisoners," he ordered. "Let the wolves go, but if they try to fight, blind them."

"Parok!" shouted Rokah. "Don't do it. Have we not been comrades? You heard for yourself what the Overlord has done. He has betrayed all of us. Let me fight him!"

"No!" cried Tok over the uproar. "It is my right!"

And now the chant grew even louder, echoing off the rocks of the pass. "FIGHT! FIGHT!"

Parok swept his cold eyes over the horde, then turned them on the Overlord. "I think, Master, that you had better fight the Enemy," he said. "That way any doubts will be laid to rest."

"Doubts?" growled Groh. "Who dares to doubt me?"

But the shouting of the horde grew louder, and even the guards were muttering among themselves.

"Could the Master be afraid?" one asked the other, with a sidelong glance at Groh.

"He should fight the Enemy. If our Overlord wins, it will prove what he has always said, that the Enemy is a liar and a coward."

"FIGHT! FIGHT! FIGHT!" screamed the horde.

Groh whirled to face his followers. "Yes! I will fight!" he cried. They shrieked their delight, and rattled their beaks and claws against the rocks.

"I declare an aerial duel, single combat, to the death," shouted Parok when they had fallen silent.

"The Master and the Enemy will climb level with the mountaintops before they begin."

Again the horde thundered its approval, as the Overlord stretched his wings and preened his flight feathers.

Gloran and the other ravens clustered around Tok, except for Rokah, who stood apart. But for a moment Rokah's eyes met Tok's. "Kill Groh," he said. "For all our sakes."

"I will do my best," said Tok. Then he turned to Karah. "Look after Parvah," he said. "She needs help."

"I will," said Karah, her eyes fierce and bright. "Good luck. If we live I will weave a Telling about you that ravenkind will never forget."

"Tok!" cried Brekka, as he turned away. "Have you no word for me?"

"Farewell, Brekka," he replied. "I thank you, brave one, for your courage and your loyalty."

He fluttered onto Selaks's back and leaned forward, speaking low into her ear. "Now, my *vóra*, you will have a chance. Everyone will be watching the duel. I'm counting on you wolves to get our ravens out — in your jaws, if they won't go willingly!"

The white wolf turned her head and gazed at him, her eyes deep pools of gold. "Fight well, *lóran*," she said.

"Let the duel begin!" shouted Parok.

The Overlord was the first to take off, mounting into the air with easy flaps of his great wings. Tok too circled upward, the storm of lies and fear and hate falling away behind him. Here, in the pure air, it was all very simple now, he thought. He would win or he would lose. But either way he would have fulfilled his vows.

A thermal was forming over the cliffs, and he spread his flight feathers, riding it. Though the air was cold, his black back soaked up the sun, warming his wing muscles as he flexed them. It should have been a day for dancing, he thought. Far below him the Valley rolled away, silver and white, to the feet of the Cloven Mountain. There was still some way to go before they came level with the mountaintops, still some time to strengthen his heart with the beauty of Skyah's world . . .

Then from above came a blow so fierce, so piercing, that he felt as if he had been run through. He screamed as agonizing pain radiated along his left wing. Then the wing collapsed and over the whine of the wind Tok heard the mocking laughter of the Overlord as he plunged headlong down the sky.

Chapter 37

To kill for vengeance is the death of kora.

— Dooms of the Kort

"Fool!" Groh's voice echoed down the wind. "I obey no rules of duelling!"

Scooping air desperately with his right wing, Tok gained a moment's lift against the thermal. He struggled desperately to force his weakened wing open and at last he succeeded, but he knew he could not flex it. He would have to glide, and could not gain much height.

But now the Overlord came down on him again, driving another agonizing blow into the wound on Tok's back. He felt warm blood soak his feathers as he rolled to one side, slashing at his opponent with his claws. Feathers tore away, and Groh screamed as a great wound opened in his chest. Banking left on his stiffened wing, Tok pivoted under the Overlord, raking him again with beak and claw. Groh grappled with him, drawing him closer and battering him with his wings, while Tok plunged his beak again and again into his enemy's chest. The Overlord's blood mixed with his own, drenching him.

Down they plunged, icy air whining through their feathers and the rocky walls of the mountains spinning past them.

Now the Overlord relaxed his hold and began to flap his wings, trying desperately to gain height. But Tok held on grimly, and tore at Groh's chest with his beak. For he knew he could climb no more.

"Let go!" shrieked the Overlord. "You'll kill us both!"

"So be it," shouted Tok, "if that's the only way to stop you."

The screaming of the raven horde below filled Tok's ears, as the cliffs rushed up at them. Then they crashed to earth among the rocks of the pass and everything went black.

His strength is his weakness.

Lost in a haze of pain, Tok's mind clung to the words, though their meaning escaped him. Who had said that? Someone . . . Part of him yearned only to sink into darkness and rest, but the words remained, pulling him toward the light.

He opened his eyes. Clear sky above him. Jagged rocks around him. The roar of the raven horde echoing off the cliffs. Panic seized him — the Overlord!

Where was he? Tok tried to move, but pain seized him. It felt like every bone in his body was broken. Somehow he got his feet under him and forced himself upright.

Groh lay not far away, one wing folded under him. Tok dragged himself forward. Pinning Groh to the ground by his shoulders, Tok glared down at him as he opened his eyes. One more blow to shatter Groh's chest, and it would be over. Tarkah's death, his ruined children, the Terror — all would be avenged. He had longed for this moment.

The Overlord twisted beneath him, but Tok held him fast. "Kill me," growled Groh. "I am at your mercy."

Tok drew his head back to strike, then a shudder swept through him. He could not do it! To kill in the heat of battle was one thing. But to murder a helpless opponent would be *unkora*. A sickening feeling of failure overwhelmed him. For he knew that if he did not kill Groh, the nightmare would begin again.

Unless . . .

"Ravens!" he shouted, and the roar of the horde suddenly died away to a silence so deep that the very rocks seemed to listen. "You saw what happened!"

"WE SAW!" The response seemed to come from one mighty throat.

"Your master broke the rules of the duel. He cheated. Just as he has cheated *you*. He is *unkora*, as he has always been."

A wordless roar echoed off the cliffs.

"Will you follow such a master? Many of your comrades have died serving him. But for what?"

There was another mighty roar.

Suddenly Groh broke from Tok's grip, twisting away and throwing him onto his damaged wing. Before Tok could scramble to his feet, the Overlord had taken to the air. Circling low, he screamed at his followers, "There is the Enemy. You have heard his lies. Kill him! Kill him!"

An awful chant burst from a thousand throats. "DEATH! DEATH! DEATH!"

With a thunder of wings, the horde rose into the air. As they did so, Tok saw the wolves bounding toward him with their riders on their backs. Rokah and Parvah flew behind them.

"I told you to go!" Tok cried to Selaks.

Her eyes blazed. "As if we would!" she said, glaring up at the gathering horde.

"Let them come," snarled Taxin. "We'll take plenty of them with us!" Beside him, Sibirok raised his voice in a howl of defiance.

Then the darkness of the horde covered them, and the air swirled with the heavy beat of thousands of wings. Tok waited for the storm of blows, the battering of beaks to fall upon them. Now, at the end, he felt only a great calm.

Then the darkness grew less, it was passing . . .

"They're going over us, Tok!" cried Karah, from her

perch on Taxin's back. "They believed you!"

"Look! They're attacking Groh!" shouted Gloran.

Gazing upward, Tok saw the lone black figure of the Overlord turn suddenly in the air and try to fly away. But the seething black mass of the horde caught up with him and closed around him. A shrill scream echoed among the mountaintops, and then there was silence. As they watched, the great mass of ravens shattered into ragged groups, which wheeled away in all directions. Farther and farther they flew, scattering as they went. The west wind rose, veiling the distant peaks in cloud, and a blood-spattered black feather drifted down to land at Tok's feet.

Chapter 38

It will come to be:
Lanna the Seer,
Raven the Teller,
Arda the Keeper,
The Three will dwell in peace.

— from "The Legend of the Three,"
Tales of the Tellers

Ice crystals danced in the air, setting rainbow arcs either side of the sinking sun. And as Tok gazed down into the Valley, the white raven flew out of the west on the wings of the coming snow and lit on a large boulder near him.

"Tunavik!" cried Tok, and his companions turned to gaze at him in wonder.

"Victory is yours, Tok," said the white raven, her dark eyes glowing.

"It is not my victory — I failed!" he replied. "For in

333

the end I could not kill the Overlord."

"But you turned the strength of his own followers against him. It was enough. And now the Valley belongs to you and your wolves."

"We owe it to you, Tunavik," said Tok. "You set me on my journey. And you told us about the Wanderers. Without them we could never have reached the Valley."

Tunavik bowed. "It was my task to bring the Lanna and the ravens back to the Valley. That task is done. Yet something remains to be revealed."

Tok's heart began to pound. "You mean what Selaks Saw back in the Barren Lands?" He turned to the white wolf. Her eyes had widened into pools of darkness as the snow swirled around them, and he knew she was Seeing again.

"Yes," Tunavik replied. "I was as startled as she was when she Saw the Sender, for I had not understood the power of a Seer of the Lanna. I feared that if she told you what she had Seen, my hope for us all would fail."

"Is the Sender so terrible, then?"

"Look into my eyes, Tok, and tell me. For it is time."

Tok gazed into Tunavik's strange dark eyes, which seemed to grow larger and larger, until he felt as though he was plunging through them. The world around him dimmed, and a deep throb like a great beating heart sounded in his ears. He saw a space with a glowing fire, and beyond it a creature, dark-haired, dark-eyed, gazing back at him. And that creature was . . .

Tok gave a great cry. "A Two-Legs! The Sender is a Two-Legs!" He tried to spring into the air, but his battered body would not let him.

Suddenly the vision was gone, and there was only the mountainside, the snow and the white raven gazing back at him.

"The Sender's people are the Arda," she said. "The Keepers of the Valley. Long ago, Lanna, ravens and Arda dwelt together here in peace. And a white raven was ever the Messenger among them. But other Two-Legs came who wished to make themselves the masters of all. Then the killing began. And the Three were killed or scattered."

With an effort, Tok stopped trembling. "It has all been for nothing, then," he said bitterly. "The Overlord is dead, but the Two-Legs will surely ruin this Valley as they have so many other places. We will be driven out again."

"I tell you it will not be so," said Tunavik. "You have seen for yourself that the Two-Legs can work for good. Did they not heal Selaks? This Valley has been set apart forever, and the Arda appointed its Keepers. Wolves may run here safely now, and ravens fly free. The Keepers will not hunt you or cut the trees or poison the waters."

"Can it be true?"

"It is true. I swear it. And in this world there are

many other Valleys, Tok, and other Keepers. In these places wild things can seek shelter from the Change. Someday, perhaps, they will go forth to claim the Earth again."

The white raven spread her wings and rose into the air, circling once above the heads of the wolves and their riders. Then she became one with the whirling snow.

Tok drew a long shuddering breath.

"You saw the white raven, didn't you?" asked Karah. "I felt something was there, though I could not see her myself."

Tok nodded, still too shaken by his vision of the Sender to speak.

"But what has frightened you, Tok?" demanded Brekka. "You are not easily frightened. And why did you talk about a Two-Legs?"

"Because this time I saw more than the Messenger," Tok said at last. "I saw the creature that sent her. It is a Two-Legs, called an Arda."

There was a moment of shocked silence. Then, "You mean a *Two-Legs* brought us here to the Valley?" asked Gloran.

"I can't believe it," muttered Kimmik. "Not one of those killers!"

"It's true," said Selaks. "For I too Saw the Messenger and the Sender."

"How can we ever trust the Two-Legs?" growled Taxin. "After all they have done to the Lanna!"

"Yet we must try," said Tok. "For what other choice have we now? The white raven swears we will be safe here."

Karah dug her claws into Taxin's mane. "Let us try to trust and hope, *vór*," she said. "For truly this is like the ending of the Legend of the Three, that Tellers have told since the days of First Raven. May it all come to pass as the white raven says it will."

Now Rokah, who had been sitting silent, spread his wings.

"Wait," said Tok. "What will you do now?"

"Why would you care?" replied Rokah. "I should never have believed Groh's lies about you. Sometimes, watching you these past months, my heart has told me that you could not have done what he said you did. But my pride was too great for me to admit I was wrong." He gave a kark of bitter laughter. "Now I am disgraced and foresworn. I betrayed you, and may not share the haven you have won. I shall return to the Cold Forest."

"Would you have the Overlord win after all, then?" demanded Tok.

His son stared at him.

"You betrayed us, yes, because you believed Groh's lies," Tok went on. "But when you learned the truth you joined us, there at the last when all seemed lost, instead of trying to save yourself. Despite everything, some remnant of your *kora* must be alive, and if it is, it can be healed."

"How?" challenged Rokah.

"You are a great leader, Rokah," Tok replied. "I saw how your followers grieved when the Overlord disgraced you. They are leaderless now and trained in evil ways. Go and find them, show them how to establish Korts and live in peace."

The Valley below was fast disappearing as the snow closed in. Tok gazed a while into the gathering dusk before he spoke again. "But there is something I want you to know, Rokah," he went on. "I always thought that ravenlaw could never change. Because I left my mate and she was killed, because I abandoned my territory, I believed I had broken that law, that I was forever *unkora*. I now know that I am not." He turned back to Rokah. "Laws can be changed if they need to be. For one thing, ravenets have never had a say in our Korts, and so they turned to the Overlord. But we can create better Korts. Will you help us do it, Rokah?"

Rokah raised his head. "I will," he vowed.

"I'll help you!" Karah broke in. "I'll teach you and the others the Tellings of ravenkind."

"We'll all help," said Tok, and the rest of the ravens quorked their agreement. "But much will depend on you."

Rokah spread his wings. "It is a worthy mission, Father," he said, lifting into the wind. "Someday you will be proud of me again." Without waiting for an answer, he flew swiftly down into the Valley.

"And you, Parvah," said Karah, turning to Tok's daughter, who was perched on a nearby rock. "Will you join us too?"

"Gladly!" she said, her eyes brightening.

Then Tulik edged forward. "Ravenlady," he said, "would you care to be my rider?"

"I would be honoured," said Parvah. With a graceful flip of her wings, she landed on his back. The little wolf turned his head to gaze at her, his eyes shining.

"Let us go now," said Taxin. For the light was failing and snow swirled thick around them. The pack gathered around their *vór*, doing him honour. Lifting their muzzles, they sang into the coming dark — wild music that wove itself among the voices of the wind. Then, like creatures out of a dream, they vanished into the falling snow.

But Selaks and Tok stayed behind.

Sibirok too lingered. "For myself, I seek a new beginning," he said, with a sidelong glance at Selaks.

"Do you?" she replied, but her golden eyes were dancing.

Then back through the storm winged a rumpled, ragged figure that landed with a thump on Sibirok's shoulders. "Oh, ho!" the big wolf rumbled. "I seem to have stolen Barator's rider." And he ran out his tongue, laughing.

Brekka shook snow off her wings. "Barator forgives me. I'm staying with you, Tok," she said, casting a defiant glance in his direction. "So there!"

Tok gave a great quork of laughter. Stubborn! he thought. But brave and loyal too. She had yelled defiance at the Overlord and faced death at his side. He would never forget Tarkah, for she would always be part of the morning of his life. But suddenly he saw that for him, too, there could be a new beginning.

He tried to spread his wings, but the pain made him flinch. Yet he managed a bow. "Welcome — my lady," he said.

The wind whipped eddies of snow around them in the dusk. In the dark woods below, the Wanderers were gathered, and two black ravens on two white wolves went down into the Valley.

SHARON STEWART says that "the most fun part of the *Wolf Rider* research was finding out about how wolves raise their families — the fact that usually only the alpha male and female breed and the rest of the pack act as loving 'uncles and aunties.' Wolves, it seems, are very emotional creatures, and raising pups is a joyous part of pack life. All members of the pack are deeply attached to the pups, and the alpha female definitely shares babysitting duties as soon as the pups are old enough."

Sharon's previous book about Tok Skydancer, *Raven Quest*, won the 2005 Silver Birch Award. She was inspired to write the story when the image of a black raven riding on the back of a white wolf in a swirling snowstorm flashed across her mind. That image is represented in the cover of *Wolf Rider*.

Sharon is the author of *Banished from Our Home* from the Dear Canada series, plus two books in the Beneath the Crown series, *The Princess in the Tower* (shortlisted for the Geoffrey Bilson Award for Historical Fiction and for the Red Cedar Award) and *The Last Duchess* (shortlisted for the Red Cedar Award). She is also the author of *The Minstrel Boy, Spider's Web* and a recent biography, *Louis Riel: Firebrand*.